Dark Coup

David C. Waldron

DARK COUP

This is a work of fiction. All the characters and events portrayed in this book are fictional or are used fictitiously. Any resemblance to real people or incidents is purely coincidental.

ISBN: 1490915265
ISBN 13: 978-1490915265

Cover art by David C. Waldron and Erin Lark Designs
Editing by Dancing Out Loud Multimedia

First printing, July 2013

To my readers,
thank you.

Prologue

May 21, 2013 - Outside Promised Land Army Base, Natchez Trace State Park, Tennessee

A weary group of refugees approached camp, huddled in the backs of a number of canvas-topped troop carriers with the sides rolled up. Their preliminary "meet and greet" had gone well, and they were grateful not to be travelling on foot anymore. They'd survived a long cold winter and, though slightly warmer, an even more brutal spring.

The residents of Promised Land and Redemption had weathered the bitter winter and late spring by circling the wagons, so to speak, and sheltering in place. Even in the dead of winter there'd been no rest with a never-ending list of chores and outdoor labor to get done. The reality of their new situation had been forcefully brought home to civilians and military personnel alike. Previously used to travelling from heated homes to heated offices in heated cars, they soon learned that any warmth at all meant splitting a stack of firewood–every couple of days, and that was just the beginning of what needed to be done in a day.

The base, along with all of its personnel, was on high alert. Through their contacts with the other military bases and installations, Major Mallory Jensen knew that Colonel Olsen wasn't resting and, while they had been relatively secure in their position up until now, they all knew that could change with literally no warning. Mallory and her command staff kept everyone on their toes with random raid drills and constant upgrades to the base and town fortifications.

Several layers of fences–topped with concertina and barbed wire–surrounded the base, while soldiers were constantly on patrol. Foxholes had been dug all along the perimeter and reinforced bunkers and gun pits dotted the landscape.

It never failed, though, that when life on base or in Redemption seemed most difficult, when no one felt like they would ever be warm or dry or comfortable again, a group of refugees showed up. They served as a stark reminder that life could be much, much worse.

Today's incoming refugees had lost roughly half of their original group over the past three weeks. They'd abandoned their collapsing neighborhood on the outskirts of Clinton, Kentucky. Staying put really hadn't been an option any longer, but leaving had opened them up to a whole new set of dangers.

There had been a couple of skirmishes with organized, roving bands. They'd lost the few supplies they'd left with, but worse, they'd lost people. Friends, neighbors, family members…children. It turns out there isn't all that much food just sitting on the side of the road, either, but you'd be surprised what you'll eat when you're starving; really, truly starving.

Now, after trudging for almost ninety miles, they were just grateful for the hope of something resembling normal. While everyone was too exhausted to be more than vaguely curious, they still looked around as the trucks made their way into Promised Land over the bumpy dirt road.

…

The trucks passed through an outer and an inner perimeter, both fences topped with more concertina wire, before approaching what looked like a tent city. In fact, it looked a lot like the 4077th on the old M*A*S*H TV show. There were large tents for communal gatherings and small tents for individual functions. People were walking around carrying firewood, which made sense, and what looked to be electronic equipment, which didn't.

They drove by a crew that was laying down a wooden floor for a tent, another crew erecting a medium-sized tent, and a third crew that was putting wooden sides on yet another tent. It looked like a mixture of military and civilians working together, side-by-side, which was a relief to the group in the trucks. They hadn't known what to expect, but had at least hoped it wouldn't be some kind of military dictatorship they were walking into.

They heard the sound of running water from a corrugated metal hut with a sign that read "showers", they heard children laughing and singing a rhyming song. They could smell lunch cooking as they drove by the mess hall, and there was the brief cackle and squawk of chickens from a large pen right behind it.

A half-a-dozen people were doing laundry in a row of metal tubs lined up by a metal faucet. It looked to be evenly divided between men and women. Some were soaping, pounding, and wringing; and some were hanging the wet laundry up to air-dry on lines stretched between poles.

At the crackle of gunfire, a hundred horrified refugees ducked in unison. Some threw themselves over children or spouses while some cried out. It turned out that they were passing the practice range. It would probably be many months, if not years, before the trauma they had lived through eased enough for that sound to mean nothing. Eventually, the trucks came to a stop and the drivers came around and opened the tailgates, lifting their hands to help their passengers down. "Welcome to Promised Land," they said to each new arrival, as they set foot on the ground. "Welcome to Promised Land."

Chapter One

As the trucks carrying the new group into camp came to a stop, Sergeant Ty Novak, Promised Land's doctor, strained to catch a first glimpse of the group he would be examining today. At first, no one moved at all, and then the drivers of the trucks got out and dropped the tailgates. The influx of refugees had all but dried up over the past few months, but when the occasional group showed up they were usually a little more eager to get out and look at their new surroundings.

Ty wondered why nobody seemed in a hurry to get off. That is, until he saw the first few people; and what he saw made his heart ache.

He'd been an Army Medic for ten years, and joined Doctors without Borders almost as soon as he'd finished his residency. He'd served in the Army in Afghanistan and Iraq, and with Doctors in Sudan, Kenya, and Niger, and it was still a shock to see anyone–much less Americans here at home–in such bad shape.

He'd grown used to seeing pretty much all men with beards, but scissor-trimmed and clean-cut. The men getting off the trucks looked like they hadn't had access to scissors in at least six months. Everyone's hair was long and unkempt. They looked like they had at least tried to rinse off when they had a chance, but he also knew they had come almost a hundred miles, and the first order of business when you find water when walking that far is to *drink*–then bathe.

As a group, they were emaciated, and showed profound muscle wasting. The women looked to have lost *all* extra body fat; they were not only flat-chested, but had no butts, either. There wasn't a single man with a gut on him. He was pretty sure he could also see some untreated ballistic trauma and crush injuries in the growing crowd on the ground. He mentally added gangrene to his growing list of concerns.

From where Ty was watching, though, one thing stood out more than anything else; the children. The children brought home just how long this whole ordeal had been going on. He could see, at their thin ankles and wrists, inches of bare skin where they had long outgrown the pants and long-sleeve shirts they were wearing. Replacement clothing was a distant dream, and these children had been living a waking nightmare. But, like children the world over, they continued to grow…and grow. Ty wondered if he was about to diagnose his first case of rickets, scurvy, or possibly even goiter, since the power had gone out.

…

Sergeant Patterson had been the one to perform the "meet and greet", and had called ahead to have food ready. The exam waiting area had been turned into an impromptu mess hall, and they were serving milk, cornbread, rice, and beans.

Joel was there to greet the group, and he took a seat on an empty table at the front of the tent. It helped make him a little less intimidating, but at the same time, everyone could still see him.

"Everyone," Joel said, "my name is Joel Taylor. I'm the Mayor of Promised Land, which is this camp, and of Redemption, which is the town about eight miles southeast of here."

"I just want you to know that there is more where this came from," Joel said, gesturing to the food they were wolfing down. "We aren't being stingy, I promise, but we know you've been through a rough patch and we didn't want to throw too much at you too quickly."

"I also want to welcome you," Joel said, "and let you know how we have things set up. First of all, we do have power, but it's limited.

We don't run it everywhere, and it isn't running all the time. We use it mostly for the infrastructure pieces; like water purification, communications, and defense—if we need it. That sort of thing."

Joel looked around and saw that he had people's attention, but they were eating while they were listening. "Second, is water. We have a fairly good supply through surface water, but we're pretty strict about anything that could pollute the groundwater. It's just common sense."

"Lastly," Joel said, "are the work details. We have agreements worked out with a number of farmers and ranchers in the area that need additional labor. We all benefit by helping out both here and there. The milk you're drinking right now came from the dairy; the corn for the cornbread came from one of the farmers."

"A little bit later we'll have folks get together with each of you," Joel continued, "to figure out where you'd be best suited to help out. It won't be right away though. You've had a rough go and need some time to rest and recover. Again, welcome to Promised Land."

Several in the crowd murmured thanks, many nodded, and it was obvious that they really were grateful. It was just as obvious they were in shock; the haunted eyes, the way that some looked over their shoulders almost constantly.

Joel noticed one father telling his teenage son to slow down and not to gulp his food and couldn't help but smile.

"What's your name, son," Joel asked.

"Matthew," the boy said, slightly embarrassed now that he'd obviously drawn attention to himself.

"Well, Matthew," Joel said. "I'm serious about there being more—right now, even—and I can understand your being hungry. I have a seventeen-year-old son myself. Your dad is right, though. Give it a few minutes and see how your stomach feels before you go back for some more, and do yourself a favor; don't get any more milk. Drink water until dinner. Trust me. If you're still hungry in ten minutes and your stomach doesn't hurt, by all means, please go back for seconds."

Matthew looked at his Dad, and then back at Joel.

"It's really ok," Joel told both Matthew and his Dad.

"Thank you," Matthew's Dad said, and held out his hand. "Paul. Paul Sewell."

"Good to meet you, Paul," Joel said, and shook both of their hands. "You too, Matthew, and I think you'd like my son, Josh."

. . .

Ty had noticed this next girl fairly early on. Her mother had been comforting her while they ate, cradling her on her lap. Ty had also noticed a moist, rattling cough–which could be anything—and that her cheeks looked flushed, even from a distance. Her name was April, and her mother was with her for the exam.

"When did your cough start," Ty asked April. He always tried to get the answer from the kids first; their answers tended to be more reliably honest. If it seemed a little *too* off-the-wall, he would get clarification from the parent, but he'd found that parents had a tendency to sugar-coat things if they had the chance.

"A couple of days ago," April said.

Ty nodded. "A couple two, or a couple three," he asked as he got the thermometer ready.

April made a thinking face and closed her eyes, which seemed too big in her gaunt face. "Three, I think," she said. "Sometimes I get allergies and they make my nose run, and I get a cough. This isn't," April started to shake her head and then held still as Ty put the thermometer in her ear, "this isn't the same, though."

Ty nodded as he read the thermometer after it beeped. "Well, you have a little bit of a fever," he said, "but you aren't the only one. It's not very high, and once I look in your nose and ears and listen to your lungs, I think I can guess why."

"Mmhmm," Ty said, in that infuriating tone that only doctors have, "mmmhmmm. Now, I need you to take a couple of deep breaths and try not to cough when you let them out, ok?"

April nodded.

After several breaths, Ty took the stethoscope out of his ears and looked at both April and Mom. "Ok," he said. "It looks like you have a little bit of an upper-respiratory infection. Nothing serious, though, and we do have some antibiotics in camp. We should be able to get it cleared right up."

April's mom smiled weakly. "Thank you," she said.

"And now it's Mom's turn," Ty said, and called a nurse to come in while April went out to wait with the rest of the group.

...

May 22, 2013 - Fort Rucker, Alabama

On his way to a meeting with the Colonel, Major Bradley Sanford was struck, and not for the first time, by the juxtaposition of the world they had all left behind and the changes they'd had to make over the last year. He didn't think he'd ever get used to the fact that central air-conditioning was a thing of the past because it just used too much electricity, but the base still used laptops, printers, and radios. He was still responsible for an IT staff of twelve on an Army base in post-apocalyptic America. The irony of the situation almost made him laugh…almost.

Fort Rucker was the home of the US Army Aviation Center of Excellence and had been the primary flight training base for the Army. Now, rows upon rows of airplanes and helicopters sat idle. What had been a busy base, teeming with activity, was now a shell of its former self. There were still over seven thousand people living on base, but the life had been drained out of it when the power went out and the world changed almost a year ago.

"Sir," Sanford said as he entered Colonel Olsen's office.

"Have a seat," Olsen said, without looking up from his papers. Life had gone on almost as usual after the power went out at Fort Rucker. He was sleeping in a regulation bed, eating regulation food. He still had hot and cold running water, and with the exception of a month or so without reliable electricity, power was no longer an issue. "How are things progressing with Major Franklin at Fort Campbell?" Olsen asked.

Sanford paused for a second.

Olsen raised an eyebrow. "I don't need you to blow sunshine up my butt, son, that's what I have Lieutenant Colonel West for," Olsen said. "It's not in my most recent reports, and I'm not stupid. Why is Fort Campbell suddenly radioactive?"

"Well, Sir," Sanford said, fighting an urge to look over his shoulder. "It hasn't been in the reports because we haven't generated them for you." Sanford went on before Olsen could tell him to quit beating around the bush. "We don't have anything concrete, but… well, Major Franklin seems to be *saying* all the right things, but we don't have proof that he's implemented any of his orders."

Olsen nodded.

"We also strongly suspect that Major Franklin is the one who supplied the Stingers to Major Jensen that are interdicting the air space around Natchez Trace," Sanford continued. "There's no way to know for sure without tipping our hand, but there is *nobody* else nearby who could have provided her with enough of them to cover the area they are protecting. And if he's helping her out, it's likely that he's helping others out as well."

"How are they communicating, though," Olsen muttered, half to himself. "And why run the risk. He has to know that eventually we'll find out."

"In the case of Major Jensen," Sanford said, "apparently they go all the way back to Basic together, so they've known each other a long time. We obviously don't have the entire records base available here, but we were able to piece that much together. As for anyone else he may be helping, who knows."

"How sure are you about the Stingers?" Olsen asked.

Sanford made a face and half shrugged. "As sure as we *can* be on purely circumstantial evidence, but I really don't think it would hold up in court."

Olsen frowned. "It'll hold up in *my* court," Olsen said.

"Sir," Sanford asked.

"I'm judge, jury, and executioner," Olsen said.

"Understood," Sanford said.

"West," Olsen shouted to his second in command, Lieutenant Colonel Howard West, whose office was across the hall.

"Colonel," West said as he came into Colonel Olsen's office.

"Close the door," Olsen said. "We have a thorn in our side in the form of Major Franklin. I want him taken out and Campbell brought under our command."

Olsen got up to watch what little activity there was on base through his office window. "I can't have one of my officers blatantly disregarding orders," Olsen said. "I didn't *ask* him to do something, I gave him an *order*. This has gone on long enough, and we are going to make an example of Major Franklin and what happens when you disobey a *direct order*!"

West nodded in agreement.

"However, it is critical that the base be taken intact," Olsen said. "There is too much infrastructure, manpower, and material to waste by simply destroying it to take out one person." Olsen turned around to look at West and Sanford, "Unless it becomes obvious that the only way to rid ourselves of his rebellion is to raze the entire base and everything around it. Do I make myself clear?"

"I believe so, Sir," West said with a nod.

"Yes, Sir," Sanford said.

"Outline the mission and have a brief for me in the next seventy-two hours," Olsen said. "Coordinate with however many other units you think it will take. West, you're in charge of this and I'm leaving it up to you, but commit whatever force you think necessary to do it in a single strike. Dismissed."

Chapter Two

May 26, 2013 - Fort Campbell, Kentucky

Lieutenant Mathis was in the communications room when the radio came to life with a call from Fort Bragg on the HAM radio.

"At some point," Mathis thought, *"I really need to tell the Colonel about those."*

The message was short and tersely worded. "Prepare for an attack," the voice on the other end said, "within the next ninety-six hours."

"We need to tell the Major," Sergeant Yale said as he reached for the board that managed on-base communications.

"I'll take care of it," Lieutenant Mathis said.

Just then one of the on-base radios came to life and Yale was happy to let the Lieutenant take care of notifying the Major.

...

"Mathis," Major Ben Franklin said as he caught up with him outside one of ammo dumps on base. "Any word from Lejeune or Bragg, or even Promised Land?" Mathis shook his head. "Nothing sir," he said. "Not a peep. I'm sure they're just as busy with the day-to-day as we are, though."

Ben nodded and looked around as they passed one of the vehicle depots. "Where do we sit as far as getting some of this equipment spread out and deployed around the base," he asked. "I don't like keeping all my eggs in one basket, and leaving the bulk of our ground equipment consolidated at the depots is just bad tactics."

"Understood, sir," Mathis said. "We've emptied three of the other depots, and I'm working on getting these last two cleared out. We've only got so much time and manpower available to redeploy everything, though." Shuffling the vehicles from one lot to another to keep Ben of his back had been a bigger pain than he'd anticipated when the Major had originally mentioned it. He was proud of the idea he'd had to put a number of their vehicles into maintenance to get them out of the depots and out of commission at the same time.

"Fair enough," Ben said.

A couple of months after the power went out, Ben had begun questioning Mathis's loyalty. Recently, however, Mathis had really stepped up and taken a lot off of Ben's plate, freeing him from to focus on managing the day-to-day interaction between the base and the surrounding area.

"Keep me in the loop and let me know if you need anything," Ben said.

"Yes, Sir," Mathis replied.

. . .

Sergeant Yale hadn't exactly been a model soldier before things went sideways with the power, but he'd learned quick enough to take his job seriously after that. Yale was disturbed that he hadn't heard anything about preparing the base for an attack, or seen any activity that indicated the Major was taking the warning from Bragg seriously. His biggest beef before the power went out had been with Officers who felt the enlisted ranks were beneath them.

It had been two-and-a-half days since the transmission warning them to prepare for an attack; over half the time the warning had given them. He really didn't have any ideas as to *why* the Major wasn't doing anything, but it was obvious that nothing was being done and he felt it was his duty to find out how come.

After his shift, Yale headed down to speak with the Major, but pulled up short when he saw Mathis at the desk outside the Major's office.

"Why isn't the Lieutenant in his own office," Yale wondered to himself, but decided it didn't matter. He walked towards the office with the intention of knocking on the door directly instead of going through Mathis.

"Can I help you, Sergeant," Mathis asked as Yale got closer, barring him from the office with the question.

"I need to speak with the Major, Sir," Yale said.

Mathis frowned. "Is there something *I* can help you with," he asked.

"No, Sir," Yale said. "I'd like to speak with the Major."

Mathis looked down at some papers on his desk and replied, "I don't believe the Major has time to speak with you right now."

"With all due respect, Sir," Yale started to say.

"I said," Mathis said as he looked back up from the desk, "the Major is busy."

Yale had seen through the window in the Major's office on the way by that he was in fact *not* too busy, in his opinion, to discuss why nothing was being done to prepare the base for an attack. He took a step back from the desk and craned his neck back towards the window to show he didn't believe what he was being told.

"Yale," Mathis said, "if I have to tell you one more time, I'll bust you all the way to Private."

"Sir, that won't matter a hill of beans if we're unprepared for an attack in the next couple of days," Yale said.

Mathis narrowed his eyes and pulled the radio from his belt. "Security to the Major's office," he said. "*NOW.*"

Yale knew something was wrong and wasn't going to go away quietly, but now time was short so he yelled for the Major.

Mathis came around the desk to confront Yale, but the Sergeant began walking to Ben's door. Mathis had to take several steps to get in front of Yale and physically block him from going further.

"What is it," Ben asked from his office and Mathis heard him get up from behind his desk.

"Nothing, Sir," Mathis said. "I've got it under control."

Yale disagreed and yelled around Mathis towards the office. "Sir," he started, "why aren't we…"

Yale's voice cut off as Mathis did the only thing he could think of to shut the man up and hit him in the jaw.

While the blow had silenced Yale, his reaction was immediate and violent. This was *exactly* the kind of crap he had a problem with and he'd had enough. Yale launched himself at Mathis and the force of the impact took them both to the ground.

Mathis didn't know what he'd expected, but being tackled by the Sergeant hadn't been on the list. He was struggling to pull his sidearm while wrestling with the Sergeant and trading the occasional blows when Ben came out of his office.

"What is going *on*," Ben snapped.

"This man," Mathis started to say, but was temporarily silenced by a jab to the gut.

Just then the MPs arrived and Mathis was able to push Yale off of himself and stand up.

"Mathis," Ben said, trying to keep his voice level. "Why were you brawling with Sergeant…Yale?"

"He wouldn't let me," Yale started to speak, but the MPs had arrived with their weapons drawn. When one of them raised the butt of their rifle to hit him, he shut his mouth with a click.

"It's a long story," Mathis said, hoping Ben would let it go for the time being.

"Yale," Ben said, looking at the Sergeant. "Care to add anything?"

"I'll take care of this," Mathis interrupted.

"No," Ben said, "you'll let me talk to the man."

"Sir," Mathis started, but was interrupted by Ben asking Yale if he had anything to say.

"Why aren't you doing anything to prepare for the attack," Yale blurted out all at once.

"Excuse me," Ben asked, suddenly tense and even more serious than he had been.

"I think I can explain," Mathis said.

"If you interrupt me one more time," Ben said to Mathis, "I may be tempted to pick up where Yale here left off. Not another word."

Mathis glared daggers at Yale, but didn't interrupt. Instead, he put his hands on his hips in a slightly rebellious pose which put his right hand next to the grip of his .45.

"We got a warning from Fort Bragg two days ago," Yale said. "Prepare for an attack in the next ninety six hours."

The MPs were behind Yale and to Mathis's side at this point.

"Why wasn't I informed," Ben demanded, looking from Yale to Mathis and back again.

"Lieutenant Mathis was in the radio room when the call came in," Yale said. "I said we needed to let you know and he," Yale motioned to Mathis with his chin, "said he'd take care of it."

Ben turned to glare at Mathis and was surprised to see one of the MPs reach out and grab Mathis's right wrist. The other guard, trained to deal with the more immediate threat first, stepped to the side of Yale and leveled his rifle at Mathis.

"He was reaching for his sidearm, Sir," the guard holding Mathis's wrist said. "I have a feeling it wasn't for Sergeant Yale, either."

Ben gritted his teeth and then nodded to the MP who took the .45 out of Mathis's holster, handed it to the Major, and then proceeded to put handcuffs on Mathis.

"Why," Ben asked, not really expecting an answer. "What could he possibly be holding over you?"

"You know nothing," Mathis said, "*nothing.*"

. . .

Mallory took the middle-of-the-night radio call from Ben in her office. "How're things holding together up there," she asked.

"I wish you'd asked me that a week ago," Ben said. "It's about to come completely unraveled. I was *just* informed that we got a warning call from Bragg almost three days ago."

Mallory was stunned and couldn't respond right away.

"The warning gave us a four-day window," Ben said, "which is just about to close."

"What happened," Mallory said.

"My mole happened," Ben said. "He has been running interference for the last couple of months and now he's intercepting messages to me. We have a general plan in case an attack happens, but we're really short on time now. We may be in trouble."

"Is there anything I can do," Mallory asked.

"Not right now," Ben said, "and I have to get to evacuating and preparing the base. I just wanted to make sure you knew what was going on."

"Let me know as soon as anything happens," Mallory said. "Don't keep me in the dark on this."

"You'll be the third person to find out," Ben said.

...

May 27, 2013 - Fort Campbell, Kentucky

"We're cutting this close," the radar operator said.

"We're operating on an imaginary timeline," Ben said. "But we have to get as many people out of here as we can. We have no idea when they plan to hit us, or really from where. Has there been any more word from Bragg?"

The radio operator, Sergeant Yale, shook his head. "And Lejeune has been silent too," he said.

Ben cursed. "Well, almost all of the heavy equipment left this morning," Ben said, "and we've been going nonstop since then. Whatever happens, the Colonel is going to get quite a surprise when he finally gains control of the base."

"I just wish we could get *all* of the civilians out of here in time," he said.

"They've been leaving at almost the same rate we have," one of the Sergeants who'd stepped up in Mathis's absence said. "The ones that are sticking around either can't leave, really don't have much to offer the Colonel without the infrastructure we're taking with us, or plan on going down in flames giving the Colonel hell."

"I'm afraid of what the Colonel will do to them," Ben said, "regardless of why they're still here. A tyrant doesn't care *why* you're in his way; you're just an obstacle that needs to be removed. These are all human beings, people *we* have sworn to protect and…we're running out on them."

"We'll bloody his nose before we go," the Sergeant said.

"And that's why I worry," Ben said, "that's why I worry."

. . .

May 27, 2013 - Staging Areas - Clarksville, Tennessee & Hopkinsville, Kentucky

"We are *go* for the final assault on Fort Campbell," came the command over the radio. "Air support will be supplied by aviation units from the 3rd ID out of Hunter and Fort Stewart.

"Roger," was the sole acknowledgement by all of the units involved.

"I really hoped it wouldn't come to this," Major Weaver from Fort Bragg said. *"And I can't even get a message to Ben at this point!"* he thought.

. . .

May 27, 2013 - Elkton, Kentucky

Chief Warrant Officer Fourth Class Diego Hobbs kept his face expressionless, but he wanted to be anywhere rather than here. He'd been tapped, not as the battalion leader, but as the entire flight leader for this mission since his bird was mission-capable again. For a month he'd been "assisting" his mechanic and had managed to keep his bird from being mission ready. But two weeks ago, command finally told him to leave it to the guys who really knew what they were doing. Luckily, his mechanic had known *exactly* what Diego was doing, and made sure to take another week to "figure out what was wrong."

"Now I'm back in the game," Diego thought, *"and I'm in charge. Curse the luck. Do or die time."*

"Buzzard Hawk flight," came the controller over the radio, "begin thru-flight. Lift-off in twelve minutes."

"Roger base," Diego said, and then began his final pre-mission briefing.

"Communications check," Diego said. "Coopers."

"Check," came the reply.

"Harris."

"Go."

"Flight channel check…"

Chapter Three

"We have contact," the radar operator said. "Spotters saw the dust plumes just after we picked up radar contacts."

Ben crossed himself.

"I didn't know you were Catholic, Sir," Yale said.

"Lapsed," Ben said. "Beginning to think I need to spend a little more time at church on Sundays. How long have we got?"

"Assuming they want to soften us up first with Black Hawks," the radar operator said, "and we'll know that in about a minute from radar, fifteen minutes on the Hawks, and another ten minutes for the ground troops."

Ben's radio crackled to life. "Major, you have an incoming call from Colonel Olsen."

"Put it through to this handset," Ben said.

"Major Franklin," Olsen said.

"Colonel," Ben answered, allowing just the right amount of annoyance to creep into his voice. "May I ask just what in the hell is going on? I just got word that I have a number of inbound aircraft. Judging by their speed, I would assume they are helicopters. And I'm now being told that there are several incoming land vehicles, from the north *and* south. If I didn't know better, I would think my base was under attack."

"Major," Olsen said, "I think you know very well what's going to happen, and whether or not your base actually comes under attack is completely up to you."

"Would you care to explain that, Colonel," Ben asked.

"No more than I'm sure you would care to explain your lack of compliance with direct orders to subdue and disarm your local civilian population," Olsen said.

"So, the gloves are completely off," Ben thought.

"Yale, I want the rest of this exchange on the PA system and rebroadcast on every channel we have the ability to broadcast on, unless I tell you to sever it," Ben said. "Everyone needs to hear this. I'm going inside so he doesn't hear the feedback.

"In that case, Colonel," Ben said, less than a minute later, "you won't mind explaining yourself at all. I'm refusing to comply with the patently illegal and unconstitutional orders of an egomaniacal tin dictator with delusions of grandeur."

Ben took a breath and checked to see if his handheld was still transmitting, which it was. He expected his radio to shut off at any second, but he was prepared for that. "Nothing in the mission statement of the US Army, or any branch of the military for that matter, gives you or I the right to do the things that have been outlined in your new 'orders.' The first thing we swear to, as both Officers and enlisted soldiers, is to uphold and defend the Constitution of the United States of America against all enemies, foreign and domestic. You are in direct violation of that oath, Colonel, and have become an enemy domestic."

Ben was still transmitting, so he kept talking. "Colonel, stand down and turn your men around. Nobody needs to die today."

Ben's transmit light finally shut off and he put in the code to allow his handheld unit to continue to function now that his satellite link had been severed. The Colonel didn't know he wasn't in the radio room.

"Bravo, Major, very well spoken," Olsen said. "I'm sure you spent quite some time on that little speech. Just so you know, it didn't go out like you had hoped, though. I'm sure your people heard it like you wanted, but I had control of your radio board and it wasn't retransmitted back to my people. Nice try, though."

"Damn, maybe it got out on UHF and VHF," Ben thought.

"Unfortunately, you don't know what you're talking about," Olsen said. "The Constitution hasn't been our guiding document for almost a hundred years now, and the oath you speak of is just so many words. If anyone is going to stand down, it's going to be you. Save your people and let us in, only a few people need to die today."

"How can you say that," Ben asked. "What do you mean it hasn't been our guiding document? Honor is alive and well, and if the Oath means nothing to you, it still means something to hundreds of thousands of men and women who won't let you destroy what they have sworn to protect."

"Then this is on your head, Major," Olsen said. "You've had your last chance."

...

"...last chance."

Diego switched to the private channel used by the flight for the mission.

"Battalion leaders," Diego said in his typical cool, no-nonsense mission voice, "check in."

After all of his leaders checked in, he asked the first of two questions.

"Did everyone copy the last transmission," he asked.

All of his leaders answered in the affirmative and even though they tried to play it as cool as Diego, there was some heat in the one-word answers.

Diego let the silence sit for several seconds before asking his second question.

"Are all battalion leaders in agreement with our current course of action," he asked.

"Coopers, negative."

"Harris, no way."

"Roger," Diego said. "Use UHF fallback frequencies in case of emergency."

Diego switched back to the general mission frequency and made his announcement.

"Control," Diego said, "Buzzard Hawk flight is aborting, repeat Buzzard Hawk flight is aborting."

"Negative, flight leader," control replied.

"Affirmative, control," Diego said with a smile. "Illegal orders will not be followed, talk to the Colonel. All battalion leaders concur."

"Negative, flight leader," control replied again. "Orders are not illegal, proceed as planned."

"No can do, Leo," Diego said, using the control operator's name instead of his call sign. "You and I both know this is wrong. We'll find someplace to land, but I doubt we'll be coming back to base any time soon. Pass the word: if anything happens to any of the families of these guys, we took off with a bunch of fully-loaded and heavily-armed Black Hawks, and we *will* exact our revenge."

"Good copy," was all Leo said, and then broke the connection.

...

"Major," the radar operator said, "the Black Hawks are changing course. South-south-west."

"What the," Ben said as he looked over at the radar operator. "Why..."

"What, Sir," Yale said when Ben trailed off.

"Promised Land," Ben said. "Get them on the radio, now!"

. . .

"Not a good time, Ben," Mallory said, "and things are only just starting to calm down after our new arrivals."

"It's not a social call, Mal," Ben said. "I'm about to be invaded, but it looks like the air support just made a left turn and might be headed your way."

"Excuse me?!" Mallory shouted.

"I didn't *send* them there," Ben snapped. "I'm just trying to give you a heads up before your radar goes crazy."

"Thank you for that," Mallory said. "I have to go shoot down some helicopters now."

. . .

Ben and his command staff had known this day would come eventually, and had drawn up several different plans to defend the base. Ironically, Mathis had been critical to many of the strategies he was now implementing, which made Ben wonder if there were hidden dangers or weaknesses that had been intentionally left open. Unfortunately, he had to work with what he had since he'd only had a little over a day to prepare.

Every approach to, and all of the main roads on base had been turned into an obstacle course for the invading force while still allowing his defenders to have fairly unrestricted fields of fire. Ben knew they would be outnumbered—and outgunned—by several orders of magnitude, but he planned to make the invaders pay for every inch they took and had even toyed with the idea of burning the base to the ground on his way out.

The invading forces came from three different directions and Ben was glad he hadn't waited any longer than he had to evacuate the base. The only way out now would be through one of the attacking forces. The initial attack seemed to have been delayed with the loss of their air support, but whoever was in charge over there had recovered quickly and the lack of helicopter over-watch only gained Ben a couple of hours.

Ben was relieved that the attack hadn't started with a barrage of artillery to 'soften him up'. That was the one thing he had no defense against and the death toll on his side would have been staggering. Instead, they led off with M1 Abrams tanks on all three fronts, followed by Bradley Fighting Vehicles. His anti-tank devices, large concrete structures that were either shaped like a caltrop or the giant '16 ton' anvils from the cartoons, kept the tanks busy long enough for his meager defense force of less than three thousand to move from point to point and engage them with medium-range anti-tank missiles.

The tanks crews also proved to be reluctant to use their main gun to clear the obstacles. Less than a dozen main guns were fired, and then only after his men had destroyed two tanks, before the tanks were called back and the smaller, more agile Bradleys began to make their way into the base.

It's true that war is a nasty business, and once it comes down to one-on-one fighting it's chaotic and all the best planning in the world goes out the window. On the other hand, a battle like the one Ben was involved in is almost orchestrated...choreographed even. Obviously neither side knew what the other was planning, but you eventually started to get a feeling for how the other side thought and what was coming next.

Ben almost felt as though the other side was being...hesitant in its attacks. It was obvious that they'd been instructed not to level the base, if at all possible.

He immobilized three Bradleys, again with medium-range shoulder-fired anti-tank missiles, but he was beginning to lose men on his side as well.

Less than an hour after the attack began, Ben's troops had expended almost a million rounds of ammunition, most of it fired at the tanks and Bradleys, which basically shrugged it off but kept the occupants' heads down and inside the vehicles. The second wave was going to be tougher, though, and Ben did his best to prepare his men to fire on fellow Americans. It was entirely possible, probable even, that many on today's battlefield had served side-by-side during their careers. Not the definition of 'friendly fire' he'd grown accustomed to, but a fitting description nonetheless.

The sun was going down by the time the infantry started its assault all along the perimeter of the base.

There was no way for Ben to defend the entire perimeter; he simply didn't have the manpower. Instead, he'd reinforced the passive defenses as much as he could; additional razor wire at both the top and bottom of fences and remotely detonated claymore anti-personnel mines, as well as unmanned sandbag bunkers to give the impression of a larger defensive force and discourage the invaders from using that avenue of approach.

Ultimately, it took less than a day for the invading force to gain a decisive advantage and Ben was forced to admit that they would have to abandon the base.

…

"It's going to be a fighting retreat," Ben told the platoon sergeants, "and we'll punch through to the west."

"Sir," one of the Sergeants said, "it's almost like they want us to do just that. The fighting has dropped off there and there's hardly any heavy weaponry on that side."

"I know," Ben said. "And I admit that I don't know for sure, but with the way this battle has progressed up to this point, I get the feeling that whoever's commanding the troops on the ground on the other side would just as soon let us go as kill us to a man. He has to know he's going to win eventually, but if he can give us a way out without making it too obvious, he'll save a lot of lives on both sides."

Ben didn't say that he also got the impression that in the grand scheme of things, the opposing commander was on their side. Sure, people had died on both sides, many more on the other side than Ben's, but the *percentage* of casualties was far higher for Ben and both sides knew it.

"First rule of an ambush," one of the other Sergeants said. "Give the other side a way out and let them see it when the time is right. Yeah, I know this isn't an ambush, but it's still true."

"What's our casualty situation," Ben asked.

"Seventeen dead, Sir," the first Sergeant said. "Eighty-one who can't be moved."

Ben closed his eyes and squeezed the bridge of his nose. "I hate to have to ask," Ben began.

"You don't have to, Sir," the Sergeant said. "Six medics have already volunteered to stay behind with the wounded."

Ben nodded.

"Let's start consolidating the forces for a final push to the west," Ben said. "We'll wait for a lull in the fighting, which should happen any time now. It's been about three hours since their last push and they'll back off before they make another attempt. When they do, we fall back and put everything we have into getting out the back. Use our Bradleys to clear the way through our own defenses."

...

Fighting retreat turned out to be an understatement. While the attacking force to the west was certainly smaller than the other two, either they didn't get the memo to let him go or it had been a feint all along.

The initial push had gone well enough and all of his forces were able to clear the final fence without too much resistance. Part of that, he was sure, was due to the fact that his counterattack had been so unexpected.

That, of course, was when his plan, minimal as it was, met reality and it turned into an every-man-for-himself run for the border–in this case, the Tennessee border.

After what felt like a week, but was in fact only about an hour, the attackers broke off their pursuit. Without air support it was just too dangerous, and the further they got from the base greater the risk of an ambush grew.

With a final shot over Ben's bow from the Abrams, which had been oddly silent during the entire chase, the pursuit was called off and the attackers headed back to the newly 'liberated' Fort Campbell.

Chapter Four

May 27, 2013 - Promised Land Army Base, Natchez Trace State Park, Tennessee

Dan knocked on the door frame of the office Joel used when his duties as Mayor forced him to spend the day in Redemption. "I see we got some new blood," Dan said.

"Yup," Joel said as he looked up from the pile of papers he was working on, "and a pretty good-sized group, too. It looks like the neighborhood or community, or whatever they were relying on, finally collapsed about three weeks ago."

"How'd they know to head here?" Dan asked.

Joel leaned back in his chair and tried to stretch some of the kinks out of his back. "Well, we've been here for almost a year, Dan," Joel said. "Word is bound to have spread that there's *something* going on in Natchez Trace."

Dan made a face. "Yeah, I guess. I mean, *we* found you and all we had to go on was a hunch based on how a bunch of postcards were arranged on a bulletin board," Dan said.

"True," Joel said and shook his head. "You know, I didn't even know about that until you told me? I had to ask Rachael about it later that night. She admitted to it but claimed that she was sure that nobody we wouldn't want finding us would be able to figure it out. I'm glad she was right."

"Me too," Dan said. "I'm really glad she left that clue or we'd have been toast. But back to this new group, where are they setting up?"

"For now," Joel said, "they're in the tents in camp. Now that we've filled the lodge, cabins, and the rest of the houses here in town, that's all we have left."

"At least they've all got wooden sides now," Dan said.

Joel nodded. "After three weeks on the move, they were just happy to have a warm, dry, safe place to sleep."

"How're Rachael and Aurora?" Dan asked, changing topics.

Joel smiled. "They're doing fine. Aurora is doing a great job of keeping us from getting a full night's sleep, like a newborn should, and we're doing our best to keep the world from seeing us at our worst."

"Spoken like a new dad," Dan said with a return smile. "Speaking of which, how are you doing? Not burning too much of the midnight oil?"

"I'm fine," Joel said, "but I really think Ty could use a hand."

Dan made a 'humph' noise and rolled his eyes.

"No, seriously," Joel said. "I think the new group may have brought some kind of bug in with them and Ty's already got a lot on his plate just dealing with the everyday stuff around camp."

"Yeah," Dan said. "Ty loves it when I offer to help. Gives him a chance to lord it over me that he's a doctor and I'm just a medic. I don't even bother asking anymore, Joel. A man's ego can only take so much."

"Well," Joel said, "he really does look like he's running himself ragged. Would you be willing to give it one more try…for me?"

Dan laughed. "Ok," he said, "for you. But seriously, unless there's someone who needs a splinter removed, or maybe an enema, he's not going to let me help out with anything."

...

"Dan," Ty said, "I appreciate the offer, I really do, but this isn't that big of a deal."

Dan was trying to remain calm. He could already tell how this was going to play out by Ty's condescending attitude. Still, he'd promised Joel he'd try, and now that he'd seen what was actually going around...he felt he had to try for his own sake.

"Ty," Dan said, "Dr. Novak, please listen to me. We had something just like this back in our neighborhood. It *killed* my only son. Only eighteen-months old. One day he was with us, the next he was *gone*. It didn't spread like this at first, but a couple of months later it came back, and it started with the kids both times. These are the same symptoms, Ty. I know they are."

"Dan, listen...I'm deeply sorry for your loss. I can't even imagine what that would be like, but you have got to calm down. These symptoms you're so worried about are also the symptoms of a lot of other mostly harmless illnesses. Which you'd know...if you were a doctor."

Dan quietly fumed as Ty continued, oblivious.

"I've got this under control. You didn't see these folks when they first arrived. At the very least they all had somewhat compromised immune systems. Children get hit the hardest with that."

"Ty," Dan started.

"Look," Ty interrupted, "I know you mean well, but I think I've been exposed to more of these things than you have. Go back to town and I'll let you know if anything comes up and I need your help, okay?"

"Right," Dan thought. *"Just like you let me know we were letting* sick people *into the community in the first place?"*

...

"April, honey, I really want you to take a nap," her mother, Jean Oliver, said. "The doctor said you need to get some rest to kick this thing. You've been out with the other children every day since we got here."

"But I'm already feeling better," April whined. "There's a bunch of kids here. I'm not tired, and lying in bed is so-o-o boring."

Jean reached out to check her daughter's forehead for a fever. She didn't feel warm right now, so she gave in. "Ok, but take it easy. Don't run around too much, and if you start coughing I want you to come right back to the tent and lay down. Understood?"

April sighed, but nodded. "Okay, Mom."

"I love you, honey, now go make some friends."

…

"How's Derek handling the transition," Jean asked Stan Bryant, one of the fathers from the neighborhood that had come in with her, while they were starting what little laundry they had.

"He was hoping to meet some of the older kids here in camp since it's the weekend," Stan said. "But he wasn't feeling well this morning. He had a headache and I couldn't get him to eat any breakfast."

Jean shook her head. "April swore up and down she was feeling better, so I let her go out to make some friends. It's probably just that everything's finally catching up with him."

"Probably," Stan said. "He would sometimes get stomachaches and have trouble sleeping when things weren't going well at school. It might just be the stress."

…

Jean came back from the laundry to find April on her cot and inside her sleeping bag.

"Change your mind," she asked with raised eyebrows–until she heard her daughter's teeth chattering. It was easily in the mid-seventies outside, which meant that April must have quite a fever to be shivering like that. Jean hurried to her daughter and felt her forehead.

"Oh, honey, you're burning up!" Jean tried to keep the panic out of her voice and was thankful, for the umpteenth time today that they weren't on the road anymore. "Stay here, honey; I'm going to go get the doctor."

April just nodded weakly and coughed a couple of times as Jean left the tent, and almost ran smack into the doctor on her way out the door.

"Doctor…," Jean looked for the nametag on his shirt but couldn't find it right away and couldn't remember his name off the top of her head. She recognized him, though, as the man who had cleared them for entry into Promised Land.

"Novak, Ma'am," Ty answered for her. "I just came from the Bryant's. It's Ms. Oliver, isn't it?"

"Yes. It's my daughter, April," Jean said as she turned around, and they both walked into the tent. "She was fine this morning, but she came back from playing with some of the kids and now her fever is back."

April was coughing frequently, and shivering hard inside the sleeping bag, despite sweating profusely.

After putting on gloves, Ty felt her forehead and then took her temperature. After checking the digital thermometer he cleared it and took it again; 103.2.

"April, I know you are shivering but I need to listen to your lungs, honey," he said. "We'll get you back under the covers as quick as we can."

April nodded and sat up slowly. Ty listened to her breathing, which was growing more rapid, when she wasn't coughing, and made a bit of a face.

"Ok, lay back down," he said, and took her pulse.

"Ms. Oliver?" Ty said, and nodded towards outside. Ty wanted to let April try to get some sleep.

"Ma'am," Ty started. "April has been on the antibiotics for four days. By now, the cough should have cleared up, and she really shouldn't have a fever of any kind unless the infection is resistant to what we gave her. Since you said she wasn't allergic to penicillin, I put her on something in that family."

Ty stopped speaking as April had a coughing fit. He wanted to listen to how it sounded. "As bad as that sounds, at least she isn't wheezing. Unfortunately, what sounded like an upper-respiratory infection a few days ago, and should have been responding to antibiotics, has settled deeper into her lungs." Ty said. "I'm worried about pneumonia at this point, and I think we need to change the antibiotics. I'd like to move her to town, where we have a more permanent clinic, as well."

Jean nodded, "Whatever you say."

"I'll go talk to the Major and get everything arranged," Ty said, and then reached into his bag and pulled out a packet of ibuprofen. "Give her these while I'm gone, we need to start getting the fever down."

"Thank you," Jean said.

"Just doing my job, Ma'am," Ty said.

…

"This is Dan," he said as he answered the radio.

"Dan," Ty said. "Have you got a minute?"

"Um, sure," Dan said, a little taken aback to receive a call from the doctor after their run-in this morning.

"We may have a situation developing," Ty said, "and I need to know if you've noticed anything out of the ordinary in town."

Dan leaned forward and rubbed his eyes. "Nothing's come up over the last week or so, no," Dan said. "It doesn't have to do with the group that just came in does it?"

"Possibly," Ty said. "I'll let you know if I need anything else."

"Aaaaand I'm back to being shunned," Dan said after the radio cut off.

...

"What's going on, Sergeant," Mallory asked, with no preamble, as Ty came into the command tent.

"I'm not entirely sure," Ty said. "We've had some lingering colds crop up over the last couple of months but…"

Mallory looked up at Ty's pause.

After a breath, Ty continued. "It looks like something came in with the last group."

"How bad is it?" Mallory asked. "And is it something that we can stop with a quarantine of the group?"

"I don't have an answer to either of those questions yet, unfortunately," Ty said. "Quarantine might be a good idea to contain whatever it is, but it might be too late, too. It's been almost a week, and there's been a lot of contact already–especially between the kids. We don't have to panic yet. Like I said, I don't really know how bad it is."

Mallory sat back and steepled her fingers. "How much contact has there been between the camp and Redemption," she asked.

"Minimal," Ty said after thinking for a few seconds, "just due to logistics."

Mallory nodded. "But not none," she said.

"No," Ty shook his head and answered the Major's next question before she asked. "Standard procedure is to isolate the sick, and quarantine those who are likely to become ill from the rest of the healthy population. I'll find out who has been going back and forth between camp and town and confine them here for the duration."

Ty sighed. "I even have the legal authority to do that."

Mallory nodded.

"Joel is not going to be happy," Ty said.

"Why," Mallory asked.

"He's been going back and forth for the last couple of days," Ty said.

Mallory kept her face blank and noticed that Ty had done the same. Both of them had come to the same realization, although Mallory had taken a little longer. Aurora.

...

"I'm *what?*" Joel shouted.

Mallory had Ty with her to break the news to Joel. Ty had been right, he wasn't taking it well. "We have a medical…situation," she said.

"Joel," Ty said, "we don't know exactly what they brought in or how it's transmitted. We don't know what the incubation period is, nothing. Your contact was fairly minimal, considering, but you have been here a lot during the day, so you're going to need to be included in the quarantine."

Joel shook his head. "I don't think you understand," he said. He looked to have aged ten years in the ten seconds since they told him. The horror was etched on his face. "I have a two-month-old baby."

"I know," Mallory said, "and I know taking care of her round-the-clock without you is going to be hard on Rachael, but this is really best for both of them."

"NO!" Joel shouted again. "You still don't understand! I have a two-month-old baby, who hasn't had *any* vaccinations, for *anything!*"

Joel looked at both Mallory and Ty as it slowly began to dawn on Ty. "I've been back and forth for the last four days," he said. "I could have already exposed Aurora to whatever it is."

By now the color had drained completely from Ty's face. "Joel," he said. "I'm sorry, I didn't even think about that until just now."

Ty looked at Mallory, back at Joel, and then at Mallory again. "I have to go," Ty said. "I have to get in touch with Dan. He needs to know everything that's going on, and possibly set up an isolation ward in town. I'm sorry, Joel, I just didn't think."

"But you did," Mallory said after Ty was gone. "Because that's what you do. The first day I met you, you were thinking about fires, and disease, and medications running out."

Mallory shook her head. "How do you do it?"

"Not now, Mal," Joel said.

"I'm serious, Joel," Mallory said. "I can't say they will be ok, but given how quickly the little girl started showing symptoms, I would think that something would have happened with your daughter by now. I hate to say that, but there it is. I know this is your family we're talking about, and your baby girl. But it's been your family we've been talking about all along."

Joel nodded but was floored by what he felt was Mallory's rather cavalier attitude about his family, specifically his wife and newborn daughter. "I need to call Rachael and tell her before someone else does," Joel said. "She deserves to hear it from me."

Mallory gave him a small smile, "You can do it in here," she said. "Let me know when you're done."

...

Rachael was crying, holding Aurora in both arms, and trying to hold the stupid radio all at the same time.

"I really wasn't around any of the new folks that much," Joel said, trying to calm her down.

"Who knows how much it takes, though?" Rachael sobbed.

"I know, hon, I know," Joel said. "Ty is going to talk to Dan and have him set up some kind of isolation ward to keep things, well, isolated, I guess. I don't actually know how it works but I'm sure they do."

Rachael wasn't in the mood to be cheered up. "How long," she asked.

"I don't know," Joel sighed. "Neither Ty nor the Major said. I can't imagine that it could go on for too long. It'll be ok. There'll be people to help take care of you. I'll insist on that. I'll find some volunteers to go into isolation with you if I can, ok?"

"What about Maya and Josh," Rachael asked.

"They're going to have to stay up here with me," Joel said. "We already have a tent for the three of us."

Rachael nodded and then realized that Joel couldn't see her, and blew a snot bubble when she tried to laugh. "Ok," she said. "You have to promise to follow the quarantine, all three of you. Stay healthy so you can come home."

Rachael barely held back another sob when she thought about her other two children. "Give them my love," she said, "and keep them safe too."

"I promise."

Chapter Five

May 29, 2013 - Promised Land Army Base, Natchez Trace State Park, Tennessee

"The raid on Ft. Campbell was two days ago," Mallory said. "We should have heard something from Ben by now. Or at least something from one of the groups that evacuated before the raid even started."

"Major Weaver, from Bragg, did check in late yesterday," Sergeant Evan 'Sparky' Lake said. "They let a pretty large group go after a little over a day of fighting. It's possible they just haven't been in a position to check in."

Mallory was visibly distressed about not hearing from or about Ben, and the fact that she was so overly interested in Ben's well-being was driving Kyle nuts. Every time she mentioned Ben, even indirectly, was yet another reminder that any possibility of a relationship between she and Kyle was slipping further and further away. The thing that hurt the worst was that she didn't even realize she was doing it, or seem to care.

"Give them time, Major," Eric said. "They may just be laying low for the time being. We have thirty Black Hawks and their crews to take care of now, it's not like you don't have enough on your plate."

...

May 29, 2013 - Fort Rucker, Alabama

Major Bradley Sanford was early for a meeting with Colonel Spencer Olsen and was about to knock on the door of his office when he heard the Colonel's raised voice. Apparently, somebody was getting chewed out inside. Sanford wasn't usually one to eavesdrop, but it was hard not to when you were standing right in front of the door, and you never knew when a piece of gossip may end up being valuable.

"I understand that, Sir," Sanford heard Olsen say through the door.

"Sir," Sanford thought. *"Who is Olsen talking to in there? For that matter, who could Olsen be reporting to?"*

"Realistically," Olsen said, "probably at *least* six months before the next phase can be implemented."

"The next phase," Sanford thought, and looked around to see who else might be able to hear the Colonel. Nobody was close enough to hear, though, as Sanford looked at his watch and continued to wait and listen, and wonder. *"The next phase of what?"*

"I've taken care of the holdout," Olsen said. "Two days ago. Fort Campbell was taken, intact, with minimal loss of life or resources on our side."

"Sir," Olsen said, obviously trying to hold onto his patience. "*I* care about the loss of life! My soldiers aren't a commodity, and they certainly can't be replaced at the drop of a hat."

"No, Sir," Olsen said after another pause. "Well, of course California has already been disarmed. It was all but disarmed *before* the power went out!"

"Heh," Sanford thought, *"good point, but what is he talking about?"*

Olsen paused again as the person on the other end of the line spoke. "With all due respect, Sir, you gave me the Southeastern United States." Olsen said. "Tennessee, North Carolina, South Carolina, Georgia, Kentucky, Virginia, and West Virginia. Sir, are you aware that there are people living in the West Virginia mountains that still don't know the power is even out?"

By now it was obvious to Sanford that Olsen was alone in his office, but on the radio with someone. That begged the question, who in the world could he possibly be on the radio *with*?

"No, I'm *not* quite finished," Olsen said. It didn't seem to matter. From the sound of disgust Olsen had just made, Sanford was pretty sure the other end of the line had already broken the connection. Sanford heard a drawer slam shut and then waited for a count of ten before turning and knocking on the door.

"Come in!" Olsen yelled.

…

"Problem, Major?" Olsen asked, once their meeting had ended.

"No, Sir," Sanford said.

"Are you sure," Olsen asked again.

Sanford realized, belatedly, he'd been wearing his emotions on his sleeve and the Colonel had picked up on his unease. He needed to cover himself to get the Colonel off his back. "Absolutely, Sir," he said. "More of a question, if I may."

"You can ask, Son," Olsen said. "No promises of an answer."

Sanford nodded in understanding.

"What's our endgame, Sir?" Sanford asked. "What are we ultimately trying to accomplish? We haven't heard from the President, or anyone else in the chain of succession, ever. We found and dusted off ARCLiTE, and deployed it basically on our own authority …so," Sanford shrugged, "what's the end goal?"

Olsen leaned forward and folded his arms on his desk. "Son," he said, "I'm going to say this one time. Things are under control. You're doing a fine job following orders, and as long as you continue to, things will work out just fine for you."

The weight of Olsen's gaze, and the only thinly-veiled threat, dried Sanford's mouth.

"Trust me," Olsen said. "You don't want to end up on the wrong side of this one."

...

May 30, 2013 - On the road between Fort Campbell and Promised Land

"Do we have a final count yet," Ben asked the current radio operator in his Humvee.

Ben had been on the move for two days and had slept for maybe four hours total since leaving the base. He still couldn't use the word 'abandon', but he was too much of a realist to use 'egress'.

"Sir," the Sergeant said, "we had to leave eighty-one that were too wounded to move. We lost seventeen. Nobody new since the final push out the back."

Ben shook his head. *"Including the walking wounded, that's almost three-hundred men."*

"Sir," the Sergeant manning the radio interrupted Ben's reverie. "The lead Humvee is requesting a destination."

The group Ben headed made quite a sight with all of their Light Attack Vehicles, Humvees, civilian vehicles, and heavy equipment. Coordinating the movements of this mixed force over deteriorating highways and side roads was quickly becoming problematic.

He had a limited supply of fuel and rations, so he couldn't keep moving forever. Ben reached for the radio.

...

"Ben!" Mallory almost shouted when she got on the radio in her office. "Where have you been? Are you ok?"

"Good to talk to you, too," Ben said. "I've been around. We've had to keep our heads down for the last couple of days to keep the heat off of anyone else. We took some casualties and," Ben paused, and then swallowed, "I ended up leaving almost a hundred men on base because we couldn't move them."

"I'm sorry," Mallory said. "But most of you made it out in one piece?"

"That we did," Ben said. "Which brings me to the other reason for this call; we need a place to call home."

"*Of course,*" Mallory almost said without thinking. Instead, she caught herself and was more realistic with her answer.

"Ben," she said. "It's complicated. I hate to have to say that but it is."

"Okay," Ben said. "Go on."

"Well," Mallory said, "a couple of things. First of all, we have an illness of unknown origin in camp, and everyone would have to be under quarantine. Second, because of the quarantine, I don't know where we would put your people. Speaking of which, how many of you are there?"

Ben was silent for several seconds and Mallory wondered if she'd lost him. "Ben," she said, "you still there?"

"Yeah," Ben said. "I've got just under forty-five hundred people."

It was Mallory's turn to be silent.

"We're not coming empty-handed, Mallory," Ben said. "We have food, fuel, heavy equipment, and munitions. We've also got everything we need to rough it for the time being."

Mallory took a deep breath and keyed the microphone. "We'll find a place, Ben," she said. "When will you get here?"

"How long do you need," Ben asked. "I've still got a lot I need to coordinate on my end."

"Can you give me a week," Mallory asked. "I may be able to have some land cleared by then."

"That'll be fine. See you then," Ben said.

"Ben," Mallory said, before they signed off, "be safe."

...

Karen was fanning herself and rubbing the back of her neck when Eric walked into their tent. "Long day?" he asked.

"No more than usual," she said. "I'm just tired, and this headache is killing me." Karen rolled her head to try to stretch her neck.

"Early bedtime after dinner," Eric said as he sat behind her on the pair of cots they kept pushed together in the corner of their tent to take over massaging, and realized her skin felt much warmer than usual.

"I'm really not hungry," Karen said.

"What have you had to eat today, babe," Eric asked.

Karen shrugged. "Not much, I just haven't been hungry, why?"

"I think you have a fever, and something *is* going around camp," Eric said, and reached around to feel her forehead. "Yup, you have a fever."

Eric opened his canteen and offered it to her. "Drink some water and get in bed, I'm going to get Ty."

"I'm fine, I just need some rest, maybe," Karen said.

Eric shook his head. "No, you are not fine," he said. "Yes, you are going to start with some rest but I'm going to get Ty. Drink the water. You haven't eaten today and I bet you haven't had anything to drink either. I don't want you getting dehydrated. Be in bed when I get back," Eric said. "You have ten minutes or you may be embarrassed when Ty walks in on you changing."

Karen acted like she was going to argue, but at the look on Eric's face she just nodded.

"Good girl," he said, and left the tent.

...

"Headache, fever, she hasn't eaten lunch and isn't interested in dinner, and I had to force her to drink some water before I left," Eric said to Ty once he tracked him down and was following him back to a makeshift office.

Ty rubbed his forehead with a hand and then asked, "Anything else?"

"I realized she was warm when I was rubbing her shoulders," Eric said, mistaking her sore neck for tight shoulders.

Ty nodded. "I'll meet you at your tent. I need to finish here first and look a few things up."

...

Eric came back to the tent to find Karen sulking in bed. "Ty will be here soon."

"This is stupid," she said.

"He looked concerned when I told him," Eric replied.

"Of course he did," Karen said and rolled her eyes. "He's a doctor, that's what we pay him to do."

Eric furrowed his brow. "He's not getting paid to do anything, Karen. He wanted to look a few things up before he came over," Eric said. "We have quarantine in camp, babe. Something's obviously going around, and I don't think he wants to take any chances."

Karen closed her eyes and took a deep breath. "I know, I'm sorry," she said. "I don't know what's gotten into me. I'm tired and...I don't know."

Eric sat down by the cots and held her hand under the covers. "It's ok. I love you. Go to sleep if you can, and we'll deal with whatever it is when Ty gets here."

Ty showed up about ten minutes later and knocked on the frame around the tent flap.

"Come in," Eric said.

Karen squinted at the streaming sunlight as the flap opened and shut.

Eric squeezed Karen's hand and then gave the seat to Ty.

"So, Karen, feeling a bit under the weather," he said.

"I guess so," Karen said. "Mostly just a headache and fever, though." Karen put the lie to that by trying to roll her head again, which Eric had been noticing her doing since he'd returned to the tent.

"How about your neck," Ty asked.

"Kind of stiff, I guess," Karen said.

"Appetite," Ty asked.

Karen frowned and shook her head. Ty picked up the canteen and shook it, noticing that it was mostly empty, so at least she had drunk some water.

"Stomach-ache," Ty asked.

"No," Karen said.

Ty nodded and pulled out his pen light. "Okay, let me check your eyes," but as soon as he swung the light towards Karen's face, she flinched and squinted, and he turned off the light.

Ty sighed and nodded.

"Eric, come sit down," Ty said.

Eric felt his stomach drop, but came and sat on the side of the cot and reached under the covers to hold Karen's hand.

"Karen, have you ever heard of Meningitis?" Ty asked.

Eric and Karen had had no warning, and both of them gasping in stereo would have been comical if the situation hadn't been so serious.

Karen nodded weakly. "How bad is it?"

"I can't put this mildly, and I don't have the tests to make a definitive diagnosis, but you are showing all of the classic symptoms of bacterial meningitis," Ty said. "The good news is that if it is, I may *finally* know what is going around camp."

Ty sighed. "The bad news is that I have no idea how far along it is, or if we have the right kind of antibiotics to treat it."

Ty reached out and grabbed Eric's hand and Karen's shoulder. "I'm going to give you the strongest antibiotic we have, but because I honestly don't know how far along it is, or even what strain we're dealing with, I can't know for sure if it'll be the right antibiotic."

Eric took a deep breath and squeezed Ty's hand. "Thank you for being honest with us. I think I speak for Karen, too, when I say that it's better than false hope or an outright lie."

Karen nodded and swallowed. "How long before I'll start to feel better?"

"I brought the antibiotics with me," Ty said, "just in case. I want you to start now. It's intravenous–sorry, an IV–twice a day. I'll start a saline IV now and add the antibiotics to it. We'll keep the IV going as long as we need to. It's at least a ten-day course, though, so it could be a week before you are feeling much better."

Ty was fighting back tears, because he knew at this point that there was a real possibility that nothing he could do would make any difference for any of the sick patients in camp or in town. The best case would be that they had caught it in time and the antibiotics they had were correct for this strain. Karen could start feeling better in three or four days. In a worst-case scenario, they all had a drug-resistant strain of streptococcus pneumoniae, causing pneumonia or meningitis, and people would either get over it on their own, be left with severe neurological damage, or be dead within the next week.

"I'll be back tomorrow morning, or have one of the medics come by," Ty said.

"Thank you," Karen said, "for everything."

Ty nodded and left as Eric and Karen hugged.

Chapter Six

Eric laid out a sleeping bag on the floor of the tent next to their cots, but didn't sleep at all the first night. He'd asked Ty if he needed to worry about catching anything from Karen, but Ty told him not to worry as long as they weren't kissing and she wasn't coughing. He'd stayed off of their cots–mostly to make her more comfortable, and so she could get as much sleep as possible.

Ty showed up at 5:45 in the morning to give Karen her meds. "It feels like your fever has come down a little bit," he said. "It's probably a little early for the antibiotics to have done too much but are you feeling any better?" As subjective as patient reaction was in a case like this, it would still be the best barometer to the efficacy of the drug.

Karen shrugged. "I was able to sleep, but I don't know if that was just being tired. I'm hungry for breakfast," she said.

Ty nodded. "That's definitely a good sign," he said. "Stay in bed, eat when you can, but get as much rest as possible."

Karen yawned and nodded and then pointed at Eric.

Ty was a little alarmed at first until Karen clarified after her yawn. "No, tell him the same thing."

"Of course," Ty said, relieved. "Eric, you won't do anyone any good if you make yourself sick by not getting any rest. Sleep when Karen sleeps, Doctor's orders. I'll talk to the Major."

"Fair enough," Eric said. "I'll get breakfast for both of us and then we'll *both* take a nap," he looked at Karen, "deal?"

"Deal," she said.

"Things are getting worse around camp so I won't be able to stop by as much as I'd like, I'm afraid" Ty said on the way out. "Unfortunately, just knowing what's causing it won't miraculously cure everyone, and more people are coming down with this, or pneumonia, every day."

"Do what you can, and try to get some rest yourself," Eric said and Karen nodded in agreement. "We need *you* healthy right now more than we need *me*."

…

Ty was right, and things really did seem to be going from bad to worse around camp. When the medic came to give Karen her antibiotics that night he was wearing a mask, and he gave Eric a handful of disposable masks, with instructions to wear them whenever he was out of the tent.

Breakfast the following morning was a surreal experience. Every cough or sniffle was followed by the sound of someone scooting over on their bench seat, or their chair sliding on the wooden floor. Nobody sat right next to or directly across from anyone else. Eric caught up to Joel after the meal and only really felt like he was allowed to talk to him because they were both wearing masks.

"How's Karen doing," Joel asked. "Rachael sends her best, and she's in our prayers. The kids are really worried."

"I think she's doing a little better, actually" Eric said. "The fever comes and goes but she's still got the headache and the sensitivity to light."

Eric held up a covered tray that he had taken out of the mess hall. "She had an appetite yesterday, though," he said, "and Ty says that's a good sign. She's tough, she'll be ok."

"How are *you* managing," Joel asked, noticing how bloodshot Eric's eyes were. "You don't look like you've been getting much sleep."

"Me," Eric asked and shrugged. "I'm fine. I really didn't have my life turned upside-down. Your family is split in half right now. How are you guys handling it? How're Rachael and Aurora?"

Eric could see the emotions warring on Joel's face until eventually concern won out. "Rachael says they're doing fine," he said. "Sheri's down there with her while Chuck is out checking on the availability of coal at the New Johnsonville Steam Plant. She's also got almost a dozen other people who went into isolation with her down in town, including another family. It's rough on the kids, though. They weren't able to bring any of their own clothes or other belongings from town up into camp, and now we're back to sleeping in tents."

"Hey," Eric said. "The tents aren't too bad now. I sleep in a tent."

. . .

"Time for breakfast," Eric said when he got back to Karen.

"Not hungry," Karen said.

Eric checked her for a fever, which she didn't have, thank goodness.

"Babe, you have to eat," Eric said. "Even just a little bit is better than nothing. You have to keep your strength up."

"I need to rest," Karen said and rolled over. "And I need for this to just be done."

Eric put the tray on a folding chair next to their cots and sat down beside her. "It's just going to take time," he said. "Ty said it could be a week before you really start to feel better."

He reached out to massage her shoulders and neck and she flinched away. "Still sore," he asked.

"The neck is, yeah," she said.

. . .

Today was Karen's third full day on antibiotics, and Ty had come by in person a couple of hours ago to switch her IV. Over the past few days, Karen had broken a fever at least a dozen times and her appetite had come and gone almost as often. It had been a long day and Karen was finally sleeping quietly, so Eric decided to move from his sleeping bag onto the cots to be closer to her. As he was drifting off, he reached over to hold her hand and felt a slight tremor to the bed frame, and in her arm.

Eric was immediately wide awake. He sat up and turned up the lantern and saw that Karen was shaking...*hard.*

Eric jumped out of bed, flipped his cot out of the way, and grabbed his radio off the pile of clothes on the folding chair. "Mayday, mayday, mayday. This is Eric; I need the doctor to my tent NOW!" Eric dropped the radio back onto the pile of clothes.

"Thank you, Sparky, for fixing these!" Eric thought.

Eric's radio crackled, "I'm on my way, Eric," and then went dead. The response registered with Eric, but only peripherally. He was on the bed now, holding Karen and trying to keep her from hurting herself as the seizure increased in intensity.

He barely heard the running boots approaching their tent, and didn't look up as three people stormed inside—Ty in the lead with his medic's rucksack.

Karen was still breathing and the seizure, although terrifying to Eric, didn't seem to be getting any worse. Ty checked Karen's eyes, but they had rolled up to the point that you could only see the whites.

"What's causing this?" Eric screamed.

"Swelling," Ty said, "against the brain. That's what meningitis *is.*"

"Can't we do something," Eric begged as he looked from Karen to Ty.

"Right now," Ty said, "we're doing all we can. The seizure isn't getting any worse and she's still breathing."

The seizure was coming to an end after less than five minutes and Ty checked Karen's pulse and breathing. Both were elevated, but not dangerously so. Her eyes were back to normal but...

"What," Eric asked when he saw that Ty was obviously concerned with Karen's eyes.

"Just a minute, please," Ty said as he checked Karen's pupils repeatedly and then swore under his breath.

Ty looked at the two medics that had accompanied him and nodded to the door. Apparently they wouldn't be needed and they were dismissed.

"Eric," Ty said, "sit down."

"I am sitting," Eric said and crouched nearer to Karen on the bed.

"Please, Eric," Ty said, "on a chair."

Eric realized that Ty was trying not to let his agitation show and slowly stood. He pulled on his pants as he realized for the first time that he was in his boxers and a t-shirt, and brought one of the chairs next to the bed.

Ty was checking Karen's vital signs again.

"What's going on," Eric asked.

Ty checked Karen's eyes one more time and then turned his attention to Eric.

"Eric," Ty said. "It's common, not normal but common, for someone to be unresponsive after a seizure. This is different. Karen is most likely in a coma right now."

"No," Eric said and started to stand up.

Ty put his hand on Eric's arm to keep him in his chair.

"I'm sorry, Eric," Ty said. "I'll do what I can, but I have to be honest...unless the swelling goes down..."

"The antibiotics," Eric asked.

"Right now it's a waiting game," Ty shook his head. "I'm sorry, Eric."

"You keep saying that," Eric said, "but she's not dead. You don't know Karen like I do. She could get better; she could come out of it. If it's possible to beat this, Karen will beat it."

"But you need to prepare yourself," Ty said. "We don't have the facilities to treat her, or anyone in camp, like we used to. You need to know that she might not."

...

Eric spent the next two days by Karen's side; holding her hand, talking to her, trying to coax her out of her coma. He was convinced that if he said the right thing, triggered the right memory, touched the right nerve, that she'd come back.

He slept fitfully in the chair, and was occasionally startled awake when one of the medics came in to change her IV. He realized near the end of the second day that the IV was the only nutrition she was getting at this point.

Twice he thought he felt her squeeze his hand, and yelled for the medics, but both times turned out to be minor seizures. Neither was as bad as the one that had put her in a coma, but they weren't a good sign.

"I'm not taking her off of the antibiotics," Ty said. "We don't know if they're working or not, and if they are, we need to give them a chance to do their job. The fact that she's still having seizures isn't encouraging, though. I'm sorry, Eric."

"Is there anything I can do," Eric asked. "I feel so helpless. I'm just *sitting* here."

"She knows you're there," Ty said. "If the antibiotics are working and she comes out of the coma, she'll know you were there. Don't underestimate the power of your presence."

...

One of the medics had brought Eric dinner when he realized that he hadn't left the tent all day except to use the latrine. If something happened, Eric wanted to be there for it no matter what it was. He ate with his eyes on Karen, watching her for some sign that she was coming out of it.

It was because he was sitting up and not hunched over her hand, and could see more of her body, that he noticed the exact moment she stopped breathing. He didn't recognize it at first, only that something profound had changed. After about ten seconds, he realized what it was and called for help—after almost dropping his untouched plate of food on the floor.

"*Karen!*" he yelled, knowing at this point that it was a futile gesture. He fumbled for her wrist to check for a pulse, hands shaking like he'd been injected with one-hundred cups of coffee. He pressed his ear to her chest, listening for any beat at all, just as Ty ran into the tent. He'd been on his way to another patient when he'd heard Eric yell.

He saw that Karen wasn't breathing right away and checked for a pulse at the throat. If her heart had stopped there really wasn't any point in CPR.

"Eric," Ty said, and gently took Karen's wrist from his hand. "She's gone."

Eric nodded and as he hung his head the first tear fell to the floor.

"I need to go get a couple of the medics," Ty said.

Eric closed his eyes for a heartbeat and then turned to look at Karen's still form; his fiancée in all but name. The woman he had wanted to marry but had never found the time or words to ask. Now she was gone.

"We need..." Ty started.

"*I* need a couple of minutes," Eric snapped and then took a deep breath. "Surely you can give me five minutes."

Ty closed his eyes and nodded and then left the tent.

Eric brushed Karen's hair with trembling fingers and tried to get some of the tangles out. Karen wasn't really that fastidious, even though she claimed to be a girly-girl. She looked calm now.

"How am I supposed to go on without you?" Eric thought. *"Wow that is so selfish. I'm sorry. I feel like I've let you down again."*

"You're beautiful, you know that?" Eric said. "You'll always be beautiful. I love you. I was going to ask you to marry me. I even have a ring, right over there…"

Eric got up and went to his trunk, got out the ring, and brought it back to the bed.

"See," he said, and showed it to Karen. "I even had it before the lights went out." Eric was starting to sob.

"I, uhm, I'm not going to be using this ever, now, and we were together for so long, and one of the things you said the night we lost power was that you were waiting for me to propose," Eric said. He had to stop talking for several seconds; the words couldn't get past the strangled feeling in his throat. Finally, he wiped his eyes and nose with the back of his hand, unable to keep up with the tears but allowing himself to see. "I'm going to go ahead and give this to you now."

Eric gently pushed the ring onto Karen's left ring finger, kissed her hand, and kissed her tenderly on the lips. "I had it the whole time, babe. I'm so sorry. I love you so much, Karen. Oh, God, Karen, I love you so much."

Chapter Seven

June 2, 2013 - Redemption

Rachael had been up since the sound of the steady rain and water dripping into buckets woke her up shortly after dawn. Sleeping in wasn't an option if she and Aurora were going to have a warm bath this morning. The fire she had going outside, under the carport, needed to be stoked, water needed to be brought to a boil, and at least a dozen buckets of water needed to be hauled in to the tub.

As Rachael was lugging buckets into the bathroom, she took a moment to appreciate the roof over her head, leaking though it was. *"At least we're in a house now,"* Rachael thought, *"and not that drafty cabin, or worse, a tent."* With the thought of the tent came the realization, again, that Joel and the kids were in tents up at the base in Promised Land. *"How miserable must they be right now,"* she wondered.

After every trip with the buckets, Rachael peeked in on Aurora who was still fast asleep in the bedroom. As much as she wanted to be able to watch her baby every second of the day, she knew there was no way she'd be able to do so. One of the first things they'd done when they moved into the house in town was to put the mattress in the master-bedroom directly on the floor so that there was less chance of Aurora rolling off of it while unattended.

On her third set of buckets, and after one set of hot water from their tea kettle and Dutch oven, Rachael heard Aurora making noise and babbling like she did every morning. She dumped the two buckets she was carrying into the tub and went to get her baby.

"Well good *morning!*" Rachael said, and was greeted with a giant, open-mouth gummy grin.

"Let's get you fed so Mommy can get back to work," Rachael said.

Rachael treasured the time she spent nursing her daughter, but hoped this wouldn't be one of her marathon sessions. The last thing she needed was for the Dutch oven to boil over into the fire, or for the tea kettle to scorch. It wasn't like she could go down to the super-center and get a new one.

. . .

As soon as Aurora was finished, Rachael carried her into the living room and laid her on a large square of blankets. Living in a house with carpet and not being able to vacuum, well, Rachael never thought the day would come that she would wish for a working vacuum cleaner.

She retrieved the buckets from the bedroom and then carefully carried the hot water from the outdoor fireplace under the carport where it had been heating, and dumped it in the tub. She set one more Dutch oven of water to heat and carried two more buckets full buckets of cold water from the rain gutter cistern at the corner of the house into the bathroom.

"You know, for as much as these weigh," she thought, *"these buckets really don't hold a lot of water."*

The tub was as full as it was going to get without cooling off too much, so she gathered their laundry and the remaining clean towel-half. Nobody used full towels anymore; it was too much work to clean a whole towel when you could use half a towel and you got just as dry.

Once everything was ready, she stripped down, added her clothes to the laundry pile, and went to get Aurora. She undressed her baby girl and then stepped carefully into the lukewarm bathwater.

...

The best part of the bath, aside from getting clean, was the soap. One of the women in town made the most *heavenly* herbal goat's-milk soap. She'd been making it almost the exact same way since before the power went out and it was amazing. All by itself it made the bath worthwhile.

Rachael tried not to think about the fact that she would never have taken a bath with her older two when they were this age. Instead, she focused on the obvious joy Aurora took in splashing and the fact that she was able to take a warm bath in the tub.

Once they were both clean and before the water was too cold, she climbed out and toweled them both off, starting with Aurora. She put her baby in her last clean towel-diaper and a long gown made out of a cut-down military blouse and took her back into the living room.

Rachael wrapped a blanket around herself, combed out her wet hair, and then set to work on the laundry in the tepid water. As she finished each piece, she wrung it out and took it to the carport where she had a clothesline set up. She couldn't hang it up in the yard because it was raining, so this was going to have to do.

Once the laundry was done, she went into the living room to nurse Aurora again on the couch.

...

Just as Aurora finished nursing, there was a knock at the door.

"Of course," Rachael said, *"and here I am looking like I'm dressed for a toga party."*

After Rachael got herself put back together, with Aurora firmly on her hip, she went to open the door, knowing it could only be one of a handful of people who were in isolation with her during the quarantine.

"Look, it's Aunt Sheri," Rachael said to Aurora, who giggled.

"C'mon in," Rachael said and opened the door all the way to let Sheri in. She hadn't taken a good look at her guest yet.

Sheri didn't say anything right away, just stood stock-still in the doorway.

Rachael had been looking at Aurora while she held the door, expecting Sheri to come right in, and when she didn't, Rachael realized something was wrong. Sheri hugged her arms tightly around herself and Rachael saw, finally, that her eyes were red from crying.

A lump rose in Rachael's throat and she had to swallow two or three times before she could speak.

"Joel," she thought. *"The kids?"*

"What is it Sheri," she finally asked as she reached out with her free hand and pulled Sheri inside and then closed the door.

"Sit down," Rachael said, and then sat next to her on the couch. "What is it?"

A tear crept down Sheri's right cheek just before she spoke. "It's Karen," she said. "Karen's gone, Rachael."

. . .

June 10, 2013 - Promised Land Army Base, Natchez Trace State Park, Tennessee

"Eric, I," Kyle paused after knocking on the tent frame around the door.

"Didn't anyone teach you it's polite to wait to be told to come in?" Eric asked without looking up.

"Sorry," Kyle said. "Are you moving into a different tent, or into the town?"

Eric did finally stop the packing he was doing and stood up, but didn't look at Kyle. "Something like that, yeah."

Kyle grabbed the closer of the two folding chairs in the tent, and took a seat. "Talk to me, Eric," he said, leaning forward. "I'm not saying spill your guts and have a good cry, but you need to talk to somebody and you need to do it yesterday."

"Not now," Eric started.

"Yes, now," Kyle interrupted. "Cut the crap and the macho bravado and talk to me."

"What do you want from me?" Eric said as he turned around, eyes red and puffy.

"Honesty and some emotion, for starters," Kyle said. "Don't hit me, but it's been a week since the funeral. You've been walking around like a robot. Nobody can get more than a half-a-dozen words out of you at a time. You're 'fine' when they ask, which you obviously aren't–nor should you be."

Eric just stood there with an undershirt in one hand, a pair of socks in the other; shoulders slumped, looking at Kyle.

"Sit down," Kyle said. "Put that down and talk to me."

Eric collapsed onto the two cots he'd been sharing with Karen until a week ago–the first time he'd sat on them, much less slept on them, since she'd died.

"There's nothing left for me here," Eric said. "I don't care anymore."

It was all Kyle could do to keep his jaw off the floor, but he didn't so much as twitch.

"About anything," Kyle prompted.

"I know it doesn't make sense, but yeah," Eric said. "Everything is up and running and there isn't really any reason for me to stick around. Mallory doesn't need *me*, specifically. The base–the military side of things–has been running smoothly for months. Frankly, I don't know that I did all that much to help get everyone out here."

"Well," Kyle said, "don't sell yourself too short. You and I both know that a large part of that semi-truck group wouldn't have come if not for you. You apparently made quite the impression on Mr. Grace that first day."

"And I haven't done much since," Eric said. "I'm a techie, Kyle, a geek. Not quite as bad as Sparky but that's really what I do. Mallory only promoted me because I had the seniority. That and she needed *somebody* with at least some command experience to back her up. Honestly though, I've been next to useless recently.

Eric sighed. "I'm done, though, Kyle," he said. "They don't need me and I really don't need them." Eric looked over at the old-school Alice pack he was filling. "I'm leaving."

"Where to," Kyle asked.

"To be honest, I'm not completely sure yet," Eric said. "I don't want to be so far away that if something happened I would be completely SOL, but I need to go, and I think it needs to be a clean, permanent break."

Kyle nodded and chewed the inside of his cheek for a couple of seconds. "Do me a favor," Kyle said. "Don't leave just yet."

Eric squinted his eyes and was about to say something, but Kyle interrupted him.

"No, I'm not going to say anything to the Major, or anything like that," Kyle said. "I'm coming with you."

"Wait a minute," Eric started.

"I'm not asking for your permission, Eric," Kyle said and held up his hand to keep Eric from talking. "I'm coming with you; I just need a little time to get ready. I'll even tell you why."

"Fair enough," Eric said. "You know why I'm deserting; I should know why you're doing it, too."

"Ouch," Kyle winced.

Kyle took a deep breath and then began. "Ben Franklin," was all he said.

"Really," Eric said. "You've got a beef with the guy who discovered electricity? I mean, sure, we all miss it and…"

"No, not that Ben Franklin, wise guy," Kyle said, "the other one, the one from Fort Campbell; Mallory's big, strong hero."

Eric was stunned for a second and then it hit him, and, grieving or not, he was smart enough to bite his tongue.

"Nothing?" Kyle asked.

"Nope," Eric said. "This is your baby, your turn to talk."

"So, what's my problem?" Kyle asked. "What's so wrong that I'd desert? I've wasted a *decade* on her, Eric. Ten years I've been in the unit. I was the one who was there for her when that POS husband of hers left. I'm the one who…convinced him that it would be a bad idea to go after her for alimony."

Kyle looked over at Eric with death in his eyes, "That does not leave this tent, ever. You don't tell anyone, you don't ever tell Mallory, you don't even bring it up with me again. Clear?"

"As glass," Eric said.

Kyle nodded. "I know I haven't been her right hand, but when something needed to get done I took care of it. She knows who she can count on, and over the last ten years I've passed up more than one promotion to stay where I am, or where I was."

"Eric, I'd even have left the Army if I had to, because of the BS regulations about relationships between Officers and Enlisted and chain-of-command. But now there's Mr. Wonderful, Mr. Super Hero, Major Ben Franklin. He had his own base, and his own command, and everything. He even saved her life."

"So," Eric said, "is this just your observation, or has something happened?"

Eric saw Kyle's hand tighten into a fist and was glad there wasn't something in it.

"It started on the day we lost access to the satellites," Kyle said. "I rounded the corner and caught the Majors in an embrace. I did an about-face before either of them saw me, but from what I did see, it was a real doozey."

"They're old friends from boot, Kyle." Eric said. "They hadn't seen each other in a long time. Plus, he'd just pulled our fat out of the fire in a big way."

"Not done," Kyle said and held up his hand. "About three weeks ago I was on my way to discuss something with the Major and I overheard a conversation," Kyle said.

"Stop, Kyle, I don't want to know." Eric said.

"I can't stop now, Eric," Kyle said.

Eric sighed. "Ok, but don't go too far."

"Fair enough," Kyle said. "She was talking to," Kyle paused and glanced at Eric, "somebody, about relationships, and at the time they were discussing Major Franklin and, well, my name came up as well. The Major, our Major, is developing a thing for Ben. And while there may or may not have been some sort of feelings under the surface for me at some point in the past, it's water under the bridge. We were both in the same chain-of-command, etc."

Kyle paused for a second and then continued, "Now she's an officer and that relationship is strictly forbidden, and frankly, apparently, I'm not showing the 'signs of growth' that she would like to see." Kyle gritted his teeth.

"I'm not showing signs of growth?" Kyle growled. "I'm not seeing signs that I need to grow. I'm not seeing signs of anything coming my way, why should I be trying to grow?"

"How long did you listen?" Eric asked.

"About three minutes." Kyle said. "It's amazing how nobody pays you any attention when you stand there looking like a guard."

"Man, that is so wrong on so many levels," Eric said.

"And I wish I had never heard the first word." Kyle said.

"Two days," Eric said after it was obvious that Kyle was done.

"I can work with that," Kyle said, "and in the meantime we need to work on your rig."

"How so," Eric asked.

"That old Alice frame you scrounged up is for the birds," Kyle said. "Sure they hold a ton-and-a-half, but if you drop the frame wrong and bust a rivet, it's all over. Before things went south, I found a modification called a 'Hellcat'…"

Chapter Eight

"Got a minute," Joel asked Eric when he saw him in camp a couple of days later.

"Sure," Eric said. "What's up?"

"Actually," Joel said, "that's my line."

Eric made a confused face and Joel shook his head. "Walk with me," Joel said, and then turned away from the more populated portion of the camp they were in without checking that Eric was following him. After a few steps Eric caught up.

"What's going on Eric?" Joel asked.

"Meaning," Eric asked cautiously.

Joel didn't even sigh. He'd been playing a similar game with his two teenage kids for a number of years, so he just laid out the evidence. "You have been in mourning, understandably, since Karen passed away," Joel said. "Now, literally out of nowhere, you are engaged in daily life again. You're talking to people, not as though nothing happened, but you appear to have either skipped four or five stages of grief and gone straight to acceptance, or you went through them at a record-setting pace."

Joel turned to Eric. "Or, you've found something else to occupy your time and energy, at least for the short term. What is it," Joel asked. "Not *which* is it, because I know which one it is. What is it, and how is Kyle involved?"

Eric didn't respond right away because he didn't know what to say. He couldn't just tell Joel they were leaving; it wasn't entirely up to him. Just then, Eric's radio came to life.

"Eric," Kyle's voice came through loud and clear and Eric closed his eyes. "I need to talk to you."

Eric grabbed his radio and responded. "Actually, why don't you meet me...?"

...

"So, I see he found you, too," Kyle said when he saw Joel was with Eric outside of the entrance to the parking lot.

Joel folded his arms and looked from Eric to Kyle and back. "What is going on with you two?"

Eric glanced at Kyle, who nodded slightly, and then took a small breath. "I'm leaving," Eric said. "And Kyle's coming with me."

Whatever Joel was expecting, this hadn't been it, and his mouth dropped open until it closed with an audible click. It was obvious he was taking a moment to think his words over before speaking. Eric started to say something, but Joel cut him off with a curt head shake. "I don't want to know. Plausible deniability," he said. "I've been married long enough to know that what I don't know can't kill me. Hurt me yes, kill me, no."

Joel took a deep breath and looked at both of them again. "Where to," he asked, "when?"

"We're not entirely sure, but," Eric paused at Joel's raised eyebrows. "I need to go, Kyle does too. We're leaving tonight."

"Tonight," Joel yelled, then looked around to see if anyone had noticed his micro-outburst. "Why so...never mind. I said I didn't want to know. Are you sure you're ready?"

"No," Kyle snorted, "but we're as ready as we're ever going to be."

"Probably about right," Eric said.

Joel's mind was racing; trying to process what he felt would be the impact of losing both Eric and Kyle. Wondering if there was anything he could do or say to keep them from leaving, or if there was anything that he could do or provide that would help his friends on their journey.

Joel let out a breath and decided on the latter. "Do you need anything from me before you go?"

Eric and Kyle looked at each other with a bit of surprise at Joel's reaction.

"I'm serious," Joel said. "I'm not going to go running to Mallory, or anyone else for that matter. If they haven't figured out that something is up then it's their loss, and frankly," Joel looked at Kyle when he said the next bit, "their lack of situational awareness is no skin off my nose."

Kyle grinned, but didn't say anything.

"Back to my question," Joel said. "Do you need anything before you go?"

"Before we go, maybe some extra MREs but that really isn't something you can get us," Eric said. "I'm going to see what I can do. Long-term, though, there might be something you can do."

"Name it," Joel said.

"Sandbags," Eric said, "empty sandbags."

Joel made a questioning face, but said okay.

"Long-term," Kyle said, "we aren't going to live in a tent. We may build a cabin, ultimately, but we may not. One of the things we were thinking of trying was building a house that is half underground, half above-ground. The above-ground portion is made of dirtbags, or sandbags, filled with the dirt from the excavated below-ground portion."

"The bags are a great insulator," Eric continued, "and with enough people, you can literally build one in a day, depending on the type of soil. It's a bit like an igloo shape for the upper walls and ceiling. You have to scout the area and make sure you aren't in a flood plain, of course, and check the water table–things like that–but they can last for years depending on the type of bag you use. Our sandbags are UV-resistant, so if this works out we shouldn't even *need* to stucco the outside of the first couple."

Joel had been all ears once he'd gotten the gist of the design. "Deal," Joel said. "On one condition, you have to stay close enough that in case of a dire emergency, yours or ours, we can contact each other. I'd also like to know how well the 'dirtbag house' works out."

Kyle groaned. "Nice legacy," he said, "the dirtbag house."

"Can it, Ramirez," Eric and Joel said in unison.

"Right," Kyle said.

. . .

June 12, 2013 - I-40 - Approaching the Entrance to Natchez Trace State Park, Tennessee

Driving down the freeway, Ben's first reaction was shock, followed by confusion, and then disbelief.

They were approaching Promised Land, located inside Natchez Trace State Park, from the west on I-40. In the southbound lanes, lined up and evenly spaced, were about thirty Black Hawk helicopters—at least three full battalions. "Promised Land," Ben said, "this is the fifth little pig. What. have. you. done?"

"Me," Mallory said, the relief obvious in her voice. "I didn't do anything. In fact, I didn't even say anything at first; they came in here on their own looking for a place to land. Said something about illegal orders, fulfilling their Oath, and defending The Constitution."

Ben was trying not to smile and failing miserably. "I assume they were painted the whole time," he said.

Mallory laughed. "Of course, and if they had a problem with that they kept it to themselves," she said. "The flight commander just requested that nobody have an itchy trigger finger. I'll fill you in when you get here."

...

"That's quite the convoy you have there," Mallory said as she looked over the assortment of vehicles Ben had assembled. Her words were muffled, somewhat, by the disposable surgical mask she was wearing to keep Ben's people safe. They had pulled through the park, skirted camp, and were now parked in a relatively flat area they had finished clearing where a forest fire had occurred a couple of years ago.

"Is this everyone from the final defense of the base," she asked.

"Not quite," Ben said with a sigh, "I had to leave behind eighty-one men that couldn't be moved."

"How many did you lose," Mallory asked.

"Seventeen," Ben said.

"I'm sorry, Ben," Mallory said.

"It's not your fault, Mallory, it's the Colonel's," Ben said, and clenched his jaw, "and it's mine. If he hadn't pushed it we wouldn't have lost anybody, and if I hadn't decided to keep a force there as a–I don't know–as a stalling tactic to let everyone else get out...or for my own stupid pride, again, we wouldn't have lost anybody."

Mallory nodded, "At least you have the Colonel to blame. All I have is a microscopic bacteria and a doctor who blames himself," Mallory said. "Six dead so far, and I get the feeling that it's far from over."

"It was bound to happen eventually," Ben said, referring to the illness running through camp, "and this, or something like it, is probably going to happen again. Times have changed."

The look on Mallory's face said she knew Ben was right, but didn't have to like it.

Ben shrugged and moved on. "So, what about those helicopters?"

…

When Ben and Mallory walked into the room, all of the pilots stood up and came to attention.

"At ease," Mallory said. "In fact, sit down. This is Major Benjamin Franklin. Yes, that's his real name. Yes, he's probably heard all the jokes. Yes, they're funny the first time. Go ahead and laugh if you need to get it out of your system."

Instead of laughing, they all started to applaud and Diego took a couple of steps forward and held out his hand. "Chief Warrant Officer Fourth Class Diego Hobbs, Sir," Diego said. "It's a pleasure and an honor to meet you. I'm glad to see you made it out of Fort Campbell in one piece."

Ben hadn't expected the reaction or the greeting, but tried to take it in stride. "Thank you, Chief," Ben said. "That makes two of us—about getting out of Campbell alive, that is."

Everyone chuckled and then sat down to begin the debriefing for the second time—this time for Ben's benefit.

…

"We were effectively locked out," Ben said, "and he'd prevented us from rebroadcasting the conversation back via the satellite. I'm just glad that what I had to say didn't fall on deaf ears."

"I know we heard it on UHF," Diego said, "but rest assured, we weren't the only ones. If nothing else, I'm sure Colonel Olsen had half-a-dozen other people on the channel, and all of their radio operators. We can't be the only ones who have a problem with what's going on."

Ben nodded, but didn't say anything about Bragg or Lejeune. Yes, these men had apparently disobeyed a direct order, either gone

AWOL or deserted their units, and defected to the other side, but they were still not an entirely known quantity. They had also increased the number of people at Promised Land by over four-hundred people which, while it wasn't an immediate strain on the resources, would eventually put a sizeable dent in their stores.

"I know what you're thinking, Sir, Ma'am," Diego continued. "While I can only absolutely speak for myself, I'm fairly confident I can speak for everyone else here. What's happening is wrong and we know it. The Colonel is out of control and I don't know what, but *something* else is going on, and I refuse to be a part of it any longer."

Diego shook his head. "If we came here to do anything but switch sides," Diego said, "we've done a horrible job of it. We allowed ourselves to be captured and we've given up *all* our weapons."

"Point," Ben said and looked at Mallory.

"They've been model guests," she said. "They were even broadcasting well before the radar picked them up."

"This is your base, Major," Ben said, making sure to use Mallory's title. "At this point, I'm an uninvited guest myself. I'm glad I made a difference, but if nothing else I would suggest getting those thirty Black Hawks off the freeway. They reminded me of Battleship Row in 1941 on the way in."

…

"And who is this," Mallory asked.

"This would be former First Lieutenant Curt Mathis," Ben said. "He's been stripped of his rank and command until a summary court-martial can be held."

Mallory raised her eyebrows at this.

"I know you didn't have any commissioned officers who were licensed to practice law in Tennessee," Ben said. "Do you since the promotions?"

"Unfortunately not," she said. "We may have to hold this off for some time."

"Or, I can accuse him of treason and just shoot him right here," Ben said and unsnapped the loop of his holster.

Mallory put a hand on his arm. "Not worth the nightmares, Major," she said. "Trust me."

Ben still had his hand on the butt of his pistol and Mallory could feel the tense muscles of his upper arm. Ben was angrier about Mathis than he was letting his face show.

"Maybe," Ben finally said and secured his holster. "We're still going to have a nice long chat Mathis."

Mathis just looked at both Ben and Mallory.

. . .

"What's going on with him," Mallory said after they left her brand new brig.

"He's my mole," Ben said. "I was fairly sure he was communicating with someone since just before I was down here last time and decided to keep my own council instead of telling the Colonel off. I also decided to keep an eye on him instead of grabbing him right away."

Ben rubbed the back of his neck and shook his head. "Something he said a couple of days before the raid, right after the MPs grabbed him has been bothering me, though." Ben said. "I remember that I asked him why and what the Colonel was holding over him. He looked at me and said "You know *nothing*," with, I don't know, some superior look in his eyes. His whole bearing changed for a minute there when he said that and it's been bothering me ever since."

"We'll figure it out," Mallory said.

Chapter Nine

The afternoon after Ben arrived, Mallory put together a meeting to discuss some plans that Chuck had been working on for Redemption, Promised Land, and any other new towns that might crop up or, as Chuck saw it, that they might just start on their own.

The low-level hum and din of ever-present activity around base came in through the unshuttered windows.

"First of all," Mallory said, as she began introductions, "I wanted to include Major Franklin now that he's here since some of what we discuss will most likely impact him and his people."

Mallory nodded to Chuck. "Ben," she said, "This is Chuck Turner. Don't call him Charles or Mister."

Chuck held out his hand at the introduction. "I'm not as picky about it since I got married," Chuck said.

"Chuck got back last night from checking something out for us," Mallory said. "I'd like him to be in on this meeting as he's basically taken on the role of civil engineer for both the base and the town. You met Joel yesterday."

Joel nodded to Ben and everyone sat down.

"Joel," Mallory said, "why don't you start us off?"

"What we're doing isn't going to work long term," Joel said.

"How so," Mallory said.

"Basically, we've been going along for a year," Joel said, "operating pretty much like we were before the power went out. We've made a few modifications but not nearly enough. We quit looking for new ways to do things six weeks into this crisis. Everybody says things have changed but nobody is *acting* like it."

"Ok," Mallory said. "I guess I can see your point."

"So," Joel said, "things need to actually change around here, on base and in Redemption. We can't keep growing like we have been, and I don't just mean doubling in size like we just did–no offense."

Ben raised his hands in a 'none taken' gesture.

"For instance, we need to rethink the communal eating idea," Joel said. "It took a little bit of work to get things situated for the folks in isolation, but once they had what they needed, they're actually more efficient cooking for themselves in their own homes."

"We also need to look at different types of construction," Chuck added. "This last winter was proof that the homes we're used to living in just aren't designed to be used without electricity, natural gas and central air conditioning, and heating. Until we have a reliable source of power, we need to construct shelters that can use coal for heat in the winters, and possibly for cooking as well."

"Ok," Mallory said. "I assume you aren't just complaining and have some solutions to these problems."

"Some," Chuck said.

"I started out by asking myself, what is it that every town is going to need," Chuck said. "I've boiled it down to four things; a reliable source of water, food, skilled labor, and a way to defend itself. You can add to that if you want, but you really can't take anything away or the town can't survive."

Mallory nodded and Chuck went on.

"First of all, we've been relying on surface water up to this point," Chuck said, "but if we can drive wells and build pumps, even hand-pumps, we'll open up a huge area for resettlement."

Chuck glanced at his notes. "Second, food," he said. "I admit I don't know much about farming but I've been talking to the groups we sent out to work the farms and the ranch. We're working well together so far, but I think that could be expanded and enhanced. From what I've been able to gather, there's no reason we couldn't be producing a surplus right now."

"I'm going to skip skilled labor for a minute," Chuck said, "because it's actually a pretty substantial category. Next is defense, which can be handled in a couple of ways, and it kind of depends on how you, the military, want to handle it."

"Go on," Mallory said.

"Is the military going to continue to be structured like it is now," Chuck asked, "or is it going to become, as we've discussed, more of a militia? If it's going to stay centralized, and keep the structure that it has now, then initially, defense is going to be up to each individual town."

"We can't answer that right now," Mallory said, looking at Ben. "We just don't know. With Olsen still out there, we can't commit to anything other than maintaining the heightened state of awareness and security within our own sphere of influence."

"We weren't necessarily expecting an answer right now," Joel said, "but it's something to consider. The other thing to consider is that by keeping everyone massed in one spot, we're creating a target that eventually the Colonel may find it too hard to resist."

"Last is the skilled labor," Chuck said. "That includes everything from craftspeople to doctors, beekeepers to masons. Obviously, no town at this point could realistically have all the skilled trades it needs, so trade between towns will be critical. Towns will most likely need to be close enough to travel between within a day, probably on foot for the time being, which would also aid in mutual defense."

"Either way," Joel said, "it's a switch from how we're doing it here, because this is just not sustainable."

"Because of that, towns will have to start specializing," Chuck said. "Ben, you brought a lot of heavy equipment with you, and not just the military variety. You also have a lot of experienced tradesmen to back that up. Potentially, it would make a lot of sense to have a town of engineers, maybe, or one that at least was more industrial than agrarian."

Joel snickered. "Kind of puts a whole new spin on 'military-industrial complex', doesn't it," he said.

"Nice," Mallory said as she shook her head. "How long have you been waiting to say that?"

"I just came up with it," Joel said, "honest. This is the first time I'm hearing some of this."

"Another thing I'm looking for," Chuck added, "which I mentioned before, is new building techniques. We could probably go back to log cabins, but those are really very labor *and* resource intensive and I'm not sure we have enough of the right trees anymore anyway."

"What, Joel," Mallory asked. "You look like you want to say something but don't know how."

"Well," Joel said. "How many sandbags do we have?"

Mallory furrowed her brow. "Why," she asked.

"Have you ever heard of sandbag, or dirtbag, construction," Joel asked.

"Not outside of a retaining wall or flood prevention, no," Mallory said.

Joel outlined the process, to the best of his limited knowledge, in a couple of minutes.

"How come you never brought this up before," Mallory asked.

Chuck didn't pester, but was wondering the same thing, since they'd already had this specific conversation a number of times.

"I don't know," Joel said. "It just didn't seem like it would work or be worth the effort. I guess now it's to the point that I'm willing to try anything."

Mallory gave him a skeptical look, but didn't push it.

...

"Any idea how many sandbags it's going to take to build one of these houses," Chuck asked as they walked away from the meeting with Ben and Mallory.

"None whatsoever," Joel said.

"Well," Chuck said, "depending on the size of the house, it could be between fifteen and forty-thousand."

Joel stared at Chuck. "Seriously," he said. "That's...I don't...do we even have that many?"

"You heard Mallory, she doesn't know off the top of her head, and I certainly have no idea," Chuck said. "Now, to be fair, those calculations are based on being completely above-ground. I didn't factor in building partially below-grade—sorry, underground. That could cut the number almost in half but we would need to figure out how to weatherproof the interior walls."

Joel bit his lip. "Any idea if anyone knows how to make stucco," Joel asked. "Or if we even have the raw materials?"

Chuck shrugged. "I don't know, but I'll start asking around," he said.

...

"Bekah looks awful happy this morning," Dan Clark said to his wife after they had dropped the girls off with the group that walked the five-and-a-half miles to the elementary school at the Natchez Trace Recreation Lodge. Once the quarantine had expanded to the town, and both Bekah and Jessie had already been exposed, they started going to school every day again.

"She is," Marissa said. "The Kid Crockett's are going out after school today. It's the first time they've been able to hunt since the quarantine started, and she's been looking forward to it all week."

"Our own little Calamity Jane," Dan laughed. "And how are *you* doing, really," Dan asked.

Marissa squeezed Dan's hand. "I'm coping," she said. "Physically, I'm actually pretty good I guess. Nobody is asking me to do too much, and everyone seems to understand my limits...so that's not an issue." She brushed a stray lock of hair behind her ear to cover her pause, and then went on. "The quarantine up in camp is bringing up a lot of emotions I thought I was mostly over. Talking about Danny's death with the Pastor helps, but...I guess I just didn't realize how much I had bottled up and locked away in there."

When their youngest son had died from a runaway fever and cough at the age of eighteen-months, a little less than a year ago, Marissa had refused to deal with the loss. Instead, she had isolated herself from the pain and grief because she'd felt she had no choice if she wanted to protect the rest of her family as their neighborhood slowly crumbled around them. She stopped and turned to Dan in the middle of the roadway, and a couple of people had to go around them. "I'm sorry, Dan," she said. "I'm sorry I made you go through that all by yourself. It was cruel and selfish and..."

Dan reached out and touched her lips with his finger and then pulled her into his arms. "And now it's in the past," he said.

Marissa nodded and swallowed, and leaned into Dan for a few more seconds.

...

June 13, 2013 - Several miles South of Natchez Trace State Park, Tennessee

"Remind me again why we're walking," Kyle said to Eric after two days of hiking cross-country.

"Kyle," Eric said, "do *not* make me hogtie you and radio back to the base to come get you once I've vacated the area."

Kyle sighed.

"We couldn't even use mountain bikes over this terrain right now," Eric said. "And somehow, amazingly, we didn't have a single motorcycle in either Promised Land or Redemption."

Kyle shook his head. "Even if there had been a few we couldn't have taken two," he said. "I couldn't have done that."

"And I wouldn't have let us," Eric said. "And a truck, at this point, would just draw attention or make us easier to find. Neither of those is a good thing. Plus, eventually we would run out of gas and we'd be walking anyway."

Eric checked his map against the GPS and his compass. When he was packing, he'd come across the portable solar chargers that he and Karen had bought at the truck-stop convenience store on the way out of town the second day after the power went out. They had picked them up in hopes that they would come in handy for recharging small electronics at some point.

Finding them brought the pain of losing her front and center again. He was constantly running across things that reminded him of her. It was a large part of why he felt he had to leave in the first place.

The chargers also reminded him that he had a half-dozen or so Apps on his smart phone that might come in handy when he and Kyle took off–like the digital compass, a second GPS, yet another flashlight, an alarm clock, and at least a dozen military and survival-related e-books. He'd recharged his phone, and suggested Kyle do the same thing, using the camp power the day before they left. From now on he would keep it charged with the solar chargers.

Eric pointed a bit to the south-south-east, "Another mile or so and we can set up camp for a while, I think."

...

"So, seriously," Kyle asked as they were pitching the tent, "what are our long-term plans?"

Eric snorted. "Your timing stinks, Kyle. Most people would have wanted to know that before we left."

"Fine, whatever," Kyle continued, ignoring the jibe. "Do you plan to hook up with a farmer at some point? We aren't going to be able to forage forever. We're really not all that far from Redemption, or from camp–probably less than fifteen miles from either. Not that we're encroaching on anybody's space out here, but we really haven't even gone that far."

Eric finished the peg he was working on and stopped for a second, looking down at what he'd just done but not really seeing it. "One day at a time for a little while, Kyle," he said after a few more seconds. "I know I'm not the world's greatest woodsman but I've seen signs of at least some game.

"We won't have to survive on MREs forever," Eric said. "We're not going to be self-sufficient because we can't be, but we also just left, so give me a little time, okay?"

Kyle nodded. "Okay, I was just wondering."

Eric sighed. "We aren't going to be here permanently, but we'll scout the area tomorrow," Eric said, "see what's around and go from there."

"Seriously," Kyle said, "it's okay. You don't have to solve it right away just because I asked the question."

"Tomorrow, then," Eric said and went back to his half of putting their tent up.

Chapter Ten

Since Eric and Kyle were sharing guard duty, one or the other took a nap in the afternoon to try to stay caught up on sleep. Eric had just sat down by the fire-pit, across from the tent, when he had to stifle a laugh. The first few bars of the song 'All the Single Ladies' drifted from the tent and he couldn't help but smile.

"Not a word, Tripp," Kyle said.

"Nope," Eric said. A few minutes later, Kyle came out looking more than a bit sheepish.

"I can't believe I left the alarm on and the volume up so high," Kyle said.

"Could have been worse," Eric said with a grin. "You could have been sneaking up on someone and gotten a call."

Kyle shook his head. "So, how do we want to scout and who wants to go first?"

"It's going to take forever with just one of us scouting the area," Eric said, "but I don't feel comfortable leaving camp unattended. I'll go first, and we can trade off every two or three hours."

"Sounds like a plan," Kyle said.

...

Kyle had been gone for about an hour on his second trip on the third day when Eric's radio came to life.

"E.T., do not respond," Kyle said. "I don't want the noise at my end, but alpha whiskey. Come to the following coordinates and bring your ruck, rifle, and sidearm, now!" Kyle gave some coordinates and then signed off.

Alpha whiskey meant all's well, instead of something else. A-Okay, or all good, meant he was in trouble. Eric really didn't want to leave the camp unguarded, but whatever it was, Kyle felt it was important enough to call him away. Eric grabbed his day ruck (which was packed with enough to survive for three days), his rifle, double-checked the sidearm that was always on his hip, and took off at a quick trot so he could come at Kyle's position from the opposite side—just in case.

Ten minutes later, he was slowly advancing on the coordinates that Kyle had given him, which overlooked some farmland. He saw Kyle about ten seconds before Kyle heard him, and crawled to where Kyle was observing the field. Kyle handed him a pair of 10x42 binoculars and pointed at the field.

Eric scanned the field and noticed that almost all of the workers were women. There was obviously one—supervisor was the only word that came to mind—but it was immediately replaced by the word bully when one of the women stopped for a few seconds to stretch her back and was slapped hard enough to knock her down.

Eric felt Kyle tense next to him and was glad he didn't have the binoculars. At ten-times magnification he was pretty sure he saw the strike draw blood, and Kyle was death on abuse...of any kind.

Eric put the binoculars down and pointed behind them to get out of sight of the field.

"Talk to me," Eric said.

"I could take him out at this range with a single shot," Kyle said, "guaranteed. I've been watching long enough to know that he's the only guard."

"That's not what I meant, Ramirez, and you know it," Eric said.

Kyle clenched his jaw, but nodded his head. "I swear I recognize that guy but I have no idea where from," he said, looking off into the distance while trying to concentrate. "It's been driving me nuts for the last twenty minutes."

"How about eight or nine months ago," Eric prompted.

Kyle snapped his head back to Eric and then almost went back to his perch overlooking the field. "Clint," he said.

"Well, no, not Clint, himself," Eric said, "but one of the people from the raid. I didn't get any of their names, but I remember him being in camp for a day. The only reason I think I remember his face, though, is I recall seeing him on the side of the road when we ran into Clint the very first time. He looked up from changing the tire as we drove by."

"Eric," Kyle started.

Eric shook his head.

"We can't, I can't, just let this kind of thing go," Kyle said. "I won't be able to sleep at night. Okay, I've been pretty sure there were people who would set up their own little kingdoms out there, but knowing there was one right in my back yard where this kind of thing is going on and then not doing something about it?" Kyle shook his head. "I can't let this slide."

"And the fact that she was pretty had nothing to do with it," Eric asked.

Kyle had murder in his eyes when he reacted, and Eric scooted back.

"Don't you ever question my motives," Kyle said, "especially when it comes to something like this. You know how I feel about abuse, especially towards women. I know I said don't bring it up again, but that's one of the things that set me off about the Major's ex."

Kyle backed off a little physically, but the heat was still there. "He threatened to go after her, and that's when I made it my life's mission to make it abundantly clear to him that it would be his last official act on this planet. It took a little convincing–it turned out he was a bit stubborn–but I can be very persuasive." Kyle made a fist which cracked all the knuckles in his hand.

"And no, it has nothing to do with the fact that she's pretty," Kyle said. "Although, I will admit I did notice that first." Kyle blushed. "It's why I was watching her when she stopped and got slapped the first time. And what are *you* doing noticing pretty women?"

"I'm not," Eric said, but didn't even bat an eye. "Situational awareness. Just making sure your judgment isn't impaired."

Kyle blushed again. "Yes, Sir."

Eric nodded. "Let's get back to camp," he said, and continued before Kyle could protest. "I don't want to leave it unattended for too long and you need to cool down before we do anything. I'm not saying we *are* going to do anything, but even if we do, we can't plan with you in this state."

Kyle nodded and took point for the trek back to camp.

. . .

"Mr. Mayor," Mallory said as she approached Joel in the roadway. "A minute if you would."

"A minute is about all I can spare," Joel said, guessing what Mallory wanted, but determined to stonewall her. "I haven't been able to leave Promised Land for almost a month. I haven't seen my wife, or baby daughter, since the quarantine began, and I'm doing everything from the 'healthy' side of camp and without my assistant."

Mallory nodded and Joel knew that even though an apology wouldn't be forthcoming, she felt for him. "Speaking of seeing people," she said, "I seem to have misplaced two of my men and apparently you were among the last to have seen them."

"Really," Joel said, "who?"

"Captain Tripp and Sergeant Ramirez," Mallory said. "Together, no less."

"I did see them, both individually and together, the day before Ben showed up," Joel said. "I'd been worried about Eric and started out by talking to Kyle first. I'd noticed that Eric had been grieving, which was to be expected, but was starting to…" Joel paused for a second to look for the right words. "He was acting engaged again, so I wanted to see how he was doing."

"So you don't have any idea where they are," Mallory asked, "where they may be headed?"

"I'm afraid I don't," Joel said, honestly. Eric hadn't given him any specifics and Mallory's questions hadn't taken the right turn for him to have to start lying yet. She was eyeing him like she wasn't quite sure what to think of his story.

"If you hear anything," Mallory said, "please let me know."

"Will do," Joel said and then continued on his way to his next appointment.

…

"Wedding Crashers calling Proud Papa," Eric said into the radio.

"This is Proud Papa," Joel answered. "Do not tell me where you are or where you're headed. The Major finally made a point of asking me about you two and I don't want to have to lie."

"Fair enough," Eric said, "any word on the sandbags?"

"I already have them set aside and can get them ready for you to pick up whenever you are ready," Joel said. "Will fifteen hundred be enough?"

"For the size we're looking at, it should. We're going to need to make multiple trips though," Eric said. "We do have a bit of intel, but now might not be the best time."

"Better now than never," Joel said, "just in case there's a problem in the future."

"Point," Eric said. "Our old friend Clint seems to be growing his group and it looks like he's settled permanently enough to be doing some farming."

"Ok," Joel said.

"The problem is," Eric continued, "we've observed a number of fields, and the majority of the work is being done by women, and the supervising is being handled by abusive men. While I have a problem with that...Kyle has a *real* problem with that. We haven't decided how we're going to handle it yet."

"Wait; come again, how *you're* going to handle it?" Joel said.

. . .

"So now we're going to take care of...what?" Kyle asked.

"A problem," Eric said.

"No," Kyle said. "Pete was a problem. A blister is a problem. Clint and his entire band of hoodlums is a collection of problems, a gang of thugs...with guns...who already attacked an entire Army base. On that first hill I was thinking one shot, one kill. What are you thinking?"

. . .

Kyle had spent four hours getting into position near the end of the first field he'd been watching a couple of days before. His face was camouflaged with grease paint and he was almost certain he was hidden from view from both the front and back. The low crawl from over the hill had taken so long because Kyle had tried to follow the land and crush as few plants as possible during his passage. The grass, weeds, and bushes that surrounded the field were at least two feet tall and had allowed him to get within a couple of feet of the field.

The young woman was working her way towards him, and was maybe fifteen feet away when Kyle decided to try to get her attention.

"Don't look up," Kyle said softly, "but try not to freak out or yell."

"I won't," she said under her breath. "I saw you a couple of minutes ago when you moved your left foot."

"And this is why I could never be a sniper," Kyle thought.

"And you didn't call out," Kyle said, as she continued to work closer to him. "Why?"

"Because you're in what looks like Army camouflage," she said. "We had a run-in with the Army a while back because of …something stupid. I heard that the people at that base, even after getting attacked, treated everyone pretty well. If you're with the Army then you're probably one of the 'good guys'."

Her eyes darted left and right while she continued to hoe the ground, and then she bent down as though to pick up a weed or a rock and Kyle could see the bruise on her face where she'd been hit. "Because someone made some stupid decisions," she said. "They're still making stupid decisions." She picked up a rock and threw it into the woods behind Kyle.

"What's your name," Kyle asked.

She pursed her lips while she kept hoeing for several seconds without saying anything.

"My name is Kyle," Kyle said. "Kyle Ramirez."

She was less than ten feet away from Kyle now and had slowed down so she wouldn't have to turn around too soon. "Amanda," she said. "Amanda Saint James."

"Do you have any family back with Clint's group," Kyle asked.

Amanda shook her head but then said, "I've kind of adopted someone. He was an orphan and nobody else was going to look out for him." Amanda had to turn around and start the other direction.

"I saw what happened a few days ago," Kyle said, "when he hit you."

"Let's just say that was nothing," Amanda said bitterly.

"How can I help," Kyle asked.

"You can get me and a bunch of other people out of here," Amanda said. Her voice rose just enough that she realized she needed to keep it down and be more careful.

Kyle could hear the desperation in her voice. There was something else there too, though. Amanda wasn't broken and waiting for rescue, which was what Eric and Kyle had been hoping for when they had decided to risk talking to her.

"How many people want out," Kyle asked.

"I don't know," Amanda sighed. "A third, maybe half." She shook her head when she realized that meant nothing to Kyle. "Maybe three-hundred people, total. Some just want things to change. I can't talk anymore."

Kyle glanced up and saw what Amanda meant. The guard was evidently making rounds and would be able to hear them talking. Amanda sped up just a bit to put some distance between her and Kyle and soon enough any chance of communication was gone.

...

"If she can be believed," Kyle said, "and I think she can, we have at least one ally in Clint's group."

"How do we use that," Eric asked, careful not to imply that he wanted to use Amanda or put her in any jeopardy.

"I don't know yet," Kyle said. "We were only able to talk for a couple of minutes, but I'll be there again tomorrow, and the next day, and the next day until we can figure something out."

Chapter Eleven

Amanda had to check herself and keep from looking too often towards the end of the row she was working to see if she could catch a glimpse of Kyle. He was getting better at staying still, and yesterday she hadn't seen him until he moved on purpose to get her attention. She found herself thinking about him more and more often, certainly more than anyone in the group she'd been living with for the last year—which was odd, considering she had just met him and had barely even seen his face.

"You are persistent, aren't you," Amanda said when she saw that Kyle was there again, but a couple of rows over, so that they could talk longer as she worked at hoeing and breaking ground on more rows.

Kyle smiled, but knew that Amanda couldn't see him so he replied, "I've been called worse. What are the chances that you could get out of camp at night for awhile so that we could talk like normal people?" He asked.

Amanda made a face, but didn't answer right away.

"Is security that tight," Kyle asked.

Amanda sighed, "It isn't that."

"I'm not proposing anything," Kyle blushed under his face paint, realizing for the first time how his suggestion might have come across.

"No, no," Amanda said quickly. "It isn't that, either."

"Then what is it?" Kyle asked, but before either of them could say anything more, they heard a vehicle approaching, and Amanda hung her head and kept working to the end of the row and turned around.

A man climbed out of the dirty pickup truck and started walking across the field. He was fairly careful not to step on the plants, but he was obviously heading straight for Amanda.

"There's my girl," he said when he got close enough, and pulled her into an embrace that Amanda appeared to return, and then he slapped her on the butt.

Kyle missed most of what was said between them, but she refused to leave with the man because she said it would set a bad example. "There's too much work to do," she added.

"Your choice," he said, pulled her into another embrace, followed by a kiss, walked back to the truck and drove away.

Kyle didn't move the entire time; he wasn't sure he breathed from the moment the guy said "there's my girl" until the truck started back up. He couldn't leave, it was the middle of the morning and he would be seen. He was stuck until they all stopped for lunch at the earliest.

Amanda kept working on her current row, got to the end, turned around and started back Kyle's direction in the next row...closer to him. Every time she looked up he felt like she was looking right at him, and laughing.

"Kyle," Amanda said softly, as she tried to peer into the tall grass beyond the field she was working in without being obvious, once she got close enough to the end of her row for him to hear her. "Are you still there?"

Kyle didn't say anything, and didn't move to give away his position.

"Please still be there," Amanda said. "Please don't leave me. That was Clint, and he's...taken an interest in me. Ever since..."

Amanda stopped talking because she was afraid she sounded like a fool talking to herself if Kyle wasn't there anymore, but then decided to talk about it anyway. She had to get it out.

"Ever since the meeting where Clint killed William's father," Amanda said, "William is the boy I've sort of adopted, ever since I took William in, Clint has been trying to, I don't know what, but really I'm afraid I do. He's an animal, Kyle. I don't want to have anything to do with him but it's not like I have any choice!"

Amanda looked around to see if anyone was close enough to have heard her.

"Why didn't you say something before," Kyle said from straight in front of her, both startling and relieving her.

"Because I hoped he would just stop," Amanda said. "Because I didn't want you to know and because I didn't want you to think I was just using you or leading you on."

"Is that why you can't get out at night," Kyle asked. "Has it gone that far?"

Color rose on Amanda's cheeks. "No," she said. "Not yet, thankfully. Not ever, hopefully. I just don't know how I would get out of camp or where to go."

"I can walk you through what you need to do," Kyle said. "And we can figure out a place to meet."

...

Kyle had been at their arranged meeting spot for three nights in a row before Amanda showed up, and even then it was after midnight when she finally arrived. The first night it had drizzled almost all night with a brief break for a minor thunderstorm. Kyle refused to leave in case Amanda showed up using the weather for cover.

"I was beginning to think you weren't going to come after all," Kyle said when he stepped out from behind a couple of trees after getting an all-clear from Eric.

"I was afraid I wasn't going to be able to make it tonight either," Amanda said. "William was restless the night before last and woke up every time I moved around in the trailer, and last night," Amanda turned away and it looked like she shuddered.

Kyle wanted to reach out to her, put his arm around her and hold her, or do something, but, they didn't have that kind of relationship, or any relationship, really; maybe someday, maybe, but not now. Instead, he moved to the side and ducked his head so his face was in front of hers and she was looking him in the eyes again and could see that he was concerned. They only had the moon for light but that would be enough since it was just past full.

"Is everything okay," he asked. "Are you alright?"

"I'm fine," she said, trying to brush it off.

Kyle wasn't going to let it go that easily, though. He very gently put his hands on her upper arms and then on her face to make her look at him again, and then took his hands away. "No, not *fine*. Did he hurt you in any way," he asked, "or William?"

The intensity in Kyle's eyes, the fact that he obviously really cared, and that he had asked about William, brought tears to her eyes. She took a step closer to Kyle, and then another, and put her arms around him and her head on his shoulder.

Kyle hadn't expected a hug at this point, but returned it gently as Amanda was now crying softly.

"Thank you," she said. "I'm really okay, and thank you for caring about William. You're the first person to ask about him since…I guess you need to know what happened."

She pulled away and Kyle was loathe to let her go, but didn't dare try to hold on. He nodded to a downed log at the edge of the clearing and they walked over to it, but ended up sitting on the ground with their backs to it instead.

"What happened," Kyle asked. "Every time you mention William and his father you get, I don't know, quiet and distant."

Amanda nodded and wiped her eyes. Kyle wished he had some tissues or a handkerchief, but realized he had a clean bandana and gave it to her.

"It happened about two months ago," Amanda said, "before we had any real gardens or farming going on. Clint had finally had it with people not pulling their weight or doing their fair share. Don't get me wrong, there're a lot of useless leeches that really don't do anything around camp, but to lump everyone in together with them is just…" She took a deep breath to calm herself down.

"Anyway," she continued, "Clint called this big meeting in the middle of the camp. He had Coop, that's Cooper, gather everyone in the center where there's a big fire pit, and a picnic table Clint can stand on, and a flag pole we don't use. I was about a third of the way back into the crowd and I heard him yell for everyone to shut up, but nobody did. He yelled a second time and everybody just kept talking and joking around and that's when he fired the shotgun into the air."

Amanda shook her head in disgust at about the same time that Kyle did. "He shouldn't have had to, but it was just such a childish thing to do," Amanda said. "It got everyone's attention, and the guy next to me actually pulled out his gun until he realized what Clint was doing. Then Clint went off about how he was sick of being ignored and that when he called a meeting and told everybody to settle down, we needed to *shut up!*"

Amanda's eyes were growing watery again and she wiped her nose. "That's when William's father, Jim, piped up and hollered 'You can't talk to us like that'," she said.

…

"Clint got a look in his eyes," she continued. "He went off about how he *was* in fact in charge and he *could* in fact talk that way to us. Jim couldn't let it go, though. He yelled out something like 'And what if we don't *want* to do it your way?'"

Amanda swallowed and closed her eyes for a second. "Clint hopped off the table and walked through the crowd to where Jim was standing, with William right next to him. Clint said something like

'And just when did you become the spokesman for the group, Jim?' and then asked him if he would come up front with him. Jim figured he would be safe up there, in front of everyone, so he followed him up and climbed onto the picnic table with Clint." Amanda reached out and took Kyle's hand. Kyle was pretty sure he could guess what happened next, and not only because of the fact that Amanda was taking care of William now.

"I remember exactly what Clint did next," Amanda said. "He said, 'Jim here has a question. What if you don't *want* to do it my way? Simple. You leave.' Jim turned to Clint and started to say he wasn't going anywhere, but only got as far as 'I'm not go…'."

Kyle closed his eyes and softly muttered a curse.

"Pretty much," Amanda said. "Clint had reloaded the shotgun while he was telling us to shut up. As soon as Jim started to talk back, Clint leveled it at his chest and pulled the first trigger. It blew Jim right off the picnic table. Clint's finger was still on the trigger and he turned back towards us, all casual, shotgun pointed right at the crowd. Then he said, 'First, I *am* in fact in charge because, second, this is *not* a democracy. Third, there are going to be some new rules around here, and they *will* be enforced. Fourth, if anyone doesn't like the first three rules, leave now'."

Kyle squeezed Amanda's hand. "Nineteen people left after that," she said, "including a family with two young kids. Even some of the real leeches couldn't stomach what had just happened, but where were they going to go? It's not like Clint let anyone walk away with any food or supplies or anything. And then there was William. His father had just been murdered in cold blood, right in front of him, and *nobody* wanted anything to do with him." Amanda shuddered. "I think that's what caught Clint's attention. The fact that I didn't think William was somehow tainted by what his father had done while everybody else apparently did."

Kyle nodded in understanding. He didn't agree with it if it was true, but could see where she was coming from.

"And all of this was because people weren't pulling their fair share of the labor," Kyle asked.

Amanda nodded. "Clint had tried to set up community gardens and they were all dying because hardly anyone was working in them."

"So how were you surviving," Kyle asked.

Amanda pursed her lips and looked down.

Kyle reached out and gently lifted her head back up. His initial assessment a week ago, that Amanda was really just a girl, was obviously mistaken. She was a woman, proud, and in a situation truly not of her choosing.

"The group," Amanda said, and then paused, "...gathers resources."

"I think I see," Kyle said. "Do you participate in the...gathering?"

"No," Amanda said, "it's always the men, but I'm just as guilty. I use what they steal and that's what it is. They raid other groups. There, I said it." Amanda pulled her hand back into her own lap.

"I'm not judging you," Kyle said. "Although it probably sounded like it just now, and I'm sorry."

Kyle twisted and took off his rucksack and reached in for his water bottle. Time to change the subject. "Again, I'm sorry," he said. "Where are my manners? Are you thirsty, hungry? I don't have a huge selection but I'm happy to share what I've got. Chocolate?"

"Don't tease," Amanda said. "Never tease a woman about chocolate."

Kyle held up two foil-wrapped packages. "Milk or dark?"

"If William were here I'd run away with you right now," she said with a small smile. "Dark, please."

"So," Kyle said, "what was life like for you before..." he looked up at the trees and made a big sweeping motion.

"I was a teacher," Amanda said. "Elementary school. I taught third grade. I was, am, single. I'm a Pisces and I like an occasional pretty sunset, but I do *not* like long walks on the beach."

"Okay," Kyle said, drawing out the 'ay'. "Did that come out like a pick-up line? I really didn't mean for it to come out like a pick-up line. If it came out like a pick-up line I'm sorry, because it really wasn't a pick-up line."

Amanda giggled and took a bite of the chocolate that he handed her.

. . .

Kyle's radio chirped twice in rapid succession and he stopped Amanda for a second. "Go ahead," he said into the microphone.

"It's going to be sunrise in about half-an-hour," Eric said. "She needs to be getting back, like, now."

Kyle looked at the radio in disbelief and then checked his watch. 4:52.

"Roger," Kyle said.

"I had no idea it was this late, or early," Kyle said, apologetically. "How are you going to be for working in the field tomorrow?"

Amanda smiled. "I'll be fine," she said. "Sometimes William has bad nights and I'm up with him and still have to work the next day, so it'll be ok."

Kyle got up, helped Amanda up, and then put on his rucksack.

"Besides," Amanda said, "it was worth it."

She leaned in and kissed Kyle on the cheek and then stopped and kissed him again.

"Thank you, Kyle," she said. "Next week, let's try for Wednesday, okay?"

"It's a date," Kyle said without thinking.

"Yes," she said, "it's a date."

Chapter Twelve

"What in the world are you doing," Eric asked Kyle when he came back from a five-hour reconnaissance and surveillance patrol of Clint's main encampment.

"Huh," Kyle said as he looked up from his phone and then put it away, "oh, nothing. Yes, I heard you coming; no, I wasn't asleep at the wheel."

"No," Eric said, "but your mind is still somewhere else."

Kyle shook his head and looked in the general direction of Clint's camp. "This is going to sound stupid," he said, "but I wish I could call her."

Eric made a noise that sounded like a cross between a snort and a sigh.

"See," Kyle said. "I told you it was going to sound stupid."

"No," Eric said. "It's not stupid and I wasn't laughing."

Eric took a deep breath after he sat down and leaned against his ruck. "It's not stupid at all, Kyle," Eric said again, "and I know exactly what you mean. If you were fifteen we would call it a crush, and if this was an office we would call it..." Eric shrugged.

"Being a middle-aged man with a crush," Kyle said.

"Probably," Eric said with a sad smile. "Look, Kyle, I know I'm the one who originally brought it up but are you sure this is really a good idea?"

"We already talked about this, Eric," Kyle said, and then sighed. The way Eric asked, Kyle wasn't sure exactly what point he was trying to make.

"There're only two of us, Kyle," Eric said. "We have no idea what we're walking into; regardless of any intel Amanda can bring us. You and I both know you'd never run an operation with your men under these circumstances."

"I have to do this," Kyle said, "even if it means going it alone."

"Why," Eric asked.

"Because it's not just a crush," Kyle said. "I think I'm in love, and I can't just walk away. I won't just leave her there. I won't abandon her."

Eric looked at the sky for a few seconds, trying to gather his thoughts. "Kyle," he said. "Listen to yourself; actually listen to what you're saying. You, *we*, still have no viable plan. We still have no idea how many people would be for or against taking Clint down. Are you really willing to go through with all of this just because you think you might be in love?"

"Maybe I can convince Amanda to just leave then," Kyle said.

"You know she won't leave without William," Eric said, "but what if she or William won't leave without somebody else, or a whole family? What then?"

"I'll figure something out," Kyle said. "It'll work out, Eric."

Eric wanted to choke Kyle. "Things don't always work out," Eric said softly.

"It has to," Kyle said. "I know it will. It sounds corny, but I want to spend the rest of my life with Amanda."

Eric froze. For a few seconds he forgot to breathe. The phrase had been like a slap in the face. Kyle honestly hadn't meant anything by it, but it hit Eric like a physical blow. Eric blinked a couple of times and then got up, turned around, and started walking out of camp.

It wasn't until Eric stood up without saying anything that Kyle realized what he'd said and how it must have come across. He felt like the world's biggest tool.

"Eric," he said, but Eric didn't react to his name. He didn't turn around, didn't wave Kyle back, nothing.

"Man, I really screwed up there," Kyle thought. *"He didn't take anything with him…I hope he's coming back. Please be coming back."*

…

Kyle was making dinner when Eric came walking back into camp. He'd been gone for almost three hours and Kyle had really started to worry. When Eric had been gone for about half-an-hour, Kyle realized he didn't even have his radio on his belt and all he'd taken with him were his pocket knife, his sidearm, and anything he'd been carrying in his pockets.

"Hey," Kyle said. "Look, I'm sorry, man. I didn't even think…"

"Don't," Eric said, interrupting Kyle who was half-a-sentence from apoplexy. "You didn't do anything wrong and I'm not mad at you. I'm not even mad, really. I'm still grieving. I will be for a long time. But I don't blame you for what you're feeling. I'm happy for you, Kyle. Really."

Kyle was still embarrassed, but nodded in understanding. "Thanks," he said.

…

June 22, 2013 - Promised Land Army Base, Natchez Trace State Park, Tennessee

"Mathis," Ben said as he sat down in the interview room—or, in this case, interrogation room.

Mathis nodded once to Ben, but didn't say anything. His attitude since his capture had been…aloof; completely different from anything he'd displayed in the eight years that Ben had known him.

"So, still nothing," Ben said. "I don't qualify for rank or even a title anymore? Just a head nod."

"As I've said, I no longer recognize your authority," Mathis said. "I never have."

"And why is that," Ben asked.

Mathis pursed his lips into a small frown and shook his head, but said nothing.

Ben leaned forward. "Today is going to be different, Mathis," he said. "Today you are going to talk to me. Today, you are going to tell me whatever I want to know."

"No," Mathis said. "It won't be any different than any other day in the last week, with one possible exception. You might finally get angry enough to make a mistake."

Ben gritted his teeth and left the room.

…

June 22, 2013 - Fort Rucker, Alabama

"Major Sanford," Lieutenant Cliff Hodges said as he knocked on the door frame. "I'm sorry to interrupt, Sir, but there's something I think you need to see."

Lieutenant Hodges had been the Colonel's liaison during the mission against Ft. Campbell a week ago. He was also one of the few people that Sanford had discussed his misgivings about the Colonel with.

"Here, or," Sanford let the question hang.

"If you would come with me," Hodges said. "It's something that was recovered during the raid."

That piqued Sanford's interest as he thought he'd already seen or heard about everything that they had found. Sanford locked his laptop in his desk and started following Hodges to the warehouse they were currently using to store everything they'd deemed of value that couldn't, or shouldn't, be left at Campbell. He was surprised when Hodges instead took him to one of the vehicle-maintenance depots, and even more surprised when it was the one furthest away from the Administration buildings.

"Dare I ask," Sanford said.

"I'm not sure you would believe me if I told you, Sir," Hodges said and led Sanford through the building and out the back.

In the lot was a HMMWV, or Hummer, with an Expanded Capacity Command and Control system. It *looked* like it was being repaired but it had several antennae fully extended, which was decidedly non-standard practice for a vehicle undergoing maintenance.

"Ok, talk to me, Hodges," Sanford said.

Hodges held up one finger and opened one of the doors to the Hummer.

…

Ben walked into the interrogation room for the second time, and this time he wasn't alone. Neither man said anything, but the person accompanying Ben was carrying what looked like a large, metal toolbox.

Ben stood across the table from Mathis and placed both hands on the table in front of him. "We're going to talk," he said. "*We*, you and I, two people. I'm going to ask questions and you are going to provide answers."

"No," Mathis said, but was cut off when Ben slapped the table. Mathis smiled ever so slightly.

Ben took out a second set of handcuffs with only one cuff attached to three links. His assistant reached into the toolbox and handed Ben a cordless drill and a screw, which Ben used to fasten the handcuff to the wooden table.

Ben then went around behind Mathis, uncuffed his left hand from his manacles and brought it to the table. Mathis was watching Ben the entire time over his shoulder and missed what Ben's assistant had been doing. Ben cuffed Mathis' left hand to the table and walked around to the other side of the table.

Mathis finally took notice of what was now laid out on the table to his left side. A dozen tongue depressors, a stack of gauze, and several strips of tape.

Mathis quirked another smile. "That's supposed to make me talk," he asked.

Ben leaned towards Mathis and for the first time, Mathis wondered if he might not be as hard as his former boss. "No," Ben said. "*You're* going to make you talk. I'm just going to help. Those are splints."

The smile disappeared from Mathis's face.

"I'm going to ask a question," Ben said, "and if you *choose* not to answer, or I don't like the answer you choose to give, I'm going to break a joint in one of your fingers."

"You wouldn't," Mathis almost gasped.

"I will," Ben said. "Whether or not I do is entirely up to you. I am perfectly capable, and at this point more than willing, to break every joint in your hand. You cost the lives of seventeen of my men, and I had to leave behind eighty-one more. I'll start with an easy one, one I *know* you know the answer to. How long have you been in contact with Olsen behind my back?"

...

"What am I looking at," Sanford asked.

"We found this," Hodges indicated the laptop and what appeared to be a homebrew radio, "powered on and running when we did a sweep of the base."

Hodges bent down to retrieve something from under the seat. "This was duct-taped on top of the laptop," Hodges said, "on the palm-rest. Right over where the hard drive sits."

"What is that," Sanford asked.

"It's a magnetic tape eraser," the Sergeant running the radio gear in the Hummer said and glared at Hodges. "And I really wish it was about fifty feet from the inside of this vehicle, Sirs."

Hodges covered his smile well, but Sanford completely understood the Sergeant's unease. One push of the button and the hard drive would have been toast beyond their ability to restore. Pre-event, maybe they could have put it back together…maybe. Now, there would have been no way.

"Duly noted, Sergeant," Hodges said. "I don't think we'll be needing it anymore. I did discharge it a number of times before bringing it anywhere near the truck."

The Sergeant wasn't mollified but didn't really have a choice in the matter and just kept silent.

"That doesn't answer the first question," Sanford said. "I see a laptop and what I can only assume is a radio of some kind. Homemade, I would assume."

Hodges turned to the Sergeant, Tuttle the nametape said, and nodded.

"It's a HAM radio, Sir," Tuttle said, "and don't let the fact that it's a homebrew fool you. Whoever designed and built it knew what they were doing. It's limited to a couple of bands but I'm impressed. The laptop though, that's the key…"

…

"So you're telling me that there is a whole separate, what," Sanford waved his hands in the air, "secret communications network going on out there? It's happening on frequencies that we can monitor right now, but all we'd hear is static unless we ran the transmission through the laptop to decode it?"

"Pretty much," Hodges said.

"And why am I just now hearing about this," Sanford asked.

"Because we weren't absolutely positive about it until we picked up a transmission," Hodges said, "and were able to decode it in real time on this rig," Hodges pointed to the laptop and HAM combination, "while getting nothing but static on Uncle Sugar's multi-million dollar state-of-the-art receivers."

Sanford sat back in the increasingly uncomfortable seat and folded his arms.

"There's one other thing," Tuttle said.

Both Hodges and Sanford looked at Tuttle, since nothing else had come up during any of the conversations Hodges had had with Tuttle.

"I've been thinking a lot about it and," Tuttle paused for a second, "there are only a couple of options that make sense. I say that because we found the laptop with the user logged in and the decoder running. The first possibility is that the person who was using this pushed the button when they left, or thought they did, and expected to wipe the drive, or they truly thought they were going to be coming back."

Tuttle looked at the Lieutenant and the Major and then continued. "The second possibility is that we were meant to find it."

Sanford didn't say anything but looked at Hodges.

"You can speak freely in front of Sergeant Tuttle, Major," Hodges said, knowing what Sanford was thinking. "We all share the same concerns."

Sanford nodded. "In that case," he said, "I don't think it matters. We have it now and we need to make sure we use it wisely, if at all. Who else knows about this so far?"

"A total of five people now," Hodges said, "including the three of us.

"There were three of us clearing the building," Tuttle said. "I told them I'd take care of the radio while they handled the rest of the building, since it was electronic. They wouldn't know the difference between a HAM radio and a toaster oven."

"Good," Sanford said, "for now we're going to keep it that way."

Chapter Thirteen

Kyle greeted Amanda with a hug the second time they met in the middle of the night, and got a kiss on the cheek in return.

"How are things going in camp," Kyle asked.

"About the same," Amanda said, "for everyone except me. Clint is really trying to turn up the heat. He was busy today—working. I mean really working for once, with one of the ranchers we've been trying to work out an agreement with. That's the only reason I was able to make it tonight. He was exhausted."

"I'm glad you were able to," Kyle said and paused. "I really missed you."

Amanda reached out and took his hand. "I missed you too," she said. "I know we agreed you wouldn't show up at the field anymore, but I kept checking as I got near the end of the row, hoping you might be there."

"You don't know how close I came to showing up," Kyle said with a smile. "Eric and I think we've come up with a way to get you out of there, though, with anyone else who wants to leave. You need to meet him, too, although he isn't going to stay for long because someone needs to be on patrol."

Amanda nodded and looked around.

Kyle keyed his microphone twice and a minute later Eric materialized out of the dark.

"Ma'am," Eric said. "My name is Eric Tripp. Technically, I'm a Captain in the US Army and this guy's superior Officer, but right now we're kind of AWOL–that's Absent Without Leave–so we'll see how long either of us keeps our rank."

Amanda really hadn't had any experience with the military before the power went out, so she just nodded again.

"How bad is it getting," Eric asked. "Or, maybe I should just cut to the chase. What's the likelihood of someone else stepping in to fill a leadership void if Clint were...no longer in charge?"

Amanda thought for a few seconds before she answered. "It would have to be more than Clint," she said. "Cooper and Tony would both have to go, too.

She made a face and then continued. "You know, six or eight months ago I would have said the same thing about Earl too," she said, "but not anymore. Earl's...changed. He isn't the creepy, aggressive guy he used to be. Clint still tries to lean on him a lot but he just isn't like he used to be."

Eric looked at Kyle and nodded.

"In that case," Kyle said, "here's what we were thinking..."

...

"Who's got first watch," Kyle asked the next night, knowing they were going to need all the sleep they could get for the next several nights.

"You sleep," Eric said. "I don't seem to need as much as I used to anyway."

Kyle nodded and chose not to get into it with Eric. Now that they were out of the base and on their own, Eric had picked up the grieving and he just needed to let it run its course.

...

Two days later, Amanda finally had a chance to bring things to Clint's attention.

Clint had been trying to spend more time with Amanda recently, although he was all but ignoring William. He'd made dinner for the two of them and they were eating in the kitchen of his trailer. Clint was running the small generator that powered the air conditioner, so they were eating inside for once.

She was struck, again, by the double standard he lived by. He ran the generator whenever he thought it necessary, like now. He had someone come in and clean the trailer once a week, but would have thrown a fit if anyone else took someone from their job to perform such menial labor. As much as she hated to admit it, he ate better than everyone else, too.

Once dinner was over she figured it was her best shot at telling Clint their story without him reacting...badly.

"Uhm," she started.

"Uhm what," Clint said.

"I did something I really wasn't supposed to do," Amanda said. "But I think it's a good thing that I did."

Clint gave her a sidelong glance.

Amanda blushed and looked down for a second and then looked back at Clint. "I thought I saw something," she said, "or someone, in the tall grass outside of the field I work in a couple of days ago. After lights-out I went back to the field and found where someone had been laying in the grass. I followed their trail back to their campsite."

Amanda looked away again. "I know," she said. "I'm not supposed to leave our camp, but it kind of had me freaked out."

She looked back at Clint who did *not* look happy. "Nobody saw me," she said quickly. "I doubled back on my own trail on the way back to make sure I wasn't followed, too."

Clint shook his head. "And this is the first I'm hearing about it?"

"I'm sorry," she said. "I knew you needed to know but I was afraid you'd be really upset."

Clint took a deep breath. As upset as he was, and it seemed like he was always angry these days, it wasn't really at Amanda. "You should have told me as soon as you thought you saw someone outside of your field," he said. "I can understand not mentioning it to Tony, but you should have told me right away."

He reached out and grabbed her chin to make sure she was looking at him. "And don't do anything like that again," he said. "Ever."

Amanda realized that if things didn't go exactly as planned, she might never see Kyle again.

...

"I could find it again," Amanda said, "but I don't think I could pinpoint it on a map."

"Going out and looking for them without knowing where they are is just asking for trouble," Coop said.

"Going out and looking for them is what we do if we don't know where they are, Coop," Clint thought. *"You have had it too easy with me for too long."*

"From the looks of the campsite," Amanda said, "there were only two people. If you, Coop, and Tony go, and you take me, that'd make it two to one. Plus, we'd have the element of surprise."

"Why do *you* want to go so bad," Tony asked.

"Because they were watching my field," Amanda said with a little heat in her voice. "I want to be there when they get...whatever!"

Clint nodded. "I can see that," he said. "We, the three of us, haven't been on a raid in a while. It'll look good if we throw something together and execute it on our own."

"Bad juju, Boss," Coop said, "but it's your call."

"Yes, it is."

...

"When are they going to show up," Kyle thought to himself. It had only been three days, but now that they had a plan it was driving him nuts that it wasn't moving forward.

He couldn't sleep and had his radio next to his head, volume down low when "–. –" came through in Morse code.

"Go. Finally," Kyle thought and relaxed for the first time since he'd sent Amanda back, hopefully for the last time.

Sure, if something went wrong some time in the next half hour or so he, Eric, or Amanda could end up dead, but at least things were moving at last.

Kyle stopped breathing.

Amanda could end up dead.

That was the first time the thought that something horrible could happen to her as a result of their plan had crossed his mind. Up until now he had only been worrying about himself and Eric–not because he was self-centered, but because he really didn't think anything would happen to Amanda. The story they had concocted seemed pretty airtight, and he was confident in both his and Eric's abilities.

For Kyle, the next fifteen minutes made the last four days seem to fly by.

...

"We're getting close," Amanda said quietly, but not in a whisper. After the failed raid on the base, Clint had taught his people just how far a whisper carried and how to communicate in a low voice.

His people had gotten better at moving quietly in the woods, too. On this trip, Cooper was by far the best, since he'd been hunting all of his life, and Tony was a close second. They'd both honed some skills while on the police force before the power went out.

After a couple of minutes she saw the orange glow of the banked coals and held up her hand.

None of the would-be raiders saw or heard anything less than fifteen feet to their right, in the woods.

. . .

Kyle's radio was in his bag with the volume turned off. When the single "." came through, it lit up a red light that only he could see, and only because he knew to look for it. His bag was unzipped and he'd practiced getting out of it at least a hundred times just in the last couple of days. He took the safety off of his .45, which was already cocked with one in the chamber, and got ready to...surprise...the raiders.

. . .

Eric was inching closer to the group and would come into the clearing behind them. Kyle was notified, and Eric was both relieved and worried to see Amanda in the group. Theoretically, it evened the odds; potentially, it put Kyle's head in a bad place and gave Clint a hostage. Eric was ready to kill all three of the men himself if necessary, though. Hopefully, it wouldn't come to that, but he and Kyle had decided that the threat to the base, Redemption, and the surrounding area came to an end tonight.

. . .

Kyle was trying to keep his heart-rate down and his breathing even, but it was a constant battle. It had been a while since he'd seen combat and the adrenaline was starting to flow. He could hear the frogs croaking in a pond that had to be at least a quarter-of-a-mile away, the ever-present crickets, and a couple of birds that didn't realize it was after midnight. Then, like someone had thrown a switch, the woods were silent. Kyle heard the footfalls of the people in his campsite and he had to remind himself that it was all part of the plan. He knew where Eric would be coming in from and was just waiting for his cue.

...

Eric could see the entire clearing and the raiding party was just beginning to spread out when he stepped into the clearing.

...

The couple of people in this camp looked to both be in their sleeping bags and asleep. The fire was going out and, if nothing else, they could simply grab a rifle and their backpacks. Clint was just about to breathe a sigh of relief when several things happened almost simultaneously.

First, someone turned on a flashlight too early and Clint's night vision was completely ruined. That registered, and Clint was about to hiss something when the second thing happened.

A voice from behind them, vaguely familiar, said "Nobody move."

As soon as the voice behind him started talking–shouting, actually–one of the people on the ground jumped out of their sleeping bag and Clint's heart stopped. He was wearing Army fatigues. Then Clint was blinded almost completely as a second flashlight was shined in his eyes and then swept over the others in the group.

Eric came up behind one of the men; it turned out to be Tony. "Give me your weapon," he said.

Tony tightened his grip on his handgun.

"Don't be stupid," Clint said with false bravado. "There's only two of you and four of us."

Clint felt something cold at the base of his skull and Amanda said, "Actually, there are three of us."

Clint closed his eyes and clenched his jaw. "You cheating bi…" he started.

"Don't finish that thought," Kyle said as he swung the flashlight back to Clint while keeping his .45 trained on the other man.

"Give me your weapon," Eric said again.

"You'll just kill me if I do," Tony said.

"No," Eric said, "that's not how we work. You *will* end up giving me your weapon, though."

"No," Tony said, "I won't."

At 'No', Eric reached down and pinched Tony's wrist with two fingers on the underside, where the blood vessels are, and his thumb on the top of the wrist. *Hard.*

Tony swore as he dropped the gun to the ground and lost control of his hand.

"The next time I tell you to do something," Eric said calmly, "do it."

Cooper was the only one who didn't have someone within arm's reach, covering him. He had just decided to make a break for the tree line when Tony's gun hit the ground. Coop started to raise his own gun and lunged towards the tree line himself, when he realized he'd made a serious tactical error. While the flashlight was pointed at Clint, the other Army guy still had his pistol pointed directly at him.

Instead of making a mad dash for the trees, Coop ended up dropping to the ground, and almost as an afterthought, dropped his own gun. He wasn't a coward, but he was smart enough to know how this was going to end and he didn't want to die.

Dropping to the ground saved his life because Kyle was a little slow on the trigger. The first bullet went about where his chest would have been, and the second where his back was heading. Eric only fired one shot, also where Coop's torso would have been.

"OKAY, *OKAY*," Cooper yelled, his face planted firmly in the dirt and pine needles. "I'm down, and I swear I'm not going *anywhere* now."

"That just leaves you," Kyle said to Clint.

Clint took his finger off the trigger and fanned his fingers while he ejected the magazine. Then slowly, as he was now being covered by three people, ejected the round in the chamber and locked the slide back. Finally, he grabbed the gun by the barrel and held it out to Kyle, grip first.

"While I appreciate the gesture," Kyle said, "go ahead and just drop it. Amanda, you can back up now too."

Clint gritted his teeth and almost bent down to set the weapon on the ground, but instead simply let go of the barrel.

Clint turned his head slightly, just enough to be able to see Amanda. "This is the thanks I get," he snarled.

Amanda lifted her chin. "It's better than you deserve."

Chapter Fourteen

All three prisoners had their hands tied securely behind their backs, with an additional length of rope leading to a slip knot around their neck. None of them could be trusted as far as either Eric or Kyle was concerned, so they were gagged as well.

"Last stop before we get to your camp," Kyle said. "We're going to take off the gags and give you some water. Yelling would be...a bad idea."

Kyle took off Cooper's gag, gave him some water, and put the gag back on. Coop had been very subdued, ever since he'd almost bought-it last night.

Eric took off Tony's gag and was about to give him some water when Tony spit in his face.

Kyle stepped in and cold-cocked Tony, breaking his nose–and possibly some teeth. As Tony created a diversion, Clint turned to make a break for it and, instead, received the butt of Eric's rifle in the kidney. Coop just stood there and shook his head in disgust. It all happened so fast, Amanda hadn't quite had a chance to react.

Kyle stooped down to put Tony's gag back in and said, "Sorry, you won't be getting any water there, pal. Next time, think before you act."

After Eric helped Clint back up, he held up his canteen and got a curt nod from a wincing Clint. He took out the gag and gave him some water.

"What are you going to do with us," Clint asked for the thousandth time since the raid had gone bad.

"Only what you deserve," Kyle answered, yet again.

…

As they approached the camp, they eventually caught the attention of one of the guards.

"Halt!" he said. "Who goes there?"

"Who actually says that," Kyle thought, and almost laughed out loud.

"It's me, Amanda," Amanda said. "I'm with Clint, Coop, and Tony. We found a couple of other people while we were out last night."

They hadn't stopped walking at the command to halt, and Amanda was in the lead. She kept the guard's attention until it was too late for him to raise the alarm.

"Bad idea," Eric said, as the guard drew a breath to yell.

When he realized he had three guns trained on him, he deflated and handed over his rifle.

Clint closed his eyes and slumped a little. If this was the best chance he had of being rescued, he was doomed. It was almost sunrise and everyone would be getting up shortly, but by then he had no doubt that his captors would have full control of the camp.

Amanda led everyone, the guard included, straight to Clint's trailer.

"Everyone inside," Kyle said. "You too, gorgeous," he said to Tony— who looked awful with all of the sticky, drying blood on his face and shirt from his broken nose.

Once they were all inside, the trailer felt extremely crowded until all of the prisoners were finally sitting down. First, they tied up the guard so he couldn't raise any kind of alarm, and then Eric started rummaging around the cabinets and drawers, clearly looking for something specific.

Once he found a BIC stick pen, he squatted down in front of Tony and said, "This is going to hurt, a lot, but it's the right thing to do. Lie down on your back."

Tony just glared at Eric until Kyle made a fist that cracked his knuckles. He'd been doing that a lot lately. Tony shot a worried glance at Kyle and then lay down on his back where the 'kitchen' table would usually go.

"You can whimper," Eric said, "you can curse under your breath, and you can mutter all you want, but do. not. scream. Do I make myself clear?"

With the gag in place, all Tony could do was nod.

As gently as he could, Eric felt for where the break was in the nose. Tony winced, but he didn't make a sound. Next, he used the pen to keep things straight inside each nostril, and then he set Tony's broken nose.

He was right. It hurt, a *lot*, but not as badly as getting it broken. It didn't even bleed that much after it was set.

Clint made some muffled noises and Kyle pulled his gag down.

"Why'd you bother doing that," Clint asked.

"I already told you," Eric said. "It's the right thing to do. I'm not planning on killing you and I'm not going to let the rest of your camp kill you either. As far as I know you're all going to live long, productive lives. Tony here is going to need to be able to breathe through his nose–simple as that."

Eric helped Tony up and then he sat down next to Coop.

"Now," Eric said, "I'm not a dentist, but let's have a look at your teeth. Bite me and I'll go back on my word. I'll blow this whole thing right now and shoot you in the head."

Tony's eyes got big and he shook his head.

"Ok," Eric said and took off the gag. "Nope, clean hit. Busted lip and nose."

Eric turned to Kyle. "Well done," he said, "don't do it again. I've been spit on by better than this. Give me a clean gag."

"Yes, Sir," Kyle said a bit sheepishly.

. . .

"Okay, Amanda," Kyle said. "It's time."

Amanda nodded and reached out and squeezed Kyle's hand and then leaned in to give him a kiss. Clint ground his teeth some more because there was nothing *else* he could do.

Amanda left the trailer and went to find Earl.

A couple of minutes after Amanda left the trailer, the old hand-crank air-raid siren that they used to signal a camp meeting started up. Everyone should be gathered in less than five minutes.

. . .

Amanda went to Earl's trailer and knocked on the door.

"Just a second," came a voice that was less than pleased to be disturbed.

After a minute, Earl answered the door. He'd lost a *lot* of weight over the last year, and was tucking in his shirt. "Yes, Amanda…isn't it?"

"Clint wants everyone gathered in the center of camp, ASAP," she said and blushed a little. "He wants to make an important announcement."

She'd been trying to think of things that would make her blush and Kyle had popped into her head just as she said the part about the important announcement. Everyone knew that Clint had been pursuing Amanda, and Earl read exactly what she hoped he would into the statement.

Earl nodded and headed over to the siren.

…

"Amanda said to give it about six or seven minutes after the siren," Eric said looking at Clint. "Long enough to get everyone there, but not long enough to have someone come looking for you."

Clint made a face around the gag, but nodded.

"Let's go, then," Eric said.

…

Eric was leading the procession of four leashed prisoners, with his .45 pointed at the back of Clint's head. Kyle brought up the rear and covered everyone with his M4.

They gave the gathered group a wide berth. Amanda saw them coming and got up on the picnic table to draw everyone's attention to herself.

"Everyone," she said, and all eyes quickly turned to her. The nasty business of William's father was still fresh in everyone's memory, and nobody wanted a repeat of that.

"We have a very special announcement to make," Amanda continued. "As of this morning, there's going to be a change," and Amanda put on a big smile.

Eric took over at this point with his Drill Sergeant voice. "Yes There Is," he boomed as the group came into view from behind a trailer. Several guns came out of holsters, but were almost immediately lowered as folks got a better view of what was going on. The guns were not, however, put away.

"Clint is no longer in charge," Eric said as he pushed for the line of prisoners to step up onto the table in front of him. "And neither are Cooper or Tony. Call it an end to a reign of terror, or a regime change, or just a coup. Whatever it is, these three will no longer be running things around here. In fact, they won't be around here at all anymore."

Mutters and mumbling came from the crowd, but Eric put an end to that.

"I'm Not Finished," he barked and everyone grew silent. Clint was in awe, even as he seethed. "I have been led to believe that some of you would have liked to leave after the last...incident... at one of these meetings, but everyone who left did so on foot and without any provisions. I have a problem with that..."

Eric was interrupted by Kyle's rifle coming down between Tony's and Coop's shoulders and aiming at the crowd and Kyle yelling "Drop It!" Kyle had been watching the crowd ever since they had all gotten up on the table, which was groaning and protesting the weight of all six men, and had seen someone starting to eye Eric. As Kyle yelled for the man to drop his weapon, he raised his pistol to shoot, but was tackled by at least a half-dozen people around him. It looked like the people formerly known as Clint's merry band of misfits were at the very least able to police themselves in time of need.

A very short struggle ensued, followed by a yelp and a few curses. The offending party was escorted to the front of the crowd, with his pants hanging loosely around his waist as his belt was now being used to bind his hands. Someone bent his knees for him to make him kneel down, and then pushed him into a sitting position so he couldn't get up quickly.

Eric tried not to acknowledge what had happened, but smiled a little before he went on. I guess you could call the two of us mercenaries, since we're doing this at the request of someone else. But, since we're doing it for free, I think I'd prefer the term freedom fighters."

Eric pointed at the crowd, "*You* need to choose someone to be in charge now."

Immediately there was more murmuring and talking amongst the crowd, until someone yelled, "Earl." Several other people yelled in agreement, and then a large part of the crowd took it up like a chant.

Eric held up his hand and everyone was quiet in just a couple of seconds. Again, Clint was amazed and furious at the same time. "Earl," Eric said. "The people are pretty clear, what do you say?"

And then it hit Clint. He knew where he recognized this guy from; that day out on the road, when we had the flat tire and I was talking like an inbred idiot. Earl getting all hot under the collar and me having to cool him down. *I've been having run-ins with the Army since day* ONE, *"* Clint fumed.

"No way," Earl said. "I don't want to be in charge. I've spent the last six months trying *not* to be in charge."

Eric interrupted him. "I didn't ask if you wanted to be in charge," he snapped. "I asked if you would do it. Our Mayor didn't want it either, but he stepped up once the votes were counted. Look around, who else is there? We're leaving, so someone has to step up."

Earl was silent for several seconds before he responded. "Okay then, they have to vote," Earl said. "Everyone has to vote. It doesn't have to be unanimous, since I'm sure it won't be, but it has to be a majority."

"By a show of hands," Eric said. "And no cheating. All those in favor?"

It looked like somewhere between half and two-thirds.

"All those opposed?"

About one-third.

Earl took a deep breath, let it out, and walked up to the table. "That thing isn't going to hold another person," he said to Eric.

Eric nodded and Kyle cut the rope between Clint and Cooper, and then led everyone but Clint off the table.

Earl considered his options for a moment and then climbed up. "Can I have you release them into my custody," he asked Eric.

"The guard, yes," Eric said. "The other three, no. You and I both know that would be a bad idea for a number of reasons."

Earl nodded and turned to Clint. "I'm sorry," Earl said.

"That's it for now, everybody," Earl said. "I have a feeling I need to chat with these folks, so don't be surprised if you hear the siren a little later. Normal work schedule until lunch. Nothing'll be decided before then."

Chapter Fifteen

June 27, 2013 - Promised Land Army Base, Natchez Trace State Park, Tennessee

Mathis was trying to ignore the throbbing from his dislocated left ring finger. He really hadn't thought Ben would have the guts to carry through with his threat. The taped splint on his hand proved just how wrong he'd been.

Mathis was focusing on what his guards were saying outside his makeshift cell, while ignoring the fire in his hand. They were complaining about "babysitting the traitor" as they changed shifts. Instead of keeping their mouths shut and doing their jobs, they were busy talking about what they would rather be doing around the base, down in town, or on one of the outlying farms. For the last week he'd been gathering whatever intelligence he could about the base and the surrounding area from their conversations, just in case he got a chance to use it.

For example, he now knew that they had three fuel dumps around camp, one of which was fairly close to the brig. He also knew that they were still using surface water from the lakes in the park for almost all of their potable water. Those two pieces of information alone could prove very handy if he ever got out of here.

...

"Dinner," the guard said, before he opened up the door to Mathis's cell. It had been replaced with a door of welded steel bars earlier in the day. Mathis was on his side, on his cot, with his back to the door…eyes closed and shivering slightly.

"Just stay on your cot and I'll bring the tray in," the guard said.

Usually they would open the door, enter his cell, and then close the door. Once the guard was in the room and a little closer to Mathis, he noticed that he was shivering. He set the tray down on the small table, the door forgotten, and took a couple of steps closer to the cot.

"Hey," he said. "Are you ok?"

Mathis didn't respond or react at all.

The guard took another couple of steps and put his hand on Mathis's shoulder. The guard didn't want to get any closer in case Mathis had somehow come down with whatever was going around the base, even with the quarantine. It was just about all he and his buddies had been talking about for the last week and now that the antibiotics were all but gone, he was wondering if he needed to call for the medics.

…

This was the opening Mathis had been hoping for. He'd listened for the door to shut after the guard came in, and when there was no clang of metal on metal he knew that this would be his best chance of escape. As the guard's footsteps came closer, he opened his right eye slightly to see if he could gauge the guard's position by his shadow. When the guard put his hand on Mathis's shoulder, he struck.

Mathis swung his left elbow up and back as he pushed himself up on his right elbow. He was rewarded with a solid impact on the side of the guard's head, immediately followed by a fresh bloom of agony in his hand from the jolt it sent to his finger. The guard was only dazed and not out, though, so Mathis couldn't take time to nurse his screaming hand.

Mathis rolled off the cot and stepped into a punch that drove all the air from the guard and dropped him to one knee. The guard was completely out of the fight at this point; he hadn't been expecting anything and the hit to the head had stunned him enough to give Mathis his opening.

After a quick glance at the door, Mathis stepped behind the guard, put him in a choke hold with his right arm, and started to squeeze. The guard put up a struggle, but he hadn't had a chance to take a breath since the first punch, so it was weak and short-lived. It took almost a minute for the guard to go completely limp, and then Mathis had a decision to make. Ben had accused him of being responsible for the deaths of seventeen men, but he hadn't seen it that way. Now, with what he was planning, he *would* be directly responsible for the deaths of heaven only knew how many; and he needed as much time as possible before someone raised an alarm.

So, Mathis kept the pressure on the guard's neck for a full three minutes.

...

The radio on the table just outside of Mathis's cell came to life as Sergeant Keeler was checking in on the guard on duty. He'd missed his check-in at the bottom of the hour and was about the get reamed out for it, but he didn't respond. The guard was lying on the cot facing the wall, under the blanket. He wasn't going to be responding to anything. Mathis had made sure there wasn't a heartbeat before he left.

Just as Sergeant Keeler was making a second call on the radio, there was a deafening explosion that shattered the window above the bed in the cell and rolled the guard's body onto his back.

...

Mathis was wearing the guard's blouse and cap, and had taken his sidearm, knife, lighter, and multi-tool. He had a rudimentary plan but not much more, and needed a few minutes alone to think things out.

He ducked into one of the latrines and took a minute to calm down. He was out of his cell but still completely surrounded. He needed to cause a distraction, even better if he could cause some damage to the base at the same time.

After a minute of trying not to breathe too deeply, he got to work. First, he thanked his lucky stars that he'd stopped in the latrine. He pulled off three squares of toilet paper and stacked them on his lap. Then he thumbed five rounds out of the magazine of the .45 he'd gotten off the guard and, using the pliers on the multi-tool, pulled the projectile from the end and dumped the gunpowder onto the toilet paper. It wasn't a huge amount, but he was sure it would be enough for what he needed to do.

Finally, he pulled the corners and sides of the square of toilet paper together and twisted the ends to seal it into a tight, compact, tear-drop shaped bundle. He dropped the casings and bullets into the latrine, opened the door, and headed in what he was pretty sure was the direction of the closest fuel dump. Or so he had gathered from the guards' constant chatting.

It took a couple of minutes to walk there; Mathis was surprised by the size of the base. On a whim, he grabbed a five-gallon jerry can and headed towards the sound of a running diesel engine. He was pretty sure it was one of the reverse osmosis units—still running after a year—and would be fairly close to their water source. The closer he got to the engine, the louder it grew, and he made another decision. If he was stopped, he'd fight his way out.

There was only one person manning the unit, and he just nodded in Mathis's direction. They weren't really close enough to see each other's faces, and Mathis nodded back. Mathis kept walking until he was around a couple of bends from the reverse osmosis unit and its operator, and then stopped.

He'd gotten lucky when he'd picked up the fuel can and grabbed one that was only partially full, but even a couple of gallons got heavy after a while. He had considered swapping hands but knew that his left hand wouldn't hold the weight for more than a few seconds with his finger in a splint like it was.

Mathis looked around to make sure nobody could see him and then took a few steps to get closer to the water. Instead of dumping the diesel directly into the lake, he decided to tip the can on its side and let it spill and run into the lake. The effect would be the same, and he wouldn't have to stand there and wait for the can to empty. He wouldn't run the risk of it splashing all over him, either. He opened the can, laid it down, and the fuel started gurgling out, running towards the water.

...

Mathis was shaking as he stepped back from the water. He had just taken a big step from escaped prisoner who'd supposedly aided and abetted the enemy to potential mass murderer and, he snorted, environmental terrorist. The reverse osmosis units could still provide water for the base and the town but their efficiency was going to be *vastly* diminished and the filters and membranes were going to wear out much quicker.

Fuel leaks and spills were always a concern when the Army moved. While he was pretty sure the amount of diesel he'd just dumped into the lake wasn't enough to destroy the ecology of the park, Mathis was positive it would be enough put a kink in their water supply, at least for a little while.

Mathis took a deep breath to calm himself, and got a lungful of diesel fumes, which made him cough. *"Serves you right,"* he thought.

He started back to the base, empty-handed.

As he approached the water purification unit, he imagined he could hear the engine running faster to work the pump harder but knew it was just in his head. The water couldn't be contaminated already; it was just his guilty conscience. He did look up and see that the operator was looking at him, though, staring at him. Why?

"Because you walked past here with a jerry can, not five minutes ago," he thought, *"and now you're empty-handed. Of course he's curious. Crap!"*

Mathis warred with himself for a second and then walked over to the unit and the operator.

"Didn't you just have a…" was as far as the operator got.

Mathis pulled the .45 and put two in his chest from less than ten feet away. The slide locked back on an empty chamber.

"Tough luck, man," Mathis said as he reached down and grabbed the other man's gun, extra magazine, and flashlight. "Wrong place, wrong time."

The sound of the generator had covered the sound of the handgun going off, but Mathis still looked around to make sure nobody was coming and then dragged the body into the woods.

…

It was a short walk back to the fuel dump and the base proper, and now that he was committed things seemed to go quickly. There were a number of fifty-five-gallon drums, jerry cans, and a short-bed fuel truck.

"Biggest bang for the buck," Mathis thought, and climbed up the back of the truck.

Once on top, he opened the observation hatch and shined the flashlight in to check the fuel level; about half full, and it was diesel.

He set his gunpowder bundle on the edge of the observation hatch, with the twisted point facing out, and then gently lowered the lid to hold it in place. With his legs hanging over the edge of the truck, he lit the point of toilet paper and then jumped off the truck, planning to make a mad dash as fast and as far away as he could before things blew sky high.

"Maybe I should go back and wreck the reverse osmosis unit," he thought as he ran.

…

The toilet-paper fuse burned until it hit the small bundle of gunpowder–about two seconds, and the majority of the powder burned quickly and harmlessly outside of the fuel truck's tank. The little bundle collapsed, however, and the observation-port lid fell shut. A small amount of burning gunpowder fell inside the tank where the diesel fuel vapor to air mixture was well within the explosive range.

Mathis got almost twenty feet away before the fuel truck erupted, spraying diesel fuel for over a hundred-and-fifty feet in almost every direction and puncturing and igniting the surrounding fuel drums and jerry cans. The area had been picked for a fuel dump because of its relatively sparse vegetation, but nobody had expected an explosion of any kind, much less this magnitude. The forest had caught fire about seventy feet to the north of the explosion's center.

There were no buildings or tents right next to the fuel dump, but a half-a-dozen vehicles had been knocked on their sides or completely flipped over, and were now on fire.

The explosion knocked Mathis down and covered him in flaming diesel fuel. Mathis, screaming and completely engulfed in flames, tried to stand up. A secondary explosion from ruptured gasoline cans peppered him with shrapnel and knocked him back down. He wasn't going to get the chance to sabotage the water filter after all.

On top of everything else, Promised Land had just lost a third of its fuel.

…

"How many more transmissions before you think you can break it," Sanford asked.

"Possibly none but most likely at least two more Sir," Sergeant Tuttle said. "I have a couple of computers working on the recorded transmissions but breaking a real-time transmission is actually easier, sometimes."

"And how many do we have recorded," Sanford asked.

"All of them, Sir," Tuttle said. "Every single one going all the way back to a couple of days after the power went out and the satellites came back online."

Just then one of Tuttle's laptops beeped and he opened it up. He typed on the first one and all of the 'activity' on the screen stopped. He opened the other two and typed on both of them and the screen activity stopped for a couple of seconds and then the activity started on all three simultaneously.

"And what did I just witness," Sanford asked, realizing that when he came to this Humvee he spent most of his time asking questions.

"There is a very high probability," Tuttle said, "that it just identified one of the words used in one of the transmissions. The one you overheard since you were able to give us a fairly good transcript of the last couple of minutes. Long story short, it's a chink in the encryption that I had to tell the system to account for moving forward."

"I have no idea how any of that works," Sanford said, "and I understood very little of what you just said but I'm going to trust you on that."

Tuttle just nodded. He'd been dealing with Major Sanford long enough to take it as a compliment but not long enough to be able to give him a hard time about it.

Chapter Sixteen

The third dinner shift in the mess hall was just ending and people were finishing their meals. Joel was having dinner with Maya and Josh for the first time in a week and trying to get a response other than "Okay" out of his daughter, when the explosion rocked the building.

Joel was momentarily stunned, but Josh pushed his sister under the table before the sound of the explosion had faded, and pulled the 9mm he'd taken to carrying.

"*Dad*", Josh yelled. "Get *down!*"

Joel shook his head to clear it and squatted next to the table, then looked around to assess the damage.

Wherever the…bomb? Whatever it was, wherever it had been, it wasn't close enough to have damaged the mess hall. They didn't have any glass in the windows, just wooden shutters to close during the winter. There wasn't any debris and nothing had blown in through the open windows or doors. Joel was pretty sure he could smell smoke now, though.

"Stay here until either I come back," Joel said, "or someone you know comes to get you."

Josh and Maya nodded.

Joel reached for his radio which came to life just as he was about to press the send button.

"Joel," Bill Stewart said, "We need some help. Grab as many able-bodied adults as you can and meet me at…"

…

Joel had gathered twenty men and half-a-dozen women on the way to meet Stewart.

"It was fuel dump two," Stewart told the group when they arrived. "I already have all the chainsaws out cutting a break around the fire to try and keep it contained. We need help shoveling more than anything since we can't use water to put it out; all it would do is spread the diesel."

Fire had always been the biggest concern Joel had about being in the forest. There wasn't much he could do to prevent it and their resources were limited when it came to fighting it. The Guard had a couple of fire trucks that had come with them, but right now they couldn't use them since the fire was still small enough that there was a real risk of the water simply spreading any unburned fuel.

Stewart started handing out shovels as Sergeant Keeler showed up to lead the volunteers away.

"Where's my shovel," Joel asked.

"I need you to coordinate and get additional volunteers," Stewart said.

"Like *hell*," Joel yelled.

"Joel," Stewart yelled right back, "I don't have time to argue. Those people are going to be exhausted in less than an hour. It's going to be hot, and we don't have any kind of breathing gear, so they are going to be exposed to fumes, smoke, and hot air. You are the Mayor, I need you to man up and get people down here to help out, not complain about how unfair it is that you didn't get to cut down a tree or dig a hole!"

Once he realized Stewart was right, he nodded and took off at a trot back towards the center of the base.

...

The sun stayed up until almost 9:00, which helped the firefighting effort immensely. They cut an initial firebreak, and felled the trees into the woods surrounding the fire. Once they completed the first pass, and the ground was cleared, they started a second pass to widen the firebreak to at least twenty feet. The first wave of volunteers was bone-tired, coated in dirt and ash, and nursing minor burns and lungs that felt lightly toasted.

Once the fire made it as far as the firebreak, they could use water to put it out, since it would no longer be fueled by the diesel. If nothing else, as long as the weather cooperated they could let the fire burn itself out within the confines of the firebreak.

Back at what remained of the fuel dump, Joel was rotating in new volunteers every thirty minutes. They started out as close in as they could get, and were shoveling dirt on any flare-ups or fires they could reach. Some fires would just have to burn themselves out, though. The remaining diesel in the fuel truck was a loss, and trying to put it out would render it useless. They had no other way to dispose of the ruined fuel, so they let it burn.

The heavy equipment that Ben had brought down from Ft. Campbell was a life-saver, and the only reason that the firebreak was complete by the time the sun went down. Once the trees were out of the way, three extra tractors and a front-end loader were able to clear the ground much faster than they could have done it by hand.

...

Allen Halstead stood with his hands behind his back, barely keeping his temper.

"Why," he asked, "was there only one guard on Lieutenant Mathis?"

Sergeant Pine swallowed. "I can't give you a good reason for that, Sir," he said.

"Can you tell me how he knew so much about our base," Halstead asked.

"I have a good idea," Pine said, "but I can't say for sure just yet. I'll know in a couple of...I'll know for sure within thirty minutes of the end of this meeting, Sir."

Halstead lowered his eyebrows. "Things are even worse than we initially realized, Sergeant," he said. "We didn't just lose the fuel dump, we have an environmental problem. Mathis dumped an unknown quantity of diesel into Maple Creek Lake."

Pine's eyes got a little wider.

"We found a five-gallon can on the bank," Halstead said, "and you can see the sheen from it on the water. Theoretically, it should all evaporate–depending on the weather–in less than a month, or decompose, and if it was five gallons or less, then as bad as that is, we'll recover from it."

Halstead shook his head. "The bigger problem," he continued, "is the several hundred, or possibly thousand, gallons that have soaked into the ground around the dump."

...

"The two dead that we've already discussed," Lieutenant Jackson said, referring to the guard and the pump operator, "plus Mathis. A number of minor burns, smoke inhalation, a couple people getting over some overexposure to diesel fumes. And we have a broken arm and three or four sprained ankles."

Mallory glanced at Halstead. "The loss of fuel is going to hurt," he said, "no doubt about it. We're going to have to pull maintenance on the reverse osmosis units more often as well, until we know the lake is clean."

"At least once we clean up the area," Mallory said and shook her head, "we have a perfect area for a new fuel dump. I want a fence and wire up around the other two. We can*not* afford to have this happen again."

"Already started," Stewart said. "The fence should be done by tomorrow, and there're guards there until the fence is complete. We're also cutting back on showers to every three days, except for the firefighters, and clamping down on any unnecessary vehicle usage."

"And now," Mallory said, "not to tempt Murphy, but what else could go wrong?"

...

"So what do you want," Earl asked, as blunt as he'd been on the side of the road, but not nearly as belligerent.

"A guarantee," Kyle said, "your word–which I'm willing to accept since I don't know you from Adam–things will change for the better around here. No more raids, no more abuse of women..."

"Now wait just a minute," Earl interrupted. "Who says there's been any abuse of the women?"

Amanda hung her head, looking pained and uncomfortable, but then she visibly gathered courage, sat up straight and said, "I do. Russell, he's the one that ended up getting hog-tied by the crowd," Amanda said for Eric and Kyle's benefit, "for one. He's been slapping the women around in the fields. He calls it 'motivation', but he's just being cruel, abusive and a," Amanda stopped herself before she said something she might regret.

She took a breath and continued. "Russell has been."

Eric was happy that Amanda had been the one to say something, because without her testimony it would only be hearsay.

"Russell will be taken care of," Earl said. Kyle noticed that Earl was unconsciously making a fist. Apparently, he really had changed.

"And as for me," Earl sighed. "I'm no saint, and I admit that I had some problems before the power went out."

Earl looked off to the side and rubbed his forehead and then the back of his neck. "I had some real problems before the power went out. Most of 'em were personal, a couple of them got me in trouble with the law. Mostly petty stuff," Earl said. "You can ask Coop and Tony, they busted me a couple of times."

"You remember me," he looked at Eric. "I was overweight. I have this damned thing on my face," he pointed to the foot-shaped birthmark, which was actually much less visible now that his color was better and he was getting some sun.

"I got busted a couple of times for being a peeping tom," Earl said, and blushed. "I was always looking at women as an object, or something to own, because; well, because I was *never* going to have one of my own."

Eric sat back and folded his arms. "And," he asked.

"It never went any farther than that," Earl said, "honest. I still gave women the creeps, though, because of how I was looking at 'em. Since then, I don't know, things have just been different. And since the botched raid," Earl shook his head.

"There's actually someone I'm kind of seeing," Earl said. "She seems to like me well enough and I'm not pushing it or anything. We'll see how it goes and, I don't know, maybe something will come of it. If not, I'm not going back to the old me. I haven't actually been in charge of hardly anything for the last six months, but for some reason my name came up. I'm not gonna screw that up."

"That's what I was talking about," Amanda said. "He's just different since the raid."

"Your people can take at least part of the credit," Earl said to Eric and Kyle. "We were only there for a day and a half, and we'd just tried to raid your base, but we were treated with respect, and decency, and kindness. Even by the women. I knew that something had to change, and it wasn't going to be the world around me."

"Well then," Eric said, "I think we can put the issue of abuse to bed. Raids need to stop though, like yesterday. You've started farming, and Amanda says that Clint was working with some local farmers and ranchers, so they shouldn't be necessary anyway."

Earl nodded. "Clint was doing it just to thumb his nose at your Major after the embarrassment of the raid and the meeting afterward," Earl said. "He wanted to prove that he could still do whatever he wanted and there wasn't anything she could do about it."

"Well," Eric sighed, "that ends now."

"Agreed," Earl said. "There's something else though, I can tell."

Kyle nodded and glanced at Amanda.

"If she wants to leave," Earl says, "that's totally up to her. I thought I made it clear that I don't work that way."

Kyle made a face. "It's a little more complicated than that."

…

The air-raid siren went off shortly before lunch finished since everyone would still be close to camp. Ten minutes later, Earl, Eric, Kyle, and Amanda were standing on the picnic table.

Earl held up his hand, and the group quieted down almost right away. Clint was sitting off to the side, still tied up, and now with his legs tied up too, to keep him from running off. He was beyond mad about how easily the group had switched allegiances. He consoled himself with the knowledge that it would all fall apart around Earl, just like it had almost fallen apart around him, unless Earl started ruling with an iron fist.

"First of all," Earl said, "thanks for getting back so quickly, I know it's a pain. Second, there's going to be a few more changes, and the first is going to affect everybody in one way or another."

"I know things haven't been perfect around here," Earl said. "C'mon now, let me finish. Yeah, they've been far from ideal, but some of that is going to change immediately and some of that is going to take some time. The worst parts are changing right now but—and this is a big but—I know not everyone is going to want to stick around if they have a chance to leave."

Clint was watching Earl take everything he'd built up and tear it right down in front of him, and he was just numb to it.

"I don't want anybody making any decisions until tomorrow," Earl said, "but the day after tomorrow, if you want to leave, Eric and Kyle are starting their own group. Amanda and William are leaving with Kyle, and she's taking her stuff with her. I'm willing to let them take some of the R.V.'s as well—Clint, Tony, and Coop won't need theirs anymore, after all. Now, it would be foolish for a dozen different groups to start out on their own because, well, we've seen what happens to small groups out there."

"Which leads to my second point," Earl continued. "The raiding stops now! We've got some crops growing, and I hope to find us at least a couple of farmers to trade with; we don't need to raid."

"If a large enough group decides to go with Eric and Kyle and Amanda," Earl shrugged, "I'm not going to stop you. I'd like to keep a large enough group together here for protection and defense, and to continue with the farms, but I won't stop you."

"And it's done," Clint thought. *"Why did I even bother? I might as well just die now."*

...

When the siren went off at 5:30 the next evening, there was a constant hum in the air, and you could almost reach out and touch the slight tension in camp.

"Everybody," Earl said, "there's really only one thing to do now and that's declare your intentions. I'm going to head over here to my left and Eric and Kyle are over there to my right. Before I do, though, I want to make a couple of things clear; first, no hard feelings if anyone wants to leave. Second, I plan on having a relationship with the other group, and the Army base, and the other town for that matter. It's not like anyone who leaves is dead to us."

Earl hopped down off the picnic table, which is something he never would have done a year ago, and walked off to his left. To his amazement and joy, he was immediately joined by Teri, the woman he'd been seeing for the last couple of months.

Chapter Seventeen

"I had no idea that this many people would want to stay," Amanda said.

"You said between a third and a half would want to leave," Kyle said. "And that's about what it looks like. Maybe a little less than a third want to come with us, but we're still looking at about one-hundred and thirty people."

Kyle looked at Eric, "You ready for this?"

"Absolutely not," Eric said. "It was going to be you and me, and then I was probably going to die doing something stupid."

"Yeah, how's that workin' out for ya'," Kyle asked.

"I don't know," Eric said with a smile. "This looks pretty stupid to me."

...

Shortly after lunch, almost fifty SUVs and their attached trailers pulled out of the encampment. Good-byes had taken a little while, but, logistically, it just took a long time to maneuver that many big vehicles around without breaking things.

Clint, Cooper, and Tony were in the back seat of Kyle's SUV, with Amanda covering them. William was in the front seat between them. She had instructions to shoot any or all three of them if they looked like they were getting loose, or going to cause a problem. The likelihood of that was pretty slim though, since they were doped up on a triple dose of diphenhydramine.

Kyle was in the lead, with Eric pulling up the rear. They were going to drop off their prisoners at Promised Land because that was, in their eyes, the logical place—being the only real law in the area.

The twenty-mile drive took less than fifteen minutes, and Kyle used his radio to call ahead when he was about five-minutes out. The radio operator told him the Major would meet him at the I-40 entrance to the park since the quarantine was still in effect, which was fine with him. He didn't want to have all these people in campers have to make U-turns in the middle of the park and then try to pass each other on the road to get back out.

...

"Sergeant Ramirez," Mallory said, when he got out of the SUV and came around to check on Amanda.

"Major," Kyle said, with a quick salute, but without coming to attention. Old habits die hard, but he wasn't on the parade ground and, frankly, she wasn't in his chain-of-command right now. Eric was pulling up to help with the prisoners.

"So, what have we here," Mallory asked.

"Mr. Clint Baxter," Kyle said, as he helped a slightly groggy Clint out of the back of his SUV, "Robert Cooper, and Anthony Roach. Also known as the unholy trinity or the three stooges of cell-block whatever you put them in."

"Excuse me," Mallory said.

"Clint has been behind the raids in our Area of Operations for at least the last eight months or so," Kyle said. "Even after the meeting at the airport. The group he was ruling elected a new leader a couple of days ago, and we have reason to believe things are going to change—for the better."

Eric was out of his truck at this point, but hadn't said anything yet.

"Well," Mallory said. "I guess that's good to know. I suppose I should be happy to have the two of you back, but we honestly don't have room for," she paused and looked to be doing some mental math, "another hundred-plus people."

Kyle was floored. What the *hell*? "Excuse me," it was Kyle's turn to say.

"That would be 'Excuse me, Ma'am'," Mallory said.

"No," Kyle said. "I think I'll pick and choose when I say Ma'am at this point. I didn't ask if we could stay here, and frankly it's quite an assumption you just made, thinking we were back to stay."

Eric folded his arms and leaned against Kyle's truck. This was completely between Mallory and Kyle, and he was going to let them have it out.

"Mr. Ramirez," Mallory started.

"That's *Sergeant* Ramirez," Kyle interrupted, "unless I've been court-martialed in absentia, and since you've already called me Sergeant once I know that hasn't happened. For your information, I've already done a far more extensive "meet and greet" with this group of people than anybody has done with any group you've brought in before, *ever*."

Mallory glanced at Amanda and smirked. "I bet you have," she said half under her breath.

Kyle took two steps towards Mallory and both she and the MPs who were there with her took a step back.

"Oh," Eric thought but kept the grin off his face, *"you have SO stepped in it now, girl."*

"You've got a lot of nerve to say something like that that," Kyle said. "I would have expected that from some people but not from you; never from you." He didn't yell, he didn't hiss, he didn't whisper, but the edge to his voice was so raw, and the fury, hurt, and disgust was so obviously barely contained that one of the MPs took another step back. The look in Kyle's eyes told Mallory that she hadn't just pushed too far, she had crossed a line that she didn't even know existed inside of Kyle.

It was then that Mallory saw the boy in the front seat of Kyle's SUV, and it sunk in that he'd said *you* instead of *we*. "Kyle," she started.

Kyle reached up and pulled off his Velcro nametape. "Save it," Kyle said. "I resign."

Kyle flicked the nametape at Mallory who caught it by reflex.

Kyle returned to his SUV as Eric reached in and pulled out Cooper. Kyle grabbed Tony and they delivered them both to Mallory without another word.

"Let's GO!" Kyle hollered as he rounded the front of his SUV.

...

"And here we are," Kyle said as he pulled onto the grounds of the abandoned Benton County Airport. This was one of the areas that had been scouted out a couple of weeks after they'd arrived at the park, and then checked on periodically thereafter. Remarkably, it had remained deserted...until now. Kyle was surprised that Mallory hadn't moved at least some of the Black Hawks up here, but she hadn't, and as far as he was concerned this was now home.

Kyle pulled around the runway and then stopped before driving out into the fields of grass surrounding the airport. The grass wasn't quite knee-high at this point in the summer, but Kyle had visions of hot catalytic converters starting a hundred fires and burning everyone out of their new home, and their trailers, within minutes of parking.

Once everyone was stopped and out of their vehicles, he pulled them all together for a quick pow-wow.

"This was a bit of a lucky break," Kyle started, "but we're still going to have to do some work before we can drop the trailers. After we cut down this grass, we're going to set up in the fields around the runway." Kyle pointed to the overgrown areas to the northwest, north, and northeast of the runway.

...

"So, what're the plans for tomorrow," Amanda asked.

Kyle shrugged, more in resignation than because he didn't know. "More of the same," he said. "We have a pretty good head start because we have food and a warm, dry place to sleep. The one thing this location lacks is a really good water supply. There's some, but not a lot. We need to work on a way to maximize what there is and minimize waste."

"You keep saying *we*," one of the members of the group that came out with them said. Kyle hadn't even come close to learning who everyone was yet and was just now realizing how much he relied on someone's name being front and center on their chest.

"Clint said we," they continued, "sometimes. It sounds different when you say it, though."

Kyle didn't know where this was headed, but the comment had made him a little uncomfortable. "I'm sorry, I'm horrible with names. I'm used to everyone having their last name sewn on their shirt. What was your name," Kyle asked, keeping his voice casual.

"James," he said. "James Dalton, but everyone calls me Jim."

"Well, Jim," Kyle said, "I can't speak for how things were run where Clint was involved, because I wasn't there. I can tell you that when I say we, I mean *we*. I also really don't mean to be in charge. Eric and I knew about this place and figured it was big enough to hold us all so we would head this direction and see if it was still free. We saw that some things needed to be done and…"

Kyle shrugged his shoulders again and this time he realized why he was uncomfortable. He really was in charge of this group, at least for the time being, and nobody was questioning it. Eric hadn't pulled rank and nobody in the group had stepped up since there didn't seem to be a need.

"And there isn't someone else above me giving orders for me to carry out," Kyle thought. He wasn't just in charge of a squad or a platoon and reporting back up. He was well and truly in charge.

Kyle took a deep breath before he continued. "I guess I *am* also a little used to being in charge," Kyle finally said, "If I see something that needs to get done, I try to take care of it. As a Sergeant in the Army, I also wouldn't ask my men to do something I wasn't capable of and willing to do right alongside them."

Kyle shook his head slightly. "Not everyone is like that," he said, "but that's how I worked and, well, I've only been out of the Army for about five hours so, bear with me. Old habits die hard."

That got a chuckle from the group and a smile from Amanda.

…

"Forty-one trailers," Eric said. "I say we break it up into three groups of seventeen. Not so many in one spot that they'll be crowded, but enough people that any one group should be able to protect itself for a short time or provide support for the others."

"How do we break them up," Amanda asked.

"Funny you should ask that," Eric said. "You know everyone here—some better than others—but you know everyone that came with us. I think we need a fair mix in each group; don't put all of the families together, or all the single people or couples in one group, that sort of thing."

Amanda nodded and bit the corner of her lip—her thinking face. "Give me an hour or so," she said, "and I think I can have a list for you of each group."

"Sounds good," Eric said, and turned to leave.

"Eric," Amanda said, before he had gotten more than a couple of steps away. "I know it's soon, really soon, but is there anyone I should…avoid, or, uhm, *not* avoid putting you in a group with?"

Eric was a bit surprised by the question but realized that Kyle must have talked to her about Karen.

"Thank you," Eric said. "I appreciate the concern, but I'm not looking for anyone right now. I'll be fine wherever you put me."

Chapter Eighteen

July 2, 2013 - Promised Land Army Base, Natchez Trace State Park, Tennessee

"Are you sure," Joel asked, for what was probably the fiftieth time.

"No, Joel," Ty said, "I'm not sure, but at this point I don't see any harm. The quarantine has held, nobody else has gotten sick in two weeks, and you haven't shown any signs of illness the entire time."

Rachael had been virtually isolated with less than half-a-dozen people for almost five weeks, and though they had been able to talk to each other every day by radio, they hadn't seen each other since the quarantine began. The kids seemed to be weathering the separation just fine, but he just didn't do well when they were apart for long stretches. It was one of the reasons he used to hate going on business trips.

"Go," Ty said.

As much as Joel wanted to drive to Redemption, he couldn't justify the fuel and was forced to walk.

...

Rachael was in the middle of cleaning up from lunch when there was a knock on the door. For the last, almost six weeks now, hardly anyone had knocked. The isolation zone around the four cabins they were using had held, and everyone had taken to simply announcing their presence a few seconds before they opened the front door–Rachael included.

Millie looked up, but didn't growl or head over to the door–so it was someone that she knew and didn't have a problem with.

Rachael's heart was in her throat as she slowly walked to the front door. There wasn't a peephole, nor were there windows on either side of the door. She hadn't talked to Joel or the kids since yesterday afternoon. What if something had happened?

"Who," Rachael started to ask, when her voice cracked and she had to clear her throat. "Who is it?"

"It's me," Joel said from the other side.

Rachael closed her eyes, put her hand to her mouth and whispered, "Thank you, God."

"Uh," Joel started, "can I come in?"

Rachael threw open the door, but stopped just short of letting it bang against the wall. Aurora was asleep, and the last thing she wanted to do was wake up a napping baby. She did throw her arms around her husband in a choking embrace.

"I. missed. you. so. much." she said.

Joel buried his face in his wife's hair and started to weep. "I missed you too," he said.

Behind them, a small crowd had gathered at the arrival of the Hummer that had picked Joel up about a mile out of town and they erupted into cheers and applause. This meant that the women and one family that had chosen to go into isolation with Rachael were finally free to move about, they hoped.

"The kids," Rachael asked, as she finally pulled back far enough to look at Joel.

"They'll be here later this afternoon," Joel said. "They've missed their friends, too, so they're getting caught up before they come home. Is Aurora sleeping?"

Rachael nodded.

"Good," Joel said with a wink.

Rachael laughed and then saw Dan walking down the road and waved.

"I see Joel beat me to it," Dan yelled and jogged the rest of the way to the cabins.

Cheers erupted from the crowd again.

"The quarantine and isolation are officially lifted," Dan said and held up his hands to keep the cheering from starting again. "I see Rachael isn't holding Aurora, so that means she's taking a nap. Let's keep the celebrating to a dull roar."

There were sheepish chuckles from the crowd, and a few blushes, but most everyone cheered again...quietly.

"I'm really glad that's over," Dan said, "and it's good to see you again."

"It's good to be seen," Joel said and looked at Rachael. "By everybody."

"By the way," Dan said. "Do you know why we had the volunteers for isolation that we did?"

"No," Joel said, after a second, with a quizzical look on his face.

Dan smiled. "Most of the women are pregnant," he said, "and they wanted to give themselves and their babies the best chance with this," Dan waved his arms, "going on."

Joel took a deep breath. "How many," he asked.

"Seven," Dan said.

"Wow," Joel said and shook his head, slightly stunned. "I knew it would happen eventually, but, wow."

"It's an affirmation of life," Dan said. "People get married and, even in tough times, they want to start a family."

Joel nodded and looked at Rachael again, "That's pretty much what we did," he said. "We really had no right having kids as early as we did but that didn't stop us."

"Same," Dan said with a smile. "Poor as church mice and living in a basement apartment, and Marissa and I did the same thing. Anyway, I'll leave you two alone. Good to have you back, though."

…

"Do you think I can ride it today," Bekah asked.

The girls were excited because it was the first time they were going to visit the horses in almost two months. Their last visit had been pretty spectacular since they had been there for the birth of a foal. By now, the foal would be almost eight-weeks old.

"No, honey," Marissa said. "He won't be ready to ride for quite awhile. He's probably grown a lot since you saw him last, but he's not strong enough to carry you yet."

"How 'bout me," Jessie asked.

"No," Marissa said, "not you either. I'll see if you can ride one of the other horses, though. But no promises, and no pouting if I say no."

Jessie and Bekah nodded in unison.

Marissa was looking forward to the break in routine and, just like the kids, getting away from town for even a few hours. Dan was stuck working out some medical stuff, but she was going to take any chance that presented itself.

"Got your backpacks," Marissa asked. Bekah nodded and Jessie turned around to show that she was wearing hers. Seeing the backpacks was a bittersweet reminder of everything they'd endured to get here in the first place, and the almost crushing loss when they'd been robbed in the middle of the night on the side of the road. When some of the items that had been taken were returned, including the girls' backpacks, it had brought a lot of the emotions from their trek back to the surface.

"Water bottles full," Bekah said and Jessie nodded.

"Let's go then," Marissa said. "It's a couple of miles and it's going to be warm today."

...

Travis Gibson had started out with a couple dozen horses when the power went out and had taken on another ten within a week or so when people realized it wasn't coming back on. Over the last year, through breeding and acquisition, he'd increased the size of his herd to just over a hundred. He'd realized fairly early on that people would most likely need horses for everything from transportation to working the fields and he'd seized the opportunity.

Keeping them all fed was Travis's biggest problem now, but a recent agreement with some of the local farmers to plant their fallow fields with alfalfa for the winter should hopefully take care of that. The ranch was up to three-hundred acres now—broken into three hundred-acre paddocks—and it seemed like he was building new stables all the time.

When the Army base that had sprung up in the middle of Natchez Trace approached him about purchasing some of his horses, he'd been open to the possibility but didn't really have enough of them to make it worth his—or their—while. They had, however, been willing to let him use one of their portable saw mills in return for being first in line for some horses once his herd was large enough. They were also supplying a fair amount of labor, since almost ninety of the horses needed to be ridden, curried, combed and otherwise taken care of, just about every day.

Travis saw the girls and Marissa heading to the stables and met them part way.

"Looks like the quarantine's lifted," he said.

"Finally," Marissa said, with only a touch of feigned melodrama. "I honestly don't know how people did it back before long distance travel was easier and communication to just about anywhere was as simple as picking up a phone."

Travis chuckled. "I'm guessing," he said, "it's because they just didn't know any different."

Travis squatted down to be at eye level with the girls. "So, you girls want to see J.B.," he asked.

"Who," Bekah asked.

"The foal that was born the last time you were here," Travis said. "You were the only ones from the town that were here, and we were running out of names. 'Horse' was already taken and we couldn't call *him* Bekah now, could we?"

Bekah and Jessie both giggled.

"We figured we'd name him after both of you," Travis continued, "and one of the ranch hands came up with J.B."

"You didn't have to do that," Marissa said.

Travis shrugged. "We really did need a name," he said and then dropped to a whisper, "and it could just as easily stand for 'just barely' since we almost lost him later that night. Besides, look at them."

The girls were grinning from ear to ear and obviously excited to go see 'their' horse.

"Let's go," Travis said. "He should be back in his stall with his mother. Now, just like always, you need to be careful and listen and do exactly as I say. He's still a baby and his mother can be very protective of him, just like your mom."

. . .

"Holy *cow*," Jessie said when they came to J.B.'s stall. "He grew fast!"

Travis smiled. "Not really," he said. "He's hardly grown at all since the last time you were here except for putting on some weight, he just wasn't walking around much and there were a lot of people around so he looked smaller."

Travis made a clicking noise with his mouth and then kissing noises, which set the girls giggling again. J.B. came over to where they were standing and put his head through the gate and nuzzled Jessie.

"You can pet him," Travis said. "He likes being scratched between the ears and along his neck."

Jessie and Bekah both looked at their mom and at a nod reached out to pet J.B. He whickered a little and shook his head towards Bekah's hand, which made her shriek and J.B. pulled away. J.B.'s mom, Sunshine, looked over at the commotion, but didn't feel the need to interfere...yet.

"It's ok," Travis said, and held out his hand to the foal. "He's as skittish as you are, so just be gentle and try not to make any sudden movements. Remember, you're as new to him as he is to you."

"Can we feed him," Bekah asked.

Travis looked at Marissa for the ok and then went to get some carrot sticks. He'd learned a long time ago that you didn't carry the treats in your pocket or let the horses know that was where they came from— that was a good way to teach a horse to nip and bite.

When he came back, he showed the girls how to hold the treat out on their hand so that they wouldn't get bitten: with the carrot stick lying flat on their hand and their fingers bent down and away from the horse's teeth. Since J.B. was still a baby, being hand fed was a new thing and he was still learning.

Travis showed them there wasn't anything to worry about by feeding J.B. first, and the foal gently picked up the carrot stick with his lips and then started chewing once his mouth was away from Travis's hand. Bekah was next, although she was clearly nervous, even though she had asked if they could feed him. She giggled a little as J.B.'s velvet lips probed around on her hand until he found the carrot stick.

It wasn't until after he moved his head away that she realized her hand was covered with horse spit and she made a face. Marissa made a face of her own at her oldest daughter, one that said 'don't you dare make a scene, especially not before your sister has fed him.' Instead, Bekah just wiped her hand on her jeans.

Jessie, after seeing that neither Mr. Gibson nor her sister had gotten bitten, wasn't nearly as nervous as Bekah had been. She also didn't listen to what Mr. Gibson had said and held the carrot stick out in her fist. Before Travis or Marissa could respond or say anything, J.B had reached out and bitten the carrot stick off just above her fingers. Next, Jessie opened her hand and let the small piece of carrot stick lay flat on her palm, like she'd been told to do, and after a few seconds of chewing, J.B. picked it up with his lips and moved his head to chew it away from her hand.

"Well I'll be," Travis said. "Lucky that didn't go worse, but for a bigger piece of food that's actually how you're supposed to do it; keeps them from taking too big a bite at first."

Travis shook his head. "I really wish you hadn't done it that way, though," he said. "You could have gotten bitten, honey."

"I'm sorry," Jessie said, and looked down while she wiped her hand on her pants. "He wasn't going to hurt me, though."

"What do you mean," Travis asked, "he wasn't going to hurt you."

"I don't know," Jessie said, "I could just tell he wasn't going to hurt me." She reached her hand out and scratched J.B. under the chin and along his neck, and he stuck his head further out to rub the side of his face against her head.

"You're a good boy, huh," Jessie said. "You wouldn't bite me, would you?"

J.B. pulled his head back and blew air through his lips to make the pbbbbh sound horses are famous for and then shook his head.

Jessie turned to her mom and Travis with a big grin. "See," she said.

Chapter Nineteen

"Dan," Ty said. "I need to apologize."

Dan was usually a pretty forgiving guy but he decided he was going to let Ty do most of the talking for a little while. He didn't know if things would have worked out any differently if Ty had listened to him or not, but he was in the mood to let him squirm a little.

"Ok," was all Dan said.

"Look," Ty said. "I was wrong, really wrong. I'm not used to being wrong. I'm also not used to being so completely out of my element. Even when I worked with Doctors without Borders, we knew what we were going into ahead of time, so we knew what to expect."

Ty paused. "I'm not used to being blindsided," he said, "or not having the right tools or the right medicine. It was a shock to the system. I'm sorry I didn't listen. You were right and I was, not right."

"This is killing you, isn't it," Dan said.

"*Yes*," Ty said, "for more reasons than you think. I hate being wrong because I hate losing. I didn't get into medicine to lose patients, Dan. I know it's going to happen but that doesn't mean I have to like it, and this was *bad*. Forget the blow to my ego, this was rough. People need to trust their doctor. I don't know if they're going to be able to do that now, and I *am* a good doctor."

"I know you are," Dan said. "Once you figured out exactly what it was, I don't think anyone could have done a better job under the circumstances. I really don't. I'm sorry I was being difficult and I wish I could have helped out more. All I knew was that it looked so similar to what we saw in the neighborhood...what killed my son, that it had me spooked."

"I've been living in a dream world, Dan," Ty finally admitted. "The world I used to live in, where I had tools and medicines and labs...that world is gone. There aren't any doctors or nurses or paramedics anymore. There are just healers now. I'm willing to work with you, Dan, if you're willing to work with me."

"Deal," Dan said. "That's all I ever wanted."

...

July 5, 2013 - Fort Rucker, Alabama

Sanford looked at the uniform hanging in the doorway as he was getting dressed and shook his head. He'd spent an hour the previous night trimming stray threads and tightening a couple of loose buttons on all of his pants and coats, but they still looked...vulgar. It was wrong, in so many ways, just wrong, and it was becoming a problem on base.

He noticed more and more equipment that wasn't being maintained like it should be. Uniforms were a particular problem, and it was affecting morale and performance. Things were starting to slip, attitudes were changing, and as ridiculous as it may sound, it was because little things like uniforms weren't being held to a high standard. People were growing sloppy and that just wasn't acceptable.

It was to be expected that the ready stores would eventually run out, but that didn't mean they shouldn't take care of what they had. If anything they should be taking better care of what limited resources remained.

Sanford looked at his coat and another thought occurred to him. The Colonel's uniform didn't look like it was really any the worse for wear after a year. Why was that? It most likely *wasn't* because he'd had dozens of uniforms before the power went out, which meant that the Colonel was still drawing from stores when everyone else had been severely restricted.

Sanford finished tying his tie and grimaced at the knot. It was starting to get shiny from always being in the exact same place and from the oil on his hands.

"We're all equal," he muttered to himself, paraphrasing Orwell. "Some of us are just more equal than others."

. . .

"Sir," Hodges said. "We've tracked them down to Denver."

"Excellent," Sanford said but with no real expression in his voice.

"They're at the Denver International Airport," Hodges said, "or, more likely, underneath it."

Sanford still looked nonplussed.

"Seriously," Hodges asked, completely in awe at how naïve his Major was. "The *Denver* International Airport. You know; the one that they built for no good reason while there was a perfectly good airport already in Denver? The one that went over budget by tens of millions of dollars and yet somehow, magically, the money just appeared and nobody said a word about it? The airport where whole buildings were built *wrong* and instead of being torn down and done again…they were *buried*, completely intact!"

"Nope," Sanford said, chuckling. "I take it there's some conspiracy theory about the Denver International Airport."

Hodges put his hand over his eyes. "Actually," he said, "yeah, little bit…, Sir. And it sounds like it wasn't actually that far-fetched after all. That's where the most recent communication, today's, terminated at. I sincerely doubt that if the President is there, he's hanging out in concourse A or some frequent-flyer's club."

"Are you for real?" Sanford asked, then continued when it became obvious that Hodges wasn't kidding. "Ok, so while we're at it, any bets on who the Colonel is working for? The Illuminati, the Knights Templar–maybe little green men from Beta Reticula?"

"They're grey," Tuttle said. "Little *grey* men…from Beta…sorry, Sir, it was on an episode of the X-files."

Sanford glared at Tuttle, but barked a laugh after a second. "Seriously, though," Sanford said. "Who do we think he's working for?"

"We need to talk, Sir," Hodges said.

Something in Hodges tone struck Sanford as a little…off. "I was under the impression that's what we've been doing, Lieutenant," Sanford said.

"Not," Hodges said, "like we have been."

Hodges took a deep breath and tried to think of where to begin. "Ok," he said, "you hadn't ever heard of anything odd about the Denver Airport, right?"

"Right," Sanford said, drawing the word out to be several syllables long.

"You made a joke just now," Hodges said, "about the Illuminati."

Sanford made a face and then said, "Oh you can*not* be serious."

"I'm not," Hodges said, "about the Illuminati, but I guess you could say I'm a little bit of a conspiracy, not theorist, but maybe more of a conspiracy buff. There're a lot of conspiracies out there, and I've read up on most of them. I'd be lying if I said all of them…but all of the major ones and most of the minor ones."

"I assume there's a point to all this," Sanford said.

"Yes, Sir," Hodges said, "if you'll indulge me."

"I have to admit," Sanford said, "you've piqued my curiosity."

"One more question then," Hodges said. "Have you ever wondered why you're still a Major, while people like Olsen keep getting promoted?"

"What does that have to do with anything," Sanford asked, more than a little perturbed.

"Trust me, Sir," Hodges said. "I'm asking for a reason. I'm older than you and I've been in the Army a little longer than you have, and I'm still a Lieutenant. I have my suspicions as to why, but haven't you ever wondered?"

"Of course I have," Sanford grumbled, finally, "all the time. I see…I see people like the Colonel get promoted, or I see good men get drummed out, and I wonder why? What's going on?"

"Have you ever heard of the litmus test," Hodges asked.

"Everyone's heard of the litmus test," Sanford said with a wave of his hand. "It's BS."

"Really," Hodges asked. "Would you fire on armed or unarmed civilians if ordered to, Sir?"

"No," Sanford said without hesitation. "Not unless I was fired on first, and then only in self-defense and only in sufficient force to suppress the Op-For."

Hodges just looked at Sanford for a few seconds.

"Oh, come on," Sanford said.

"Who has been responsible for every raid that's been conducted so far," Hodges asked.

Sanford didn't answer.

"Was it you, or Lieutenant Colonel West," Hodges asked.

Sanford still didn't answer, but was growing uncomfortable with the direction the conversation was headed.

"I already know the answer, Sir," Hodges said. "West was in charge, not you, because West has passed the test and you haven't. Both the Colonel and West passed the test and they've been promoted, and that's just the tip of the conspiracy iceberg."

"Go on," Sanford said, leaned back and folded his arms.

"I know," Hodges said, "*personally* know, a high-ranking officer that was drummed out because he wouldn't toe the official Administration line. They ruined his career. They ran his name through the mud, and they tried to destroy his marriage by claiming he had at least two affairs."

"You can never know what's going on in someone else's personal life," Sanford said.

"I went through OCS with his brother," Hodges said. "I know the family, I know his wife. These two were college sweethearts and he would have died before being unfaithful."

Sanford looked sideways at Hodges.

"Think about it," Hodges said, "do you really think that a scandal couldn't be created if a four-star general didn't pass the litmus test."

"Wait," Sanford said as he sat up. "You aren't talking about…"

"I am," Hodges said, "and it was a set-up, pure and simple. He quit saying what they wanted him to say and so he had to go. I know him personally and I tell you the affairs never happened."

Sanford sat back in the seat again, trying to accept the massive paradigm shift that was occurring. The more he thought about it, the more certain things made sense, though. The early retirements, all the missed promotions, non-judicial punishments for minor infractions that resulted in separation from the service–all of it seemed to make a sick sort of sense now. And it had been speeding up over the last several years.

"There's a lot more," Hodges said. "It just depends on how far back you want to go."

"Well," Sanford said, "they always say it's good to start at the beginning."

"Ok," Hodges said. "I assume you've heard of J. D. Rockefeller."

"I lied," Sanford interrupted. "Don't go back that far."

Hodges stopped and looked up, quirked his mouth like he was mentally reciting or flipping through a giant book, and then started over. "I think the key things to touch on," Hodges said, "are population control, manipulation of the economy, and governmental influence far beyond anything you've ever dreamt of, all with an end goal of consolidated wealth and power for a select few."

"This is for real," Sanford asked. He was having a hard time not shaking his head but Hodges didn't even notice.

"Potentially," Hodges said. "Yes."

"No," Sanford said. "We're wasting our time here on blue skies and BS if this doesn't have a point."

"Yes," Hodges said. "I really think this is for real. I can't prove it beyond a shadow of a doubt—nobody but the people on the inside can—but when I've laid out what I believe are the facts, the evidence is pretty damning."

Sanford nodded for Hodges to continue.

"The Council on Foreign Relations was founded in 1921," Hodges began.

…

"Stop," Sanford said almost two hours later. "I can't hold any more. I'm not questioning or second-guessing you, because I've seen and heard a little too much crazy recently, but I can't process anymore right now."

"I'm surprised you didn't stop me sooner," Hodges said.

"I cried uncle after about forty-five minutes the first time," Tuttle said.

"I've heard the old saying that the love of money was the root of all evil," Sanford said, "and that power corrupts, but this, this is…"

"Astounding," Hodges suggested. "Mindboggling, staggering, overwhelming, inconceivable…"

"You're not helping," Sanford said. "Control for the sake of control. Power for the sake of power, no other reason; it's obscene."

"I haven't heard it put that way before," Hodges said, "but that's a really good description."

Sanford shook his head. "What about this HAM network," he said after a few seconds. "Is anything happening there?"

"Actually, yes, Sir," Tuttle said, "quite a bit in fact. Nothing of any substance, but there's been a lot of traffic. Either they have no idea that the system's been compromised or they're doing a great job of keeping me busy with bogus routine traffic."

"How many…locations have you identified so far," Sanford asked.

"At least six distinct locations," Tuttle said. "And I can positively ID three of them by voice as well. One of them participated in the raid on Fort Campbell."

Sanford shook his head. "That had to be rough," he said. "Knowing what they knew going in, not really being a willing participant. Damn."

"I notice you haven't asked for the IDs yet," Hodges said.

"Have you," Sanford asked.

"No, Sir," Hodges admitted. "Probably for the same reason you haven't. I can't disclose what I don't know."

"Plausible deniability," Sanford said and looked at Tuttle. "And you *believe* you *may* be able to *possibly* ID three of them by voice, is that correct?"

"Yes, Sir," Tuttle said, "that's correct. Three at most, maybe."

"We're going to have to make contact with them at some point," Sanford said.

"Yes, Sir," Hodges said. "And we risk blowing the whole thing. Eventually though, you're right, we're going to have to work together."

Chapter Twenty

It was late, but Olsen checked the door of his office to make sure it was locked. Once he was sure he was alone, he picked up the radio at the agreed upon time, just before it came to life in his headphones.

"This is Pillar Four," Olsen said. "You know my voice by now, I'm not going to authenticate."

"We have protocols for a reason," the voice on the other end said.

"No," Olsen said. "*I* have protocols for a reason. You have protocols because you think you need them or they make you feel important. This line is so heavily encrypted that unless one of us is compromised, authentication is a waste of time. So quit wasting my time and get to the point of this week's meeting."

"My, getting awfully full of yourself, aren't you," the voice said. "Remember, you can be replaced at any time."

"Actually," Olsen said, "I don't think I can or you would have done it by now. You threaten and you bluster, but so far that's all you've done for over half a year. If you had someone else that could take my place you would have had them do it by now, so let's cut the crap."

"Temper, Colonel…" the voice started.

"Is the President still alive or not," Olsen interrupted.

"Excuse me," the voice was obviously not used to being cut off.

"I asked if the President was still alive," Olsen repeated. "The plan was that Air Force One would land and he would be taken to where you were. You've said he's been briefed but that's all. It's been a year since this thing started and I want to know if the Commander-in-Chief is still alive. Yes or no. One word."

"Colonel Olsen…"the voice began again.

"Is *not* a yes or no," Olsen said. "I'm beginning to lose patience with you people. The next word that comes out of your privileged, entitled, overindulged mouth had better be either yes or no or I'm closing this connection and I'm locking out your location. Don't try my patience."

"Yes," the voice said, but obviously through gritted teeth. "Colonel, do not interrupt me. Your President, your Commander-in-Chief, has all but abdicated his responsibilities. When we explained the situation to President Clement he was…reluctant, at first, to accept the reality of the situation. It didn't take long, however, to convince him once we reminded him of who his main campaign contributors were."

"Of course," the voice said, "we have contributed heavily to both sides over the years, but it has been an effective insurance policy that has kept both the executive and legislative branches in our pockets for quite some time now."

Olsen was silent. He already knew some of what he was hearing, and had suspected much of the rest, but to hear it blatantly laid out like this–he didn't dare interrupt again.

His handler sighed. "This contingency plan was just that, a contingency plan. It was never intended to be a primary course of action. The seed vault in Norway, useless to us right now. The fifty-square-mile self-sustaining cities sit idle and incomplete on every continent. This plan was only in place in case of a sudden disaster; a worldwide pandemic for instance, or perhaps a worldwide power outage."

"What good is this contingency plan if you can't use it long term," Olsen asked.

"The plan is fine, Colonel, the voice said. "It still allows us to carry out our long-term agenda. We'll just be a little less comfortable while the world is prepared for us to return. Understand this, Colonel, your actions are not accidents, you are part of a plan and we *will* see that plan through to completion. We are fully prepared to wait this disaster out, if necessary, but when we emerge, it will be into a world of *our* design, *our* making. Things simply happened earlier than planned. And after all, that's why you hire the best and most capable, isn't it?"

"What about everyone else," Olsen asked, "the Senators and Representatives that were with the President when he arrived?"

The voice laughed mirthlessly. "They have been put to work," he said. "Everyone must find their place and we really have no use for politicking."

Olsen was disgusted by what he'd learned, but no matter what, he was still just a small part of the plan as a whole.

"It's still going to be months before…" Olsen started.

"Too long," the voice interrupted. "It's already been a year and the plan was for eighteen months to two years. The other regions are making much faster progress and Europe is almost completely pacified. Asia took a bit longer but, except for Japan, that is almost completely pacified as well. Africa is taking longer but there are large portions there that, like your mountains of West Virginia, are unaware that the power has even gone out. You see, I *was* paying attention during your last outburst."

"Africa doesn't have nearly as many guns to manage as I do," Olsen said.

"Deal with it, Colonel. Soon," the voice said. "Make examples and the rest will fall in line. Liberty and the Pursuit of Happiness are empty platitudes without a Life to pursue them with."

"I want to talk to the President," Olsen said.

"I'm sorry," the voice on the other end said. "That won't be happening."

"Then this conversation is over," Olsen said and reached for the power switch on his radio.

"Don't," the voice said, "cut the connection, not yet. You need to learn the fine art of negotiation."

"I'm not negotiating," Olsen said. "I'm dictating terms."

"No," the voice said, "you're expressing wants and desires, which is the only thing you are in any position to do. Don't try to change your tactic at this point, it's too late. Now, what is the status?"

Olsen sighed into the open microphone.

"What," the voice said, "is the problem, the real problem?"

"Potentially," Olsen said, "dissention in the ranks. It isn't something I can't handle, but it's spreading. Slowly, but it's spreading. Nobody thinks I'm aware of it but not all of my information comes from official reports."

"Then deal with it," the voice said.

"You keep saying that," Olsen said, "like it's no big deal. You have no idea what you're talking about."

The voice laughed again and this time it was in true amusement. "You seriously believe that," he asked. "I have been 'dealing with it', whatever *it* was for the last forty years. I have made and destroyed careers at the highest levels in both the public and private sectors of every country of importance on this planet. I have manipulated public opinion in a matter of days, *days*, over something as insignificant as a personal slight. I don't use individuals as pawns, I use corporations, governments and yes, militaries."

"*I* know," the voice said, "how to *deal with it.*"

"I thought you could rely on your people's sense of duty and honor," the voice continued. "I thought you said that they would obey and get the mission done."

"There's obedience," Olsen said, "and there's blind obedience. We cultivate at least some sense critical thinking in our men. They aren't going to jump off a cliff just because I say so."

"Then your people need direction," The voice said. "They need an enemy they can see, touch and feel. You say you have been holding the threat over them for too long with nothing to show for it. Give them an enemy."

"*Who,*" Olsen said, almost plaintively and hating the sound of his own voice.

"Haven't you been listening," the voice asked, scorn obvious even over the radio. "It doesn't matter who. It doesn't matter how. All that matters is how you present it. Were there weapons of mass destruction in Iraq? It doesn't matter. Was the U.S. Government complicit in the attacks of 9/11? It doesn't matter. Are there UFOs at Area 51? It...doesn't...matter!"

The scorn was gone now as the voice continued. "You control what media remains," he said. "Say it often enough and convincingly enough and it becomes the truth as far as the masses are concerned. Once again, though, what is the status?"

Olsen gritted his teeth, but answered the question. "Taking Fort Campbell has finally had the desired effect," he said. "More of the bases are falling in line and being less...difficult about it. Things should speed up from this point forward."

"And what of your other little...problem," the voice asked, "that rebellious group camping out in the park?"

"Now that Campbell is ours," Olsen said, "they are next on the list."

"Excellent," the voice said, "and you are mistaken, Colonel. You can be replaced at any time, remember that. Also remember that if the time comes that you need to be replaced, you know far too much to be allowed to simply walk away."

Then the connection was cut from the other end.

"No more," Olsen said after he turned off the radio and locked the drawer. "That was the last time you do that to me. We play this game by my rules from now on."

...

"Major," Lieutenant Hodges said, as he passed Sanford in the hall. "When you get a moment?"

With a nod, Sanford continued to his office to prepare for yet another briefing with the Colonel. Olsen's behavior was becoming increasingly erratic and unpredictable. He was lashing out at people for no reason, and his obsession with consolidating authority with the military had risen to fanatical levels. Today's briefing was about Fort Bragg and, of all places, Shaw Air Force Base–which had been giving them the least trouble of any installation, bar none.

Not that Sanford equated "no trouble" with blind obedience...not anymore. The modified HAM radio had opened their eyes to just how large the rebellion against the Colonel and his increasingly draconian orders was. Sanford shook his head to clear it, and focused back in on the briefing. The last thing he needed was to give away something that they hadn't learned through standard channels.

...

"Talk to me, Lieutenant," Sanford said, once they were outside earshot and on their way to the garage. They'd had to minimize the number of meetings they had at the communications truck, but Hodges was adamant that they meet there today. "And make it good news. Olsen is considering going after Lejeune next. I do *not* want to go head-to-head with a base full of Marines."

"As long as you promise not to react," Hodges said.

"Believe me," Sanford said, "I'm beyond anything you could say to surprise me."

"Tuttle finally broke the encryption," Hodges said.

"I won't say about time," Sanford said. "I know it couldn't have been easy. I will say the timing is just about perfect. We need *something* to work with."

"You aren't going to believe who, or what, he's working for," Hodges said.

Sanford only made a slight face. "Who or what he's working for, that sounds a bit melodramatic," he said.

"Like I said, you aren't going to believe it," Hodges said, "even after you hear it."

…

Hodges held the door to the Humvee and then closed it behind them once they were both inside.

"First of all," Hodges said, "I've had to increase security on our little clandestine radio-intercept operation. If someone comes snooping around other than Tuttle or the two of us, they'll be intercepted at first, and if they don't take the hint, and still try to get into the Humvee, one of two hidden positions will take them out."

Sanford raised an eyebrow.

"Yes, Sir," Hodges said. "It's that serious. The Colonel wouldn't hesitate a second to take any of us out if he found out that we know what you're about to hear *or* that we didn't disclose the existence of either the backchannel communications network or the fact that we have one of their radios."

"Dissention in the ranks is growing, Sir," Tuttle said as the only enlisted person in the truck. "The only reason it hasn't gotten out of hand yet is NCOs who agree and catch it before it gets to the wrong ears, and Officers such as yourselves who are working to do something about it. I'm afraid some kind of action is going to have to take place, though, and sooner rather than later. The Colonel is going too far."

Hodges nodded. "Go ahead and play the ones we agreed on," he said.

"Wait," Sanford said, "agreed on? Who agreed on? I need to know what's going on."

"Absolutely, Sir," Hodges said. "What I meant by agreed on was the portions of the transmissions where it's made clear who the Colonel is working for. There are over five hundred transmissions, some of them over an hour long. Tuttle has listened to almost all of them and I've listened to about half. We just thought…"

Sanford interrupted Hodges' apology. "Ok," he said, "understood, continue."

…

"If I wasn't sitting in this truck right now," Sanford said, "after a worldwide power outage caused by the Sun, that we as a country actually had a *plan* for but failed to implement *at all*–much less in time. If I wasn't here, dealing with a megalomaniacal Colonel, I would call all three of us nuts and be laughing at what I just heard."

The selected transmissions took just under an hour to get through and the longer Sanford had listened, the more surreal the situation became.

"I feel like I should look around for Rod Serling," Sanford said. "I know he's dead, but at this point that doesn't matter!"

"I understand, Sir," Hodges said. "There are some other transmissions that refer to Agenda 21, and even one where, and I won't say I told you so but, the other guy actually mentions both the Georgia Guidestones and vaccinations."

Sanford closed his eyes and sighed. "Before a couple of days ago I would have said it had to be a joke," he said.

"I don't think these people joke about much," Hodges said. "And they've certainly been serious enough about everything up to this point."

"This is insane," Sanford said, "utterly and completely. We're talking about the mother of all conspiracy theories all wrapped up into one and...what, they've somehow figured out how to trigger sunspots and CMEs too?"

"No sir," Hodges said, "what I'm saying is that they have had plans and an agenda in place for decades to take advantage of a...convenient catastrophic event, regardless of the source, whenever it happened. Now that it's happened they've scurried to their hidden bunker to wait for the world to finish burning. Once their faithful lackeys have reshaped the world to their liking, they'll come out and take the reins of their perfect little planet and its newly docile inhabitants."

"Sirs," Tuttle said, interrupting Hodges's tirade. "You need to hear this."

Tuttle had been listening to decoded transmissions in one ear at 125% speed as the conversation went on, and had just finished the most recent transmission between the Colonel and whoever it was pulling his strings.

"Go ahead," Sanford said even before Hodges could.

The playback took just a couple of minutes and then all three of them were left with more questions than answers.

"No comment on the C-in-C," Hodges said.

"Then I will," Sanford said. "He waived his right to any authority he had when he landed and walked into wherever they are. If what they say is true, and we have no reason to believe it isn't yet, the President is no longer issuing orders, and even when he *was*, he was bought and paid for. They *all* have been for the last," Sanford made a dismissive gesture with his hand, "who knows how long."

Hodges nodded. "Information is power, Sir," he said. "In this case, what the Colonel doesn't know *can* hurt him. We just have to figure out how."

Chapter Twenty-One

July 6, 2013 - Promised Land Army Base, Natchez Trace State Park, Tennessee

"Mr. Baxter," Mallory said. "Welcome to my home, well, you know what I mean."

Clint sighed and looked up at Mallory through bloodshot eyes. He hadn't had a decent night's sleep since he got here and now this…thing was taunting him. He knew he was going to die here, just not how or when. Why they were putting it off was what kept him up at night.

"I'm sorry you aren't sleeping well," Mallory said. "I assure you it isn't anything my men are doing intentionally. If there's something we can get you, please let us know."

"Oh can the good-cop, bad-cop routine," Clint snapped. "When's the firing squad? Are you just whittling down the numbers to a manageable number from all the volunteers or what?"

Mallory turned the carved wooden chair around backwards, sat astride it, and folded her arms across the top. "Since you asked," she said, "yes, there were a handful of volunteers for a firing squad. They've all been turned away. I'm not going to shoot you, Mr. Baxter. You haven't been convicted of anything and even if you were, I wouldn't shoot you."

Clint grimaced and Mallory went on. "To answer your question," Mallory said, "it's taking so long because we don't have a court yet, or, at least, we didn't until yesterday. At least we have a judge now, and we have a couple of people reading up on the law to act as both prosecution and defense. Since this is a civilian matter, it will be handled as such. I'm just here to provide room and board to the prisoners."

"Seriously," Clint asked. "Is this for real? I'm going to get tried in some kangaroo court by people who've never practiced law, in front of someone who's just been appointed Judge?"

"Two minutes ago you were asking what was taking the firing squad so long," Mallory said. "Now you're concerned about a miscarriage of justice? Make up your mind, Mr. Baxter; you can't have it both ways."

. . .

"Before we get started," the newly appointed Judge said, "is there anything you'd like to say to the court. Keep in mind that you are on the record at this point, Mr. Baxter."

Clint stood up; hands cuffed in front of him, and looked around the large tent. There were only a dozen people in attendance, which surprised him a little. He thought there would be more people there. Then again, most of his victims– if you could call them that–wouldn't be able to identify him, so he didn't really have any accusers to face him.

"I *could* say that I don't recognize the authority of this court," Clint said, "but that would be kind of pointless. After all," he held up his hands as far as they would go, given that they were chained to his waist, "it doesn't look like I'm making the rules anymore. I'd like to face my accusers. I've heard the charges and I say I was just providing for my people. You don't know the circumstances surrounding the tragedy at the camp meeting."

"How do you plead," the Judge asked.

"Usually on my knees," Clint said with a chuckle, which nobody else joined in on. Clint sighed. "Does it matter?"

"Yes," the Judge said. "It matters, Mr. Baxter. How do you plead?"

Clint thought back to his talk with Mallory a couple of days ago. *"I'm not going to shoot you, Mr. Baxter. You haven't been convicted of anything, and even if you were, I wouldn't shoot you." "What have I got to lose,"* he thought. *"Why would she lie to me?"*

"I'll save you all some time," Clint said. "Guilty."

The look of shock on the Judge's face was almost worth it, Clint thought. "Are you absolutely sure," he asked. "You can still change your plea."

"No," Clint said with a smirk, "I'm sure."

The gavel came down with a flat "BANG!"

"Let the record show that the defendant has entered a plea of guilty," the Judge said. "Sentencing will now begin. Pursuant to the laws voted on and established…"

Clint tuned out until he heard the actual sentence.

"…hang by the neck until dead. May God have mercy on your soul."

"What," Clint said. *"But…"* he thought, and then realized that all the Major had said was that she wasn't going to shoot him.

…

"What are our options," Cooper asked.

"Well," his legal counsel said, "you aren't up for the death penalty. If you plead not guilty then it goes to trial. Without having spoken to anyone who would be a witness for *or* against, I can't say one way or the other. If you plead guilty, you get life in prison with hard labor, but you get three square meals and a roof over your head. You'll work for your living, though; it isn't like it used to be."

"What about Tony," Cooper asked.

"Doesn't matter," his counsel said, "it's a different case. You need to worry about you. The chances of you getting out of it in a jury trial are pretty slim. If you're convicted, you get the same sentence and people despise you for taking up their time on a jury. Mr. Cooper, things have changed, and while we voted on the laws and everyone understands what's required of us, nobody wants to have their time wasted. I'll be honest; it takes all the time we've got just to keep up with the basic labor it takes to survive right now. I'm not trying to talk you into one thing or another, but if you know you're guilty, do us all a favor and plead guilty."

. . .

"Anthony Roach," the Judge said. "How do you plead?"

"Guilty, Your Honor," Tony said.

"Do you understand what that means," the Judge asked.

"Yes, Your Honor," Tony replied. "Life in prison, no parole, hard labor."

"Very well," the Judge said and brought the gavel down. "Let the record show that the defendant has entered a plea of guilty and the sentence…"

. . .

There was a single gallows set up behind the tent used as the courthouse. The trapped-door was four feet off the ground and the condemned would fall just over two feet before the slack in the rope was taken out and, in all likelihood, they broke their neck.

As there was no appeals process, Clint had been hung the morning after his trial. It was a short, no-frills affair that took less than fifteen minutes. His last meal was a breakfast of pancakes, eggs, sausage, bacon and milk.

The pastor offered to counsel with him the night before, but Clint refused, graciously. His lower lip was quivering a little when they placed the black bag over his head, but he didn't cry, or close his eyes, or struggle.

The noose was placed over his head, and he flinched a little–which was to be expected since he couldn't see it coming. Then it was tightened, with the knot placed behind his left ear, along the jawline.

The gallows were well-constructed, and only creaked a little under his weight when the trapped-door dropped. He fell two feet and there was a sickening snap as the rope went taut and Clint's neck broke. His body twitched a couple of times and finally relaxed. The body was allowed to hang for ten minutes to ensure that he was, in fact, dead.

Ty and Dan both verified a lack of pulse and breath, and then the body was raised back up and removed from the noose. Clint had requested that he be cremated, if possible, rather than being buried. A pyre was built, and later that evening a dozen or so people gathered for a brief service. The pastor, Sergeant Marci Stanton, had refused to let him simply be cremated–or least set alight–since the fire probably wouldn't be hot enough for full cremation. Everyone deserved a funeral and a few words.

"It is not for us to judge a soul," Marci said. "That is up to God. At best we can hope to carry out justice. Clinton Baxter, we commit your soul to the care of God the Father, may you find peace."

The fire burned for about an hour and when it was out they buried what bones were left in the recently dedicated cemetery.

. . .

"You did *what*," Mallory said, not so much asking a question as demanding an answer.

"I got the answers I needed," Ben said. "And ultimately I only had to dislocate one knuckle."

"I'm," Mallory started to say and then stopped. "I don't know what to say. I'm a little bit in shock, Ben. How could you do that? How did you justify it?"

"The needs of the many," Ben started.

"Is the exact same logic that Olsen is using," Mallory interrupted.

Ben's teeth clicked as his mouth slammed shut.

"You realize you never would have gotten anything out of him again," Mallory asked. "You couldn't have trusted anything he said from that point on. He was useless as a source of *any* information."

"I had to do something," Ben said. "I had to find out what he knew, and I did, Mallory. This is huge, and even Mathis didn't know everything, but what he did know is scary."

Ben felt like he needed to defend himself under Mallory's stare so he went on. "Mathis hasn't felt any loyalty to me or the U.S. Army for almost ten years," he said, which got Mallory's attention. "He wasn't just reporting back to Olsen, he was reporting back to a handler, who wasn't in his military chain-of-command; someone completely outside the military."

Emotions were warring on Mallory's face. She still didn't agree with what Ben had done, but the fact that Mathis had been conspiring with someone outside of the military was more than a little disturbing.

"I had to do *something*," he said. "When the Colonel decided you had to be dealt with and came in loaded for bear, I had your back. When you needed help with the HAM radios, I helped you out. I even called, in the middle of a raid on my *own base*, to give you a heads up that the Black Hawks were headed your way."

Ben leaned forward in his chair. "Nobody had my back," he said and slapped the table. "Nobody was there for me when the chips were down and that weasel, that snake, Mathis, stood there and talked out of both sides of his mouth while the attack was literally mounting."

Ben slumped backwards. "Nobody had my back, Mallory," he said. "I did what I had to do, for my men and for myself."

Mallory came over and sat on the corner of the table and took one of Ben's hands in hers.

"Where are you, Ben," Mallory asked. "Look around. Where are your people, the ones that didn't *choose* to stay behind and defend the base?"

Mallory squeezed Ben's hand to keep him from interrupting until she was done and then reached up to brush a stray small braid of hair behind her ear. "Ultimately," she asked, "would it have mattered if everyone had stayed to defend the base? Would it have made any difference if I, or anyone else, had come charging up the road in the middle of the battle? You have a place to go and so do all of your people. Olsen didn't get much when he finally took the base. And standing with you, side by side, isn't the only way for people to have your back."

Ben shook his head.

Mallory reached out and put her hand on the back of his head, running her fingers over the tight curls of hair where it had grown out from his typical military buzz cut. Ben froze for a second and then relaxed and leaned into her hand, into the comfort she was offering, and then stopped. Ben put his hand on hers and then brought her hands together in front of him.

At Mallory's look, Ben sighed.

"What's going on with Kyle," he asked.

Mallory tried to pull her hands away from Ben, but he held on and she quit pulling after a second. "I don't want to talk about Kyle, Ben," she said.

"I don't either," Ben said, "but I need to, and I think you do too. What happened?"

Mallory shook her head. "Nothing happened," she said, "that's the point, and nothing was ever going to happen. Kyle thought something could, or would happen, but…"

Ben waited for Mallory to continue after she collected her thoughts.

"I think it started during my divorce," Mallory said. "He was there for me, no matter what. I could talk to him about anything and he wouldn't judge me. He didn't make any demands of me or expect me to get over it sooner rather than later. He just accepted me for who I was and made sure that everybody else did too."

Mallory snorted a short laugh. "I remember right near the end of the divorce," she said. "My ex was making less than I was, even on my meager salary, and he threatened to bring up alimony at our next court date."

Mallory looked off to the side as she remembered the events. "Kyle could tell I was having a bad day and we went out for a beer after work," she said. "I told him my ex was threatening me with an alimony request and he got all hot under the collar. I told him not to worry about it, I had it under control, but he was really wound up when we left the bar."

"He was off the next day," Mallory said, "but when I saw him the day after that he seemed to be in a good mood so I didn't think any more of it. I figured it was just the alcohol talking and he'd taken my advice and calmed down."

"When I went to court about a week later," Mallory continued, looking at Ben, "my ex shows up and he's walking like he's really sore. I asked him what happened and he glared at me for a split second and then covered it by looking away and saying he slipped coming down a flight of stairs at work. He's fine. When we get in front of the judge, my ex dropped his contest of the divorce and no mention was made of alimony."

"His lawyer pulls him aside and started asking him questions, and he just kept saying no until he threatened to fire the lawyer right there, in court, in front of the judge, for cause." Mallory smiled a little. "The lawyer shut up at that point until we were in the room to get the papers signed," she said. "He asked 'What made you change your mind about…' and my ex said, 'One more word out of you and I'll *own* your practice!' He literally didn't say another word the entire time."

"You think…" Ben started to ask.

Mallory nodded. "I didn't put it together until almost a year later," she said. "Which is stupid, or wishful thinking, or, I don't know. Kyle didn't do or say anything. I was at home, going through some things, and I came across the divorce papers and I remembered those last couple of weeks, and things finally clicked."

"And you never said anything to Kyle about it," Ben asked.

"No," Mallory shook her head, "and he wouldn't have wanted me to. He wasn't like that. He never said anything and assumed I didn't know. If he'd wanted me to know he would have told me, so I kept it to myself." She looked Ben in the eyes, "You're the first person I've ever told, and if you ever tell Kyle I knew," she let the threat hang in the air between them.

"Not a word," Ben said. "Believe it or not I understand. So why didn't anything ever happen there?"

"Aside from the fact that I was in his chain-of-command," Mallory asked.

Ben gave Mallory a look that spoke volumes.

"Okay," Mallory said. "Because at first I wasn't ready for a relationship–any relationship–and then I wasn't ready for a relationship with someone who knew all about my previous relationship. Then, eventually, Kyle was just a really good friend."

Ben winced. "Ouch," he said. "Relegated to the friend-zone and he never even knew it."

"That's not fair," Mallory said. "I never gave him any reason to think otherwise."

"Really," Ben asked.

Mallory was silent for several seconds.

"You know," Ben said, "I wanted to ask you out in the worst way when we were in boot."

"Why didn't you," she asked.

"Well," Ben said, "even back then you were a little intimidating."

"Moi," Mallory asked, taking one of her hands back and touching her chest and feigning shock.

"Yes you," Ben chuckled. "Private Jensen who could do more push-ups than anyone else in the squad, and probably than the Drill Sergeant, who consistently ran everyone else into the ground when we had a 'fun run', and outshot the Range Master, using his *own gun*."

"To be fair to the Range Master," Mallory said, "I'd been shooting an M1 Garand since I was nine."

Ben rolled his eyes. "Like any of us nineteen-year-old raw recruits gave a damn how long you'd been shooting," he said. "You were out of our league, woman! Most men would probably still feel that way."

Mallory made a small frown.

"So," Ben said softly, "I have to ask. Am I in the dreaded friend-zone too?"

Mallory stood up as if to walk away, but instead of pulling her other hand free, she pulled Ben up and out of the chair. Then, she put Ben's hands on her waist and both of her hands on either side of his face, and for the first time since her ex-husband left, kissed someone. Ben didn't wait to be invited twice, and was soon fully in command of the kiss that she had initiated.

"No, Ben," she whispered, when they came up for air, "you are definitely not just a friend."

Chapter Twenty-Two

July 8, 2013 - Fort Rucker, Alabama

Sanford tried to keep the sour expression off his face as he headed to Colonel Olsen's office for the morning briefing with West and the Colonel. West still had no usable information on how Ben had been warned about the impending raid of several weeks ago, nor did he have any leads on where the missing vehicles or supplies had been squirreled away.

Sanford, on the other hand, was full of information he couldn't use or share with the Colonel. Yesterday's session in the communications truck had been an eye-opener and he was dreading today's briefing more than usual.

Every morning ended the same way; with Olsen fuming and Lt. Colonel West storming out of the office, yelling for this aide or that assistant so he could look like he was getting something done. Nothing would change, and the process would repeat itself the next morning. Lieutenant Colonel West was living proof of the Peter Principle; he had risen to the level of his incompetence and would rise no further.

West was already waiting at the Colonel's door and Sanford followed him into the office. Colonel Olsen was standing with his back to them, overlooking the base through his office windows.

"Have a seat, gentlemen," Olsen said.

"Major Sanford," Olsen began. "Tell me what you know about the state of the morale of our troops."

For a split second, Sanford thought the Colonel knew about his meetings with Hodges and Tuttle and was on a fishing expedition. Then he remembered that morale and well-being of the troops were his responsibilities and started breathing again.

"Sir," Sanford said, stalling, "that's a tricky question to answer at the best of times. Right now, there's a lot that would go into the answer. Is there something specific you are referring to?"

"I'm referring," Olsen said, as he turned around and leaned on his desk, "to the overall morale of the troops; here and at the other bases that don't seem to be in active revolt against the directives we've sent out regarding ARCLiTE."

Sanford nodded slightly as he swallowed. "The longer this goes on," Sanford said, "the more questions they're asking, Sir. More and more in the enlisted ranks are questioning how long we're expected to keep this current posture, or when we're going to start moving *forward* with whatever the next steps should be."

Olsen was clenching his jaw by the time Sanford was finished and it had taken less than a minute to put him into his normal state—just shy of raving.

"They don't have to understand," Olsen said through gritted teeth.

"With all due respect, Sir," West interrupted, "there comes a point where they *do*. What they don't have to do is *like* it. They aren't automatons, Sir. These are people; many of them men and women with families here on base. They understand the need to follow orders and know what it takes to get the job done but there's a difference between obedience and blind obedience."

Olsen winced just slightly at the last remark from West.

West, who was surprising Sanford with his insight, continued. "We put a lot of trust and faith in our NCOs because we know that they, more than the rest, know the importance of discipline and duty.

They've been putting out fires for the better part of six months, though, and even they are starting to ask some of those same questions now."

Olsen stood back up and started pacing in front of his window; a thoughtful expression on his face, hands clasped behind him.

"They need a mission, Sir," Sanford said.

"We're at *war*," Olsen snapped.

"Sir," West asked. "I'm sorry, but with whom? American citizens, the other bases that aren't implementing ARCLiTE, zombies, *who*? I'm not even questioning the *fact*, sir," although the 'fact' could certainly be up for debate in just about anyone's mind.

Olsen had turned on West when he'd been challenged, but backed off a little once he realized that it wasn't so much his assertion of war that was being questioned, but who they were fighting.

"*Is* it really a war," Sanford asked, "and if so, are we even going about prosecuting it correctly?"

"Yes," Olsen said as he stopped behind his desk and glared at Sanford and West. "It's a war in every sense of the word, against everything you mentioned."

Sanford realized, almost too late, that West had included zombies in the list of things they were at war against and Olsen had said yes to everything, and had to literally bite his lip to keep from smiling. This really wasn't a laughing matter, but the Colonel was all. over. the. map!

"Then we have to treat it like one," West said. "Quit *telling* the men that we're at war and let them go fight in some actual battles instead of just these, these one-off skirmishes that don't mean anything."

West shook his head for a second. "But they're going to need a reason to fight at this point," he said. "This has been going on for long enough that even though they'll do what they're told, they won't be as effective unless they have a reason."

"Then give them one," Olsen said.

"But what," Sanford asked.

"I honestly don't care," Olsen said. "Make one up if you have to but do it, do it now, and make it convincing."

Sanford's stomach lurched.

"Sir," West said into the uncomfortable silence that followed Olsen's order. "In some cases, an enemy isn't going to be enough. Again, we've been at an elevated state of readiness for so long that simply putting a face on the opposition may not do it for some of the troops."

Olsen glared at West but didn't say anything, so West continued.

"We," West indicated the three of them, "have been Officers, and out of direct fire and combat, long enough to have forgotten what it's like to live on the edge for an extended period of time. They either need to stand down for a while–which they clearly can't do–or be presented with something so overwhelming that they're willing to crank it up a notch one last time."

Olsen didn't like what he was hearing, but he knew West was right. He'd mavericked from enlisted to his commission over twenty years ago and even though he hadn't seen combat in almost that long, he could remember the feeling West was describing without too much effort.

"We'll come up with something else, too," Olsen said. "Not just the face of the enemy but a real threat, a threat to *us*, not just the country or our way of life. I don't care if you even have to stage a crisis *right on base* to get their attention, but get it done."

...

"Put the President on," Olsen said.

"I told you last time," the voice on the other end said, "that isn't going to happen."

"I don't care about last time," Olsen said. "This is now, and you're putting him on."

"Much better," the voice said. "No room for misunderstanding, taking charge of the situation. Not at all like last time…"

"Put," Olsen said, cutting off the other side, "the. President. on."

"No," was the response.

Olsen was taken aback by the icy venom in the tone.

"Don't ever interrupt me again," the voice said. "I have been as patient with you as I am willing to be, but even that has an end. You may deal with your underlings and your peers however you wish, but I am neither. I am your Better and you will *never* forget it."

Olsen didn't dare respond.

"Better," the voice said. "Now, what is the meaning of this call? We weren't scheduled to speak again for another week."

"I may still have…issues with some of my own people," Olsen said. "Just putting a face on the enemy, giving them someone to finally fight, isn't going to be enough. Like you said last time, this threat has been out there for so long that they're going to need a reason to attack, they're going to need something specific to defend."

The voice laughed. "This," he said, "should *not* be a problem. There will always be dissention, skepticism, those that won't be completely on-board. There's nothing you can do about that. What you *can* do is mold the perceptions of those that *want* to believe."

"I know that, but *how*," Olsen asked.

"The same way we have been doing it for decades," the voice said. "You've already determined that you control what remains of the media, in all its forms. Propaganda is a tool that comes in many shapes and sizes."

Olsen was silent and considering what should be obvious, but still wasn't.

"You have men and women under your command with families," the voice asked.

"Of course," Olsen said.

"There are schools," the voice said. "Use them. A child's mind is a fertile field; sow it with the seeds of *your* choosing."

Olsen nodded, not conscious of the fact that he couldn't be seen by the person on the other end.

"And should all else fail," the voice said, "have them do it for the children. They are, after all, our one true hope for a better world, a shining tomorrow, the future."

The voice had said the last with such passion, such conviction; Olsen was asking his question before he realized he was speaking.

"Do you have any children," Olsen asked.

"Absolutely not," the voice said. "Don't be ridiculous. They are an utter waste of time and money."

Olsen was shocked back to reality and realized how quickly he'd been lulled, simply by the right words at the right time.

"I see," Olsen said.

"Yes," the voice said. "I believe you do."

"What happens if I can't get things under control in time," Olsen asked.

"You don't want to know," the voice said. Something about the way he said it bothered Olsen. It sounded like a cross between eagerness to tell and disgust at having to contemplate it.

"I think I need to know," Olsen said.

The voice was silent for several seconds before responding.

"We have a contingency plan for our contingency plan," the voice said. "We refer to it as The Outbreak."

Olsen could hear the capital letters, even over the radio, and it gave him the chills.

"I will not go into details right now," the voice said, "but suffice it to say, you don't want to fail. Even *we* would prefer that you not fail, but we will do what we must."

"I understand," Olsen said.

...

Sanford was rubbing his temples. "Can the man not think for himself," he asked. "He didn't even wait twenty-four hours before parroting back what his handler said to West and I when he ordered us to begin a propaganda campaign. He even used the exact same words as his handler when he did it."

"As disconcerting as that is," Hodges said, "I'm more concerned with their alternate contingency plan."

Sanford looked up at Hodges. "You don't think that was just a threat," he asked.

"No," Hodges said. "Not given the history of the CDC."

Sanford closed his eyes. "I have a feeling I don't want to know," he said. "On a scale of one to ten, where ten is little *grey* men," Sanford looked at Tuttle who made a show of looking anywhere in the truck but at Sanford, "where does this one sit for unbelievability?"

"Probably a six," Hodges said, "unless you're willing to believe the worst of humanity, then it's more like a three."

"Go ahead," Sanford said.

"First, you need some additional background on the CDC," Hodges said. "It was originally called the Communicable Disease Center and was founded in 1946. Initially, its sole purpose was the eradication of malaria and it was based in Atlanta due to the prevalence of malaria in the Southeast."

Hodges leaned forward and looked back and forth between Sanford and Tuttle as he got into his lecture. "Over the first several years," he continued, "the CDC, as a branch of the U.S. Public Health Service, which would later become the Department of Health and Human Services–which is important–sprayed as many as six-and-a-half-million homes with chemicals–including DDT–in an effort to kill mosquitos that *might* have been carriers of malaria."

"Wasn't DDT considered safe for use in the 40's," Sanford asked.

"Yes and no," Hodges said. "By the early 40's, scientists were already questioning its safety, but when the CDC was started, only seven of the 369 employees were medical officers. Even if one of the doctors had had questions about the use of DDT around people, it wouldn't have gotten any traction because the bulk of the employees were entomologists and engineers."

Sanford cocked his head to the side as though to ask a question.

"Yeah," Hodges said, "but remember, when they started they were only tasked with eradicating malaria."

"It didn't take long for them to take over a lot more though," Hodges said. "After less than a year, the CDC 'bought' fifteen acres of land from Emory University for a new headquarters. Supposedly, employees of the CDC collected the money to make the purchase, which was for ten dollars, but the real benefactor was the chairman of the board of one of the largest soft drink manufacturers on the planet."

"And that's bad because," Sanford prompted, gently reminding Hodges that he wasn't nearly as steeped in this conspiracy stuff as Hodges was.

Hodges paused for a few seconds to, once again, prepare a short history lesson. "Okay, more background. How many companies, would you say, controlled the majority of the food production in the United States," he asked.

Sanford shrugged. "I don't know," he said, "a couple dozen?"

Hodges shook his head. "Less," he said.

"Fifteen," Sanford asked.

"Ten," Hodges said. "Ten parent companies, including said soda manufacturer, controlled over ninety percent of *all* prepared food and 'health' products manufactured and distributed in the U.S. before the power went out."

"What about organic foods," Sanford asked.

Hodges couldn't help but bark a short laugh. "That's either almost as bad or far worse, depending on how you look at it," he said. "As of 2009, seven of the top-twelve distributors of organic food were the same companies that owned ninety percent of the prepared food industry."

Sanford rolled his eyes.

"The point is," Hodges continued, "that over the course of the last hundred years or so, more and more aspects of our everyday life were being managed and controlled by a smaller and smaller group of individuals. Sure they owned companies, but those companies were run by people. The same 'power elite', if you will, that funded virtually all of the SuperPACs, lobbied Congress for more restrictions on our rights, and ultimately were waiting for an event just like this to put their final plans in motion."

"I'm not making this up," Hodges said. "It's for real. But back to the CDC, the reason for the new digs was because the director of the CDC had pushed to extend their responsibilities, which was really their control, to a bunch of other communicable diseases, including STDs, Tuberculosis, and eventually immunizations."

"Most people would think that was a good thing," Sanford said.

"Most people don't see it for what it is," Hodges said. "While I can grant you that having some entity try to eradicate as many diseases as possible *would* be a good thing, that isn't what happened. The chicken pox virus, which causes shingles in adults and can *kill* you if you get it for the first time as an adult, has been around how long?"

Sanford shrugged.

"The *fourteenth century*," Hodges said. "Five. hundred. years–and we still haven't eradicated it. The first vaccine didn't show up until 1974 and wasn't available in the U.S. until 1995. *Why?*"

Sanford had no response.

"Now," Hodges continued, "the CDC, which most recently had its name changed in 1992 by Congress to include 'and Prevention', has broadened its scope to include threats to environmental health, chronic diseases, disabilities–which are many times neither the result of a disease, nor are they preventable–and, of all things…terrorism preparedness. Can you explain to me, again *why*? What possible reason could there be for this agency, the Center for *Disease* Control and Prevention, to take on *Terrorism Preparedness?*"

"That can't be right," Sanford said.

"It's right there on their website," Hodges said. "Or, at least it was. When you really stop to think about it, even their name gives away their true ulterior motive, Disease Control. You don't *control* a disease–at least not the ones they've taken on–you eradicate it, you destroy it utterly and completely."

Hodges took a breath to calm himself down. "That's the history," he went on, "now for the meat. There are very few Biosafety Level 4 labs in the US–somewhere between ten and fourteen. The CDC, National Institutes of Health, Department of Health and Human Services, or the military are involved with almost all of them in one way or another. The location in Atlanta also holds one of only two 'official' samples of smallpox in the world."

Sanford raised an eyebrow. "Who has the other one," he asked.

"Russia," Tuttle chimed in.

Sanford looked at her in disbelief. "How did we let that happen," he asked.

"Like we could have stopped it," Hodges said. "They had smallpox over there. We're lucky that nobody else has it, assuming they don't.

That's not really my point, although it makes my point. What else do they have in there that they aren't telling us? Ebola or the Marburg virus, probably; AIDS, definitely; smallpox we already know the answer to."

"Yellow fever, bubonic plague, hantavirus," Tuttle added.

Hodges nodded. "And again, that's just the ones we know about," he said. "What if they've concocted something new, something we haven't seen before by mixing a couple of things together?"

"But *why* would they do something like that," Sanford asked. "It just doesn't make sense."

"Haven't you been paying attention," Hodges asked. "Did you miss the part about spraying millions of people with poison in the form of DDT? Or how about encouraging people to just accept being injected with barely tested and generally useless immunizations? Sir, smallpox was certified as *eradicated* in 1980. Why in the *world* would *anybody* still have samples of it when what they really ought to have, if they had anything at all, would be millions of doses of one of the few vaccines that actually *worked*?"

"What do you mean the few vaccines that actually worked," Sanford said. "You mentioned immunizations before."

"Two things," Hodges said. "First, why does the CDC say we need a new flu vaccine every year?"

"Because seasonal flus don't respond to the vaccine of previous years," Sanford said.

"And when did we have the swine flu seasonal-flu scare," Hodges asked.

"Um…2009 I think," Sanford said.

"Exactly," Hodges said with a sly smile. "So why has every *seasonal* flu vaccine since 2009 had the H1N1, or swine flu, vaccine included in it if the 2009 swine-flu 'pandemic' was seasonal in nature? What did they put in that specific vaccine that they want to keep putting into people year after year?"

"Second," Hodges continued, "how effective is the annual seasonal-flu vaccine?"

"I have no idea," Sanford said, trying not to roll his eyes again.

"How about 1.5%," Hodges said.

But," Sanford said. "That can't be right. Tens of thousands of people die from the flu every year."

"No," Hodges shook his head, "they don't. That 'tens of thousands' number is for 'influenza and pneumonia' combined. When they break it down, the number of reported flu deaths is usually under two hundred."

Hodges stopped Sanford from interrupting. "They report the two together to *massively* inflate the numbers to scare more and more people into getting the shots," Hodges said. "In fact, of the couple-hundred deaths each year, less than ten percent are *confirmed* through lab testing. They literally assume that the other ninety percent are from the flu because that's how they were reported…by family members or doctors that never ran tests in the first place, simply diagnosed it as flu based on vague symptoms."

"I would normally ask how anyone could justify claiming flu deaths without even *testing*, but we're talking about the CDC so…" Hodges shrugged.

Sanford shook his head. "Ok, but now that the power is out," Sanford said, "how are they even still a threat?"

"I didn't mention that the CDC has a location in Fort Collins, Colorado," Hodges said.

"Which is only…" Sanford started.

"About seventy miles north of the Denver International Airport," Tuttle finished.

Chapter Twenty-Three

"Something's been eating at you ever since we got here," Kyle said as he and Eric walked around the perimeter of the hangars at the airport. "Your head hasn't really been in it, and I don't mean like before we left the base."

"I'm fine," Eric said.

"Oh," Kyle said and rolled his eyes. "I see. You're fine. And I suppose you just want to be friends now, too. It isn't me, it's you…"

"Knock it off, man," Eric said.

"Then cut the BS and tell me what's going on," Kyle said. "You obviously aren't happy here."

"No," Eric said. "I'm not."

Eric's frankness surprised Kyle. "Ok," he said. "Admitting you have a problem is…"

"It's not a problem," Eric interrupted, "and it's not a joke. When we left, when *I* wanted to leave, it was to get away from everything–from all this. Now what are we doing? We're still right here, not very far from where we started, and we're building another town."

Eric shook his head. "This isn't what I wanted, Kyle," he said. "I needed some space. I didn't want to be alone, but I didn't want…" Eric shrugged and looked around. "I didn't want *this*."

"I'm sorry," Kyle said.

"You don't need to apologize," Eric said. "I'm a big boy, I could have said no at any step of the way. I'm glad you found Amanda. She and William *need* you and I think you need them too. I'm happy for you, I really am. At the same time this just isn't what I wanted, what I want."

Kyle shook his head as he looked around. "I don't know that *this* is going to work anyway," he said. "At least not here."

"Probably not," Eric agreed. "The buildings here are no better than the ones in Redemption, or anywhere else for that matter, and log cabins just aren't going to happen."

"Nope," Kyle agreed. "Wrong kind of trees and not nearly enough of them for the numbers we need."

"And we can't live in the trailers forever," Eric continued. "Although they certainly didn't skimp on the ones they picked."

"True," Kyle said. "You're getting at something, though. Spit it out."

Eric stopped between the hangars and the maintenance building. "We both know this is temporary," he said, "everything about it. The location, transportation, the food situation; none of it is going to work long term. You said it when we first got here. We were lucky that they hadn't dropped the Black Hawks here already, but what if they had?"

Kyle frowned and looked around. "So where do you think we should go," Kyle asked. "I agree. This isn't ideal."

At the look on Eric's face Kyle gave in. "Okay, fine," he said. "We have hardly any water or food, no livestock, no fields for crops—and no seeds anyway. Obviously we have to do something, but I'll be damned if I'm going to go beg at the base...at least not yet."

Eric shook his head. "Furthest thing from my mind," he said.

...

"So how are things going," Joel asked, "wherever you guys are?"

"We're not dead yet," Eric said, "which is a plus. But where we are isn't going to work long-term, and frankly, I think Mallory is going to want to take this place over eventually. I'll tell you where we are when we're ready to leave."

Joel snorted. "Fair enough, I guess," he said. "So, to what do I owe the honor?"

"How is The Barge doing," Eric asked, referring to the Bar-G horse ranch. The Barge was what Travis was constantly telling people to call it. "The last time I was down there was a month or so before…" Eric paused for a second, "before the quarantine."

"Travis is doing pretty well," Joel said. "We've got probably a hundred people down there more or less full time to help the ranch hands he had before. He's up over a hundred head in his herd at last count. Mostly Quarter Horses and maybe a dozen draft horses; Percherons, and a team of Belgians with an additional mare, I think. He's complaining that they'll eat him out of house and home, but that hasn't stopped him from breeding every last mare this year."

"Is he ready to start doing business, do you think," Eric asked.

"Uhm," Joel said, stalling, "I don't know. But you need to know that the base is first in line, because they loaned him the portable mill and the manpower."

"Hmmm," Eric muttered. "I can see the portable mill, but unless Mallory's footing the bill for room and board, I don't see how she can hold manpower over his head, or at least not much."

"Fair point," Joel said. "I'll let you be the one to bring that up, though."

"If I can work it right," Eric said with a laugh, "I'll let *Travis* be the one to bring it up."

…

"Mr. Gibson," Eric said as he got out of his truck.

"Please, call me Travis," Travis said.

"Okay, Travis," Eric said and stuck out his hand. "Eric Tripp, I don't know if you remember me or not. I've been here a couple of times but we've never actually met."

"I do," Travis said, "but last time it was *Captain* Tripp if I'm not mistaken. I don't see any insignia or do-dads on the uniform, though. I assume there's been a change in situation."

"There has," Eric said. "As far as I know it was amicable and no, I didn't get kicked out. I won't bore you with the details but..." Eric gave Travis a brief history of why he'd left.

Travis nodded. "I'm sorry to hear that, Eric," he said. "You have my sympathies and condolences. Believe me; I know how fragile life is and how quickly things can change. But that's not what brings you out here today, is it?"

"No, sir, I'd like to talk to you about some horses," Eric said as they walked towards an arena and numerous paddocks where colorful horses were grazing, exercising, resting, or being groomed. "I know the base has first dibs because of the saw mill and maybe because of the manpower..."

"Maybe not so much on the manpower," Travis said. "Most of these folks live here full-time now, and I'm providing for them. Don't get me wrong, while the initial influx of helping hands was great, it isn't like the Major is sending down food and clothing for them on a regular basis or helping to build the bunkhouses or family cabins."

It was Eric's turn to nod. At least he wasn't going to have to convince the rancher that the base's initial take of horses wasn't going to be as big as Mallory might have hoped.

"I understand you've got mostly Quarter Horses," Eric said, "with a few draft breeds. Has the Major indicated what she's most interested in to start with?"

"She's said she would like the Quarters at first because they're the most versatile," Travis said, "although they are *not* draft horses. You can only work them so long in harness or pulling something before they have to be switched out. What are you looking for?"

"A combination," Eric said, "but I understand that you've got to keep your breeding stock intact. Before I get into that though, I assume you have a blacksmith?"

"I have a farrier with *some* blacksmithing capabilities," Travis said. "We make our own horseshoes and a few odds and ends."

"How are you set for coal," Eric asked.

"I'm almost completely out," Travis said, "but we've been making and using our own charcoal. It's not nearly as efficient, but it gets the job done. Can you get me actual coal?"

"Possibly," Eric said. "If I can, can your farrier make iron rims for wagon wheels?"

Travis's eyes lit up. "He may very well be able to, yes," he said and then stopped. "We're going to need some additional metal stock though. How many are you thinking?"

"Honestly," Eric said, "I don't know for sure. Not less than ten, but it could be as many as forty."

Travis's jaw dropped. "A hundred-and-sixty wheels," he almost shouted. "Are you crazy? I'll definitely need more stock...like, a *lot* more stock."

Eric grinned. "Actually," Eric said, "since I *don't* have anyone with blacksmithing experience, it'll probably need to be more like two-hundred-wheels. You know, a spare for each wagon."

Travis just looked at Eric. "This is going to take some time," he said, "and once it starts, word is going to get out, you know."

"Oh, I'm sure it will," Eric said. "In fact, you could become a very wealthy man in short order by making wagons *and* selling the horses to go with them. It's my job to come up with something to sell back to *you*."

"Aside from the idea," Travis asked.

"This was just to get you doing what *I* need you to do for me," Eric said. "Now, here's what I think I can do for *you*…"

…

"How'd it go," Kyle asked when Eric got back to the airport.

"Pretty good," Eric said. "I may have created a monster though. You should have seen his eyes light up at the mention of wagon wheels and wagons in general, and he was almost as interested in getting his hands on actual coal for his forge as anything else. He's shrewd, I'll give him that."

"Any idea on time frame," Kyle asked, "on anything?"

Eric shook his head. "Unfortunately not," he said. "He's let the base know that the herd is to a point that he's willing to start trading, but hasn't heard anything back. He's going to let them know that the window for them to exercise their first right of refusal is finite because he can't just let the herd keep growing while they sit there and can't make a decision. He's even willing to hold onto any horses they want for as long as they need since the base is most likely not set up to take care of them yet, but they need to figure it out, and soon."

Kyle grinned. "Why does that warm my heart," he asked.

"Because you hold a grudge like nobody I've ever met," Eric said, "and you've been looking for a way to stick it to Mallory."

Kyle put on a pained expression. "What on earth could make you say such a thing," he asked.

"April 7, 2003," Eric started. "We were on the outskirts of Baghdad…"

"Don't you say another word," Kyle growled. "That was *not* my fault."

"It never is," Eric said with a grin.

"I hadn't even had anything to drink yet," Kyle said with a slight whine to his voice.

"And yet seven years later…" Eric poked.

"He deserved it," Kyle said. "Pure and simple, and now it's forgiven…and had been forgotten until just now. Thanks a lot, three years of therapy, pfft, gone!"

"Right," Eric said his grin wider than ever.

…

"I know nothing about horses," Mallory said to her command group, "but we need to make some decisions or we're going to lose our place in line with the Bar-G. Apparently, Mr. Gibson's herd is up to the point that he can start making trades and doing business and we're holding up the works."

Stewart and Jackson looked at each other then looked at Halstead, but avoided looking at the Major directly.

"What," she asked. "What am I missing this time?"

"Well, Ma'am," Halstead said, being the most senior in the room, "what everybody is trying to avoid saying, and failing miserably at bringing up, is that none of us really has any experience with horses either."

"But…" Mallory prodded.

"But," Halstead continued with a sigh, "we used to have someone who grew up on a farm."

"Who," Mallory started to ask and then cut off the question in mid-breath. "Oh for the love of… That man will be the death of me."

"We'll ask around and see who else can help out," Stewart said.

"Where are we going to put them," Jackson asked, being a bit more practical.

"They'll stay at the ranch for the time being," Mallory said. "And Mr. Gibson will keep the saw mill in trade. We also talked about the fact that he's providing for the people that are working there and, frankly, it's a load off our backs that we don't have to worry about them, so I'm not pushing for the labor to be included in the deal."

The three men nodded. That seemed only fair.

"We'll get to it and should have at least one person who can tell a mare from a stallion by tonight," Halstead said.

...

"I can get you the coal," Eric said as he got out of his truck.

"Before you say anything more," Travis said, "we need to talk." Travis didn't look upset, but he didn't look like he was pleased with what he was going to have to say either.

Kyle and Eric had already made a run to the abandoned power plant and grabbed a couple full truckloads of coal and Eric was planning on coming down in the next day or two to drop it off. He even had a couple of burlap sacks in the back of the truck now as a gesture of good faith. He hoped he wasn't going to have to learn how to build coal-burning fireplaces to use what he and Kyle had gone out and grabbed.

"So…" Eric prompted after they'd walked away from the bulk of people and towards one of the newly-constructed outbuildings.

"My farrier isn't going to be able to make the wheel rims," Travis said. "We discussed it and he just doesn't have the skill or the tools. The forge isn't large enough, and although he's seen it done a couple of times, it was a long time ago and there was a bunch of, well, special equipment used to forge it and put it on the wheel."

Eric bit his lip.

"Even building the wheels and hubs is a specialized craft," Travis continued. "I had no idea when I tentatively agreed what I was getting myself into."

Eric nodded. It looked like he may be learning how to build fireplaces after all.

"However," Travis said as he started walking towards the building, "all is not lost. I can't put iron rims on wooden wheels, but who said they had to be iron rims or wooden wheels?"

Travis opened the door and ushered Eric into what was apparently a workshop. It took several seconds for Eric's eyes to adjust, but when they did he couldn't help but smile.

In front of him lay the beginnings of a wagon. The skeleton showed that it would have a wooden bottom and sides, and it obviously had wooden axles. What was just as obvious was that it had been fitted with four automobile wheels and tires. More precisely, they looked to be off of a truck or SUV.

"How did you…" Eric began and then trailed off as he approached the wagon and started inspecting the work.

"One of the reasons the rims were beyond my farrier," Travis said, "was because of their size. Another was because of the type of steel he would have had to use. For this, though, all he had to do was make a couple of connecting pieces to attach a wooden piece to a metal piece that bent the wrong way. He says that he should even be able to re-use the leaf springs to soften up the ride a little and take some of the jolt off the axles."

Eric shook his head. "Any idea how that will translate to ease of pulling for the horses," he asked.

"Considering the big wheels on the wagons they used way back when," Travis said, "the Conestoga or the Schooner were upwards of fifty pounds each and didn't have nearly the friction reduction on the axles that a packed bearing has, it should make quite a difference."

"So now I need to be able to do something for you," Eric said. "Besides the coal, which you won't need nearly as much of right away."

"Oh I'll still need coal," Travis said. "It's not like it spoils over the winter or goes bad if it gets wet. What do you have in mind, though?"

"How are you doing for electric and water," Eric asked.

"I could do with more of both," Travis said.

"Water I think I can help with fairly quickly," Eric said. "Electricity is going to take a little longer, but it'll be a longer-term fix."

"I'm listening," Travis said.

Chapter Twenty-Four

July 16, 2013 - Fort Rucker, Alabama

Sanford was beginning to hate the inside of their communications Humvee. It was cramped. He felt vulnerable every time they were in it. It seemed like all he got was more bad news whenever they got together there and, possibly the worst of all, was the funky smell a place starts to get when it's been closed off for too long with people inside.

"We've sat on this long enough," Sanford said. "It's time to reach out to someone on the other side."

Hodges nodded. "Do you have anyone specific in mind," he asked.

"I do," Sanford said, "but I'm open to suggestions."

Tuttle and Hodges were both silent for a few seconds and then Tuttle spoke up.

"Sir," Tuttle said, "if I may. I suggest we contact the National Guard group at Natchez Trace. The base they've dubbed Promised Land."

"Why them and why now," Sanford asked. "I'm not opposed to it; I just want to hear your reasoning."

"Well," Tuttle said. "From what I've been able to gather, they and Ft. Campbell have been coordinating the communications. I can't go so far as to say they're behind the rebellion, because that honestly seems to be pretty much an organic phenomenon."

"Hodges," Sanford asked.

"It does seem like the majority of traffic either goes through Promised Land," Hodges said, "or is destined for there. I would agree that while they aren't the source of the rebellion, they haven't been shy about organizing it now that it's happening."

"In that case," Sanford said, "it sounds like we're in agreement. Promised Land is who I wanted to contact in the first place. Now, exactly what do we say?"

Hodges frowned. "That's the tricky part. If we don't play it right, we could end up spooking them. The last thing we want is for them to either switch the security keys without us knowing or simply stop using the radios altogether."

"I think I should be the one to make contact," Tuttle said. "It's my job after all. I'm the most familiar with their system—not that it's super complicated—and I've at least heard their procedures a number of times."

"While I see your point," Hodges said, "I think it should be someone in a command position. We have no idea who will pick up on the other end."

Tuttle nodded at his logic.

"Agreed," Sanford said. "No time like the present,"…

The rain had finally let up after three days and Mallory was in her office with Ben, going over some of the proposals that Chuck had made regarding starting new towns. The morning had started off cool, but as the day progressed it had grown sticky and humid.

"I miss air-conditioning," Mallory said.

"Don't start," Ben said, not looking up from a brief he was reading on the people that had come with him out of Ft. Campbell. "You'll never stop if you do."

Mallory glared at him from across the room, but realized he was right. She was just wondering if she needed to conduct another raid drill when the radio behind her came to life.

"Auxiliary S Three calling Canaan Six," said a voice that Mallory didn't recall hearing before on their network.

Ben harrumphed.

"What," Mallory asked.

"Somebody's trying to be cute," Ben said. "Canaan is another name for the Promised Land. It sounds like you have a call from their S3."

Mallory looked at the radio for several seconds and noted that nobody else was responding. She knew that nobody manning a radio in Promised Land would respond to an unknown outside unit.

"Aren't you going to respond," Ben asked. "You're Canaan Six."

Mallory shook her head. "Who is Auxiliary," she asked, "and why is their Operations Officer the one on the radio?"

Ben shook his head and then paused. His brow creased and he tapped his fingers on the desk a couple of times, then he pulled out his radio, but paused in the act of calling someone and put it back.

"Who were you going to call," Mallory asked.

The call came through the radio again.

"Mathis," Ben said. "He was a WWII buff. I enjoy history but he was a walking encyclopedia. We used to talk about the resistance movements during WWII and Auxiliary rings a bell, but I can't remember why."

Mallory thought for a second and called Sergeant Cox on her radio.

"Sergeant Cox," Mallory said, "does the name or term Auxiliary mean anything to you, in reference to WWII?"

"Yes, Ma'am," Cox said. "In the Second World War, they were specially trained units set up by Churchill to act as British Resistance in case the UK was ever invaded and occupied. They were set up in 1940 and disbanded in 1944."

Ben was nodding his head.

"Thank you Sergeant Cox," Mallory said. "That was both enlightening and very helpful."

"Okay, now I remember," Ben said. "There was a credible threat of a German invasion, Operation Sea Lion, and the Auxiliary Units, or GHQ Auxiliary Units, were established as a preemptive move."

"So," Mallory asked, "who is this Auxiliary that's calling me?"

…

Mallory didn't want to wait too long, but she called in Lieutenant Halstead and First Sergeant Stewart. She didn't want to take the call alone, or with only Ben there, because she just didn't feel it would be right, and Ben wasn't in her chain-of-command. She also had Sparky come to her office because he was the one who had designed the network, along with Sergeant Hale from Ft. Campbell, as she needed to know how someone may have gotten through their security.

When the next transmission came through, Mallory responded.

"This is Canaan Six," she said, referring to her position as the commanding officer.

Everyone in the room was sitting on the edge of their chairs, leaning forward.

"C6," the other side said, "first of all you deserve an explanation. I assume you know what Auxiliary Units are or you wouldn't have answered the call. This has specific reference to the Bulldog."

Mallory nodded to herself. Even she knew that Churchill had been called The British Bulldog.

"Affirmative," she said. "Go ahead."

"Against my better judgment," the other side said, Mallory was thinking of him as S3 now, said, "I was involved in the raid on Ft. Campbell."

Mallory could see Ben tense and put a hand on his knee.

"At the end of the raid," S3 said, "during a sweep of one of the buildings…"

…

"Well," Sparky muttered a couple of minutes later with a sigh, "that explains how they got into the network."

"Yes, it does," Mallory said. "And thank you. You and Hale did a great job. We'll take it from here."

Sparky saluted at the dismissal and left, relieved that his network was still secure.

"It's easy to say you're rebelling," Mallory said, "but I need some sort of proof."

"Understood," S3 said. "I don't know how long it will take you to verify this, but if you can get in contact with Major Franklin, he has a mole. Lieutenant Mathis has been in contact with Colonel Olsen since shortly after the power went out without the Major's knowledge, although he's been silent since the raid. We have a number of their conversations on tape, and I would be happy to play them for you if necessary."

"Give me a minute," Mallory said.

Mallory looked at the group in the room and held out her hands. "Would the Colonel have given up Mathis," she asked Ben.

"I don't think so," Ben said. "He really doesn't gain anything by telling me that I have a mole and he already knows where you are. If he had the radio, why risk telling us?"

Mallory looked at Halstead and Stewart.

"I agree," Halstead said. "They have nothing to gain and everything to lose by tipping their hand like this. There is no good reason to contact us unless they are serious and want to coordinate with us."

"That makes three of us," Stewart said. "If they've had it this long and nothing has happened, but they're finally contacting us, I think it's legit. I don't want to be naïve but, again, they have nothing to gain and everything to lose. They don't know how we have the system set up, what back-doors are in place, what secondary security keys are on the laptops, none of that. For all they know we could be locking them out right now."

Mallory nodded and picked up the microphone.

"I can confirm that Mathis was a mole," Mallory said, "so now what?"

...

"So now what," Major Jensen said.

The three in the Humvee were listening via speaker and Hodges got ready to hand the microphone to Sanford.

"Please hold for my Six," Hodges said, "but not my SIX."

"Major," Sanford said, "I know who you are, it's only right that you know who I am. I'm Major Bradley Sanford. We can keep the names of everyone else to a minimum, but I felt you at least deserved to know who you were talking to. I guess you can call me Auxiliary Six."

"Thank you, Major," Mallory said. "Why are we talking, though?"

"Because we need to share information," Sanford said, "and, ultimately, I think we need to work together to get rid of a bigger threat. The Colonel isn't the problem; he's simply a tool being wielded by a much larger threat. He's a dangerous tool, to be sure, but he's being used, mostly willingly, to advance an agenda that needs to be stopped."

"That's pretty vague," Mallory said.

"And you don't know me from a hole in the ground," Sanford said. "If I tried to tell you everything I know right now, this conversation would be over in five minutes and we would probably never speak again."

There was no response from Mallory, so Sanford went on. "The orders aren't legitimate," Sanford said, "which obviously isn't news to you, but they also aren't coming from the President."

"This much I knew," Mallory said. "And by knew, I mean I actually knew. When I say Mathis was a mole, the emphasis is on past-tense. He may not have sung like a canary, but he did let on that the President wasn't in charge anymore, and that ARCLiTE was not only *not* what we thought it was, it's *more* than what we thought it was."

"Understood," Sanford said. "Did Mathis know where Olsen's handlers are?"

"All he said was an underground base," Mallory said. "He claimed he didn't know where, specifically."

"What do you know about the Denver International Airport," Sanford asked.

"Aside from the fact that it's in Denver," Mallory said, "nothing."

"We need to have a longer conversation," Sanford said, "but before we do you need to hear some of the conversations between the Colonel and his handlers. We can't do it right now, though."

Now that they were actively participating in the rebellion, or at least in contact with a rebellious group, Sanford didn't dare either stay on the air for very long or be in the radio truck too often.

"We'll contact you again in two days," Sanford said, "at 1600 hours."

…

Sparky had listened in to the exchange on the secure rig he had in his tent. Unlike the Major, he knew at least a little bit about the Denver International Airport and the conspiracy behind it. He'd flown through there a couple of times to visit family and the disturbing murals in the terminals and near the baggage claim area had piqued his curiosity in a morbid kind of way.

While he was wondering how far off all those theories had been, he was more intrigued with how they had intercepted some of the Colonel's communications. Now *that* was a question he *really* wanted an answer to.

After the call broke up, Sparky watched for the Major to leave her office and then made a call of his own. He'd heard the call for Canaan from Auxiliary so he figured he might as well continue to use the same call signs.

"Canaan S Six calling Auxiliary S Six," Sparky said into the microphone, not knowing if anyone was even manning the radio on the other end. He was surprised by the sound of a female voice.

"This is Auxiliary S Six," Tuttle replied.

"Oh," Sparky said, stupidly choosing to depress the mic button while he was fumbling for words. "Uhm, this is Canaan S Six."

"I gathered that from your broadcast," Tuttle said. "Are you new to Ham radio or just radio in general?"

"Ouch," Sparky thought. *"S6 is Communications for crying out loud. I really AM the S6 for this bunch and I'm acting like I stole my Dad's CB."*

"Negative," Sparky said, "just got caught a little off guard."

"Weren't expecting a woman on the other end," Tuttle said. There was no question in her voice but there wasn't any venom either. She'd been encountering it for years and it's just the way it was.

Sparky sighed. "Roger," he said. "Not that there's anything wrong with it."

Tuttle laughed. "It's ok," she said. "The boys actually like hearing a female voice when they're coming back from a mission or when they have to fly blind or by instruments alone. They prefer our calm, cool, no-nonsense voices to the...alternative."

Sparky was nodding his head at what she was saying. It kind of made sense when he thought about it.

"You play video games," Tuttle asked.

"Pardon," Sparky said.

"Video games," Tuttle said. "Did you play any first-person shooter video games before the power went out?"

"Some," he said, "why?"

"Most of the AI or communications interface voices," Tuttle asked, "were they male or female?"

Sparky's eyebrows went up. "Female now that you mention it," he said.

"I know," Tuttle said. "I was approached about doing a voice-over for a couple of games about a year and a half ago."

"And," Sparky asked.

"Couldn't find the time to work it in," she said. "Would have been cool I guess but in hind sight kind of short-lived."

They both laughed.

"So," Sparky said, "who found the Ham rig up at Campbell?"

"Actually," Tuttle said, "I did. Women don't go to the front lines but the fighting was over and they needed someone with *real* comms experience so I was there to go in after the fact." There was a pause as she caught herself from using names.

"My Lieutenant was there when I found it and we kept it under wraps for a week or two until I figured out how to use it," she said. "I came close to losing everything when the battery almost died. I wasn't sure if I had all the passwords changed to get back into the system yet and the power cable had come unplugged and I hadn't realized it. Linux needs a better low battery indicator, or at least the window manager that this guy chose needed a better one."

Sparky snickered to himself. Grounder was notorious for disabling as many popups and widgets as possible to make his working environment 'clean'. In this case it could have been great had the laptop fallen into the wrong hands.

"And I assume you didn't just stumble onto the Colonel's private communications with his handlers either," Sparky asked.

"Um, yeah," Tuttle said. "That was quite a bit more work, but I try not to dislocate my shoulder patting myself on the back for that one."

"Do tell," Sparky said.

Chapter Twenty-Five

The plans that Chuck had handed over to Joel and Mallory were just a rough draft–basically outlines for what he thought each town might provide. They also focused on what he thought the strengths of their existing populations were.

"The more I look at what you've put together," Mallory said, "the more I like it."

"I'm sensing a 'but' coming," Chuck said.

"Well," Mallory said with a shrug, "up to this point we, Joel and I, have tried to stay out of people's daily lives as much as possible. I agree with the general direction of what you've drawn up and I think we're going to need pretty much everything you've outlined here, eventually. What I don't necessarily agree with, is the three of us deciding how and where everyone is going to live and what they're going to do for the rest of their lives."

Chuck nodded. "I can see that," he said, "any suggestions?"

"Actually, yes," Joel said. "We need a community-wide activity where we get everyone together to talk about your proposals. Allow people to offer up suggestions, what skills they have that aren't being used right now, that sort of thing."

Joel looked at his watch and muttered a curse. "We did it again," he said.

"What," Chuck asked.

"While the quarantine was going on," he said, "we missed Independence Day!"

"There is one thing *we* need to discuss," Mallory said, "and that's our fuel situation. We need to talk to Mr. Carlisle about planting more soybeans for bio-diesel. It's the one renewable fuel that we seem to be able to control. I just wish we had more diesel vehicles. After the loss of the one fuel dump and the expenditure of the extra fuel to put out the fire, we're in bad shape."

"Eventually, we're going to have to find an alternative," Joel said, "either to petroleum, or to the cars and trucks that run on gas. Even the gas we had in storage is going to go stale without re-treatment soon."

"Agreed," Mallory said, "and I hate to use this as an example, but until we get something else usable online, we're in the same predicament we were in before the power went out. We need something better, but we can't put time, effort, or resources into something better because we need all the resources we have just to maintain our current standard of living."

"I think we're finally to the point," Joel said, "where it's critical, though. We have to take the time; we have to devote some resources to it. We don't have the luxury of not doing it right the first time and just doing it 'right now' because there may not be a second time to fix it. I'm not hugging trees; I'm trying to save my own butt!"

"I know what you mean," Chuck said. "We can use coal for a good long while, and as we're able to raise our technology base it'll be cleaner and more efficient. Unless we make a jump directly to electric vehicles though, coal power isn't going to cut it for transportation. We can't even use it for rail transportation since the closest line is probably the power plant where we're getting the coal *from*."

"And that doesn't even take into account the fact that the roads will eventually start to deteriorate," Joel said, "if they aren't already."

"So we need to talk to Carlisle about more acreage for soy," Mallory said with a sigh, "and we really need to find some alternative energy sources, sooner rather than later."

"We've got to be more open-minded about alternative methods of transportation, too," Joel said.

Mallory shook her head. "It's a good thing Mathis blew himself up with the fuel dump," she said, "or I'd kill him myself."

…

Joel and Chuck were walking back to the section of camp where the Chuck and Sheri were lived after the meeting with Mallory. The cooling breeze outside was nice after being cooped up inside Mallory's office. Inside, Joel had longed for even a ceiling fan to circulate the stuffy air.

"Can we build a coal-fired power plant here in the park," Joel asked suddenly.

"Can we," Chuck repeated, "theoretically, yes. Should we? Absolutely not, no question about it. It doesn't make sense when there's one already built only twenty miles away."

Joel's shoulders slumped.

"Why," Chuck asked. "The way you asked just now, it almost sounded like a spur-of-the-moment question."

Joel scratched his chin and made a face before he answered. "Mallory's right," he said. "We're in a catch-22 with regards to power. We have *got* to find alternative resources but both until we do and in order to develop new and renewable energy, we need electricity."

Chuck nodded. "I didn't spend a *lot* of time while I was there," he said, "but I did take a look at the power plant itself while we were picking up the first load of coal. It may be possible to get one turbine back online using good parts from the others. My biggest concern is the windings."

Chuck explained a little, without going into too much detail, when he saw Joel's confused look. "A turbine generator works by transforming mechanical energy, spinning," Chuck said, "into electrical energy, either by passing the wound wires through or over a magnetic field or vice versa. Unless you want a science lesson, just accept it as fact and one of those scientific laws, just like the one that shorted out the grid last year in the first place."

"Fair enough," Joel said. "So why are you worried about the windings?"

"Because the wires need to be a few things," Chuck said. "They need to be clean and free of oxidation, carbon deposits, that sort of thing. They need to be a solid, continuous wire from beginning to end in the winding and the winding needs to be, well, a winding of wire and not a chunk of copper. My fear is that the windings have either become fouled—which will *really* cut down on their ability to induce a current; there's a break in the wire somewhere from when they shorted out; or there're points where things have fused together."

Chuck shook his head. "If the coil is shorting out," he said, "then you won't get any current out of the generator and just end up shorting everything out internally again and have to start over."

"Is it something you think you could take on," Joel asked.

"It would be a full-time job," Chuck said. "I'd have to get back to you on that. It's not just my decision to make."

…

"The gear assembly's been busted for a couple of years," Ian Fowler said to Eric, nodding to the stationary windmill blades at the top of the tower.

"We had a real bad windstorm and the brake didn't get set ahead of time," Ian said. "I don't have the tools or the spares to fix it, but if you do can have both it and the tower. I suppose you could use it as a template for more if you wanted to."

Eric had approached a dozen farmers with windmills, or more accurately wind pumps, on their land, driving one of the smaller pickup trucks they had whenever walking was out of the question. He'd siphoned some gas from each of the remaining vehicles they'd brought from Earl's group to top off the tank in this truck, but knew he wouldn't even be able to do that much longer.

Ian had been the first to have one that he would be able to take a look at and reverse engineer. He'd had a general idea of how they worked, but having never actually seen one in action or taken the transmission head apart, he was at a loss as to how he was going to put one together for the horse ranch.

"Mr. Fowler," Eric said, "if I'm able to fix this one and duplicate the gearbox, I'll be more than happy to give you this one back. I'm not here to take advantage of you; I just want to figure out how the blasted thing works and find out if I can make another one."

"Well," Ian said with a chuckle. "I'd appreciate that, but I won't hold you to it. We have the other one for now, and the solar backup is working ok. When do you think you'll start taking it apart?"

"I'll be out tomorrow with somebody who actually knows what he's looking at," Eric said, thinking of Kyle, "to take the cover off and see how broken it is. He'll want to get a good look at it before we start disassembly."

Ian nodded, they shook hands, and Eric headed back to the airport.

...

"Any idea how deep the well is at the ranch," Kyle asked.

"Travis said it was less than eighty feet," Eric said. "I think he said they hit water at thirty and they drove the well another forty or so and they were still in the aquifer."

Kyle looked like he was doing math in his head. "A lot is going to depend on how badly the gearbox is damaged," he said. "It's been a long time since I've even seen one much less tried to fix one.

Travis's farrier may have to end up fabricating some replacement parts before it's all said and done."

"If he ends up with a working wind pump," Eric said, "I don't think he'll complain too much."

"What," Kyle asked when it looked like Eric was thinking of something new.

"Just thinking of things we could do," Eric said, "different skills we could provide on the road. How much does one of those gearboxes weigh?"

"Depends," Kyle said, "could be up to a couple hundred pounds for a really large, high-volume pump. Why?"

"Carrying full heads would be heavy," Eric said. "But carrying full-size wooden templates that we could manufacture on-site…"

Kyle was nodding. "It could even be fully assembled so we could prove that it works and we know what we're talking about," he said. "Of course, they would need to have a blacksmith or the tools locally to make the parts."

"How else could we make the parts," Eric mused aloud, relishing the chance to sink his teeth into a problem he knew he and Kyle could solve. "Or do we need to just find a blacksmith and bring along a portable forge?"

…

"I can't fix it up here," Kyle said, "but we should absolutely be able to fix this."

Eric craned his neck around Kyle to get a look at the gearbox and see if he could figure out what was wrong without having to ask. It took him a minute, but he finally saw the disconnected arms between two large gears on either side of the housing and a sliding pulley at the end of a rod that should obviously rise and fall.

"Ok," Eric said. "So tell me what happened."

"You said that they didn't set the brake before a bad windstorm, right," Kyle said.

"Right," Eric nodded.

"This model," Kyle said, pointing at the still stationary blades, "has a brake that you engage from the bottom." Kyle pointed to a rod that locked the hub of the wind wheel.

"See the spring here," Kyle asked as he pointed to the base of one of the blades.

Eric nodded again.

"That keeps a certain amount of tension on the blade," Kyle continued. "But when the hub is locked, it allows the blade to do what is called *feather*, or twist out of the way. That way the tower doesn't blow over in a really bad storm when the hub is locked or…"

"Or the gearbox tear itself apart because the wind wheel is spinning too fast," Eric said.

"Exactly," Kyle said. "Usually the blades will feather if the wind gets too strong, even if the hub *isn't* locked, but it looks like that didn't happen in this case. The pitman arms, those're the long arms here that actually do all the work and pull the pump rod up and push it back down, they broke at the end where they connect to the main gears."

"Do we have to take the whole thing down to fix it," Eric asked.

Kyle shook his head. "Technically, no," he said. "But we need to disassemble it to make sure nothing else is cracked or broken and see if there is any way we can cut copies with the torches at the airport. It would really be best if the pitman arms were forged, too, so having the farrier make those would be ideal."

"And then the ranch has a working water pump," Eric said.

"And we'll have something we can sell," Kyle added.

…

"How's J.B. doing," Jessie asked when they saw Mr. Gibson.

Travis laughed. Dan and Marissa took turns bringing the girls out and they'd been to the ranch at least every other day since the quarantine had lifted and asked the same question each time. "He's fine," he said, "just fine. He's out in the paddock with his mother if you want to go see him."

Jessie and Bekah both looked at Marissa and then took off at a run when she nodded. "They do love that horse," she said.

"The feeling seems to be mutual," Travis said. "I've been around horses most of my life and while it isn't unheard of, it's the first time I've ever seen one so young be so…attached to people, least of all kids."

Travis shrugged. "It doesn't hurt that Jessie and Bekah are well behaved," he said, "but Jessie really does seem to have more of a bond with him than anyone else."

"They're going to be heartbroken," Marissa said, "when he's old enough to be sold."

Travis had a twinkle in his eye. "Well now, about that," he said. "That's still a long way off and even then he may not sell, or I may just decide to keep him. I can't get rid of all my stock or I'd be out of business."

Marissa nodded. She and Dan had been talking about what it would take to get a horse and how much work it would be to keep it. They hadn't bothered asking how much a horse would cost because everything was pretty much barter and they didn't feel like they had much to barter *with*.

The first thing they'd need to do is get out of the house they were in now and build something that was on a good chunk of land. Marissa almost laughed out loud at the thought. *"Here we are,"* she thought, *"a year into the apocalypse and I'm still thinking about a different house and getting some land."* She shook her head.

"I see you're still building a lot," she said as they walked over to the paddock where the girls were. "The Army doesn't need the saw mill back?"

"We had some negotiations a couple of weeks ago," Travis said. "I basically bought the mill for a few horses and their continued care and feeding since they don't have anywhere to keep them, or really anyone to take care of them. Seemed like a pretty good trade at the time and now I don't have to worry about when they're going to want it back."

"How many more stalls are you planning on," Marissa asked. She'd been amazed when Travis had told her that he could theoretically double the size of his herd every four to five years.

"Short term," Travis said, "I'd like to get up to five-hundred stalls. Eventually, I'd like to have a thousand, but I'm not going to need that many for at least another twelve to fifteen years. Assuming I'm still around, knock on wood."

He'd lost his wife to a car accident a few years before the power went out and although he didn't *think* anything would happen to him, the drunk driver had proven that it wasn't always up to you when you checked out.

"Oh c'mon," Marissa said. "You're as healthy as a …" She stopped when she realized she'd been about to say 'healthy as a horse.'

"Horse," Travis asked. "Dan certainly seems to think so. He made a point to get out here once a week during the quarantine to make sure we were still here and doing ok. We were pretty lucky, though, since we hadn't had any contact with the new group and almost none with the rest of the base."

"I'm glad it worked out," Marissa said, looking at the girls who were now petting J.B. and feeding him apple slices. "For everybody."

Chapter Twenty-Six

July 10, 2013 - 16:00 - Promised Land

The group gathered around Mallory was the same as before–with the addition of Joel–when the radio came to life. After a brief introduction, Mallory mentioned the fact that their conversation was secure, but not private.

"Understood," Sanford said. "That's the nature of HAM radio, and since we could pick up all the other units using it, we assumed that everyone could hear what we were saying. We took that into consideration when we finally made the decision to make contact."

"You obviously have a plan," Mallory said, "or at least some idea of what you would like to accomplish; aside from the end goal."

"I want to play some of the Colonel's conversations first," Sanford said, "and then yes, I have a few suggestions."

…

After twenty minutes of listening to the Colonel argue with, get chastised by, and ultimately threaten his handlers, as well as finally get some useful information out of them, the recordings were done.

"That was…enlightening," Mallory said. "Disturbing, but enlightening."

"The question that remains, for me at least," Sanford said, "is what is *really* going on in the rest of the country? How is the rest of the United States really doing, civilian and military? The Colonel has been told repeatedly that the rest of the country has basically already been subdued and that the Southeast is the last holdout."

Mallory snorted. "I find that hard to believe," she said. "I've never lived there, but I just can't see Texas rolling over any quicker than we have."

"My point exactly," Sanford said. "Or Utah, Wyoming, Montana or a half-a-dozen other states I can think of off the top of my head. On the surface it sounds good, but if you think about it for just a few minutes it starts to fall apart. I don't think they planned on anyone else hearing their conversations *or* having time to really consider the implications of what they're saying."

"So," Mallory said. "What do we do about it?"

"I think we need to make contact with them," Sanford said. "We need to make direct contact with other bases and groups of people around the country."

"Okay," Mallory said. "And I suppose you've thought about how we might do that?"

"Actually, yes," Sanford said.

. . .

"I'm not sure," Mallory said, "if that's just risky, bold, or outright insane. I'm leaning towards the latter."

"Yes," Sanford said, "it's risky, but it's a calculated risk. Sitting here and not doing anything is what's insane. We know what's going on is wrong. The Colonel has you squarely in his sights, and we *need* to know what's really happening everywhere else. This is at least doing *something*, and you can't just hunker down with the civilian population there. We *have* to take the fight to the enemy."

Mallory knew Sanford was right, not that she needed convincing. Everything they did, every move they considered, needed to be in light of the fact that they weren't safe…they were, in fact, at war.

"I know," she said. "I didn't say it wasn't worth doing, just that it was nuts. They'll be going in blind with no prior contact and no idea what the situation is on the ground ahead of time."

"I'm open to suggestions," Sanford said. "And ultimately it's not my call to make. They won't be coming from Rucker, they can't. They're your birds."

Mallory paused as she thought about their options.

"So we send them out with a cover story," Joel said with a shrug.

"Go on," Mallory said.

"Well," Joel said, "I just came up with the idea so give me a minute."

Stewart stifled a chuckle but he, too, started thinking about what cover story would pass muster.

"We have a suggestion," Mallory said over the radio, "but haven't fleshed it out yet."

"I'm all ears," Sanford said.

"We craft a couple of cover stories for them," she said, "at least two. One for groups that seem to be loyal to this…cabal in Colorado, and another for groups that look like they're pushing back."

"And a way for them to tell the two apart," Halstead added.

There was silence on the air for several seconds as both sides began trying to work out details amongst themselves.

"How about Diego and his men say they represent the group in Colorado," Sanford finally said. "I'm pretty sure we have enough information to put together a convincing cover, at least until or unless a group actually tries to verify their origin."

"They're from a unit that was overrun by rebelling civilians," Stewart said. "Wait, no, bad idea. Worst-case scenario is the group they are in contact with decides the rebels need to be put down…never mind."

"They're just in transit from one base to another," Joel said. "They just need to fill up on the way to transfer the Black Hawks."

"How about the truth," Stewart added, trying to make up for the bad idea he'd just had. "Assuming it ever happens, once it's obvious that the base is in the rebel camp they could just be honest about why they're there."

Halstead nodded and added, "They may even be in communication with other bases," he said. "It'd probably save time in the long run."

Mallory shared their ideas with Sanford.

"Yeah," Sanford said. "I think that'll work."

…

"Where in the world," Travis asked, nodding to the two pickup trucks full of coal, "did you get all that? I know it wasn't my old supplier because he cleared out months ago and there weren't more than a couple of pounds left when I went by."

"For the time being," Eric said, "that's for me to know and hopefully you to never find out. I've got a couple of pieces that I need forged though, and I figured a hotter forge would probably be better and now was as good a time as any to bring this to you."

"He's in the shop now," Travis said, "working on some horseshoes. Let's take him some coal and show him what you need done."

Eric reached into the cab of his truck and pulled out the two pitman arms with the broken ends and then grabbed a burlap sack with about fifteen pounds of coal from the back.

"Looks like a linkage of some kind," Travis said when he caught sight of the broken pieces.

"Pitman arms for a gear assembly," Eric said.

"Whatever it was must have been pretty rough," Travis said, "or they weren't taken care of for the ends to come apart like that."

"They're from a windmill gearbox," Eric finally said. "I guess there were some really bad storms a couple of years ago and the wind wheel hadn't been locked like it should have been. It could have been worse; the gearbox could have torn itself apart."

The smithy had an open front and they could hear the farrier hammering on what Eric assumed was a horseshoe as they got closer. Travis waited until a break when the metal needed to be reheated and got his attention.

"How's this batch of charcoal working out," Travis asked.

The farrier shrugged. "About the same as the last," he said. "I'm finally getting used to the difference in how long things take, that's all."

Travis held out the bag of coal. "Will this help," he asked.

The farrier opened the bag and shook his head. "Travis," he said, "your timing is abysmal, you know that? You wait until I'm finally getting into the groove with the charcoal and then you show up with real coal. How much can we get?"

"I'm pretty sure we can get you as much as you need," Eric said. "I've got two pickup truck beds full outside right now."

The farriers face lit up. "I think I'd be willing to forget everything I've taught myself about using charcoal if that's the case."

"There's something Eric needs you to look at," Travis said. "See if you can fix or replace a couple of pieces."

Eric handed over the pitman arms.

The farrier examined them for about a half a minute, including tapping them on the anvil and striking them with a hammer in a couple of different places to see how they sounded.

"It sounds like cast iron," the farrier said, "but it's lighter than I would expect it to be. I'm positive I can make replacements but I won't know if I can repair them until I heat 'em up. I'd want to have the replacements already made before I did that. How quick do you need them?"

"They're for the ranch," Eric said.

"In that case," the farrier replied, "do you have a couple of hours to kill? I've got some stock that I can use for the replacements this afternoon."

…

Kyle and William were in the hangar Kyle had set aside as a workshop. William slowly spun the axle for the wind wheel with a handle to check the function of the gearbox now that it was reassembled. The pitman arms had fit almost perfectly and required just a little filing to clean up the hole on one end.

After examining everything in the gearbox, Kyle took over and cranked the wheel as fast as he could for a minute. As far as he could tell, it all seemed to be working properly. The last thing to do was fill the oil reservoir and make sure the oil rings were working right to keep things lubricated.

"How's it going," Eric asked as he walked into the hangar.

"Pretty good," Kyle said. "He did a good job and I'm just about ready to button this up. We have wooden templates of all the parts so, theoretically, we should be able to build more."

Kyle looked over at William and said, "Couldn't have done it as quick without William here."

William blushed but didn't say anything. He'd been very quiet ever since the group had split off from Earl's group. Every once in a while Kyle could get him to break out of his silence, and it was happening more often the longer they were on their own and the more time they spent together, but it still took a lot to get him to talk.

"Let's make a couple more sets of templates," Eric said

Kyle nodded. If anything happened to the set they had he'd be taking this one apart again to make new patterns. The workshop now had a drill press, table saw, and band saw powered by a propane generator from one of the RVs. Eric had also gotten several wood planks in different thicknesses appropriate for their templates from the ranch the last time he was down there.

"Up to giving me a hand on the blanks," Kyle asked William.

"Yeah," he said with a small smile.

He was warming up to Kyle, but it was going to take time.

...

Randy Carlisle, the farmer who had been their initial contact with the loose-knit group of farmers and ranchers frowned.

"Maybe," he said, "probably even. The problem is the catch-22 we've been facing all along. We need fuel to plant more of the crop to give us more fuel but we won't get any kind of return on that investment for at least four months. We have a longer growing season here than some states, but we're still looking at a net deficit for several months."

"What if we could supplement the current fuel supply with petro-diesel," Joel asked.

Randy just looked at Joel, his expression showing that he knew about the loss of the fuel dump on base.

Joel sighed. "Yes," he said, "we lost some fuel." Joel quickly corrected himself when Randy looked like he was going to interrupt.

"Ok," Joel said, "more than some. The point is that we might be able, probably *will* be able to replace what we lost, at least this time."

Randy nodded. He didn't expect the military to tell him what they had up their sleeves, but it was obvious they had something in the works.

"There're a couple of farms outside the immediate area that have been abandoned," Randy said. "A bunch of us have been trying to decide if we need to start cultivating them or not. Looks like we're gonna make use of them after all."

"How big," Joel asked.

"One is about one-hundred-and-twenty acres," Randy said, "and the other is almost two-hundred. We won't use it all, though—we can't. We don't have the seed stock to plant more than the first farm. Probably closer to a hundred acres or so."

Randy made a face as he thought about the logistics and did some quick math. "We need about five percent of the seeds from each crop for next year," he muttered, "but we're using almost all of the remaining seed stock to plant so let's call it fifteen percent and give us a buffer."

"If we can get it in the ground in the next couple of weeks," Randy said, "we can add another fifty-five-hundred gallons of diesel or so, maybe a little more, but not much."

"How much of that do we lose back to production," Joel asked.

"About twenty percent to run the machinery and the plant," Randy said.

"So a net gain of almost forty-five hundred," Joel said. "When do you think you can start?"

"I get the feeling that now that I know about it," Randy said, "I'm late."

Joel shrugged.

Chapter Twenty-Seven

It was two-o'-clock in the morning, but Diego was wide awake. He and the crews of the six Black Hawks on this raid had spent the last three days sleeping during the day for just that reason. Adrenaline would only work for so long, and they all needed to be as close to their peak performance as they could be.

Originally, he had wanted to head back to Ft. Stewart, but the Black Hawks just didn't have the range without their external fuel tanks. The new plan instead called for them to take on Ft. Campbell, whose air-defense capability Ben repeatedly assured them had been disabled before he left. Nevertheless, Diego still kept one cautious eye on the threat indicator as they approached the base from the north.

Each Black Hawk had been topped off with fuel from the other helicopters they'd left behind, which left the remainder literally sitting ducks if Diego's raid wasn't able to get back with what they came for. The goal: get as many ERFS, or Extended Range Fuel Systems, as possible–which included four two-hundred-gallon external fuel tanks and, if the opportunity presented itself, one or more fuel trucks of JP-8 aviation fuel.

Before the Colonel's attack on Fort Campbell, Ben had initially focused on getting as much diesel as possible out of harm's way, and had only been able to get about half of the fuel trucks off the base before the attack commenced. He'd brought one tanker truck with him, but, again, it was diesel and not JP-8. It was also the truck that Mathis had chosen to blow up.

Ben also hadn't considered the ERFS to be worth taking since he'd disabled all of the helicopters through various mechanical means, and he didn't know that Diego had defected to the other side at the time he'd finally had to abandon the base.

Ben had given them the correct transponder code for the base's Identify Friend or Foe system, in case it had somehow been re-enabled, but the closer they got to the base, the more tense everyone in the cockpit grew.

"Bandit flight," Diego said over the mission channel, "this is Bandit One. We didn't get a whole lot of practice on this one, but we take turns dropping off the infantry and then back up to provide cover for the next guy. We should be down over the LZ in less than five minutes."

They already had maps of the base from the initial raid they'd abandoned, and Ben had provided the detail they needed to pinpoint where the stores of supplies *should* be and where the fuel trucks ought to be parked. As his mother had been fond of saying while he was growing up, they'd crossed all their Is and dotted all the Ts. No plan ever survived contact with the enemy, though.

They could see lights on the horizon now, which would hopefully help them identify individual buildings. No activity…yet.

"Two minutes to landing zone," Diego said. He was flying half by instruments and half by sight from the three-quarter moon. He hated night-vision, and avoided it at all costs unless he absolutely had to use it. The eerie, flat green, with no depth perception always freaked him out and it took him a good couple of minutes to get used to normal vision again when he took off the headset.

The threat indicator was still silent; so far, so good.

His co-pilot and navigator started picking out landmarks as they got close enough and calling out directions.

"Bandit flight on me," Diego radioed. If this went south, it would be his fault and no one else's.

"Starboard," the co-pilot said, "thirty degrees."

The one concession Diego had agreed to was the visor on his helmet. It would allow him to see the infrared laser designator his co-pilot was using to mark buildings so there was no doubt as to which one he was talking about. In this case, a green triangle appeared on a building to his right and he headed in that direction. His co-pilot was even pretty good at keeping the marker centered as he changed course.

Diego could see a number of other Black Hawks on the tarmac now, arrayed in their normal pre-flight parking pattern. There would be plenty of room to set down and unload one at a time, but not more than that. Unfortunately, guards were already trickling out of the building.

Diego flipped the switch for the external loudspeaker. "Stand Clear," he said, his voice booming over the pavement. He could see the guards flinch at the volume. "You're outgunned and probably outnumbered at this point. Nobody needs to die tonight."

The first guard started to back up a little, but the second stood his ground. *"Your funeral,"* Diego thought to himself and brought his bird in to hover just over the LZ. Just as he was almost down, the guard who refused to back up brought his rifle to his shoulder.

"Fine," Diego said, and pulled back on the collective just a touch to raise the nose of the Black Hawk, bathing the guard in prop wash, which knocked him down and caused him to drop his rifle.

A few seconds later and Diego was back in position, the doors were open, and the infantry were out of the hold. A few more seconds and the landing zone was as secure as it was going to get in hostile territory, as the guards were now prisoners.

Diego took off and took the place of Bandit Two. The process was repeated five more times, and sixty heavily-armed members of the Third Infantry Division began looking for things to loot.

...

Helicopters cannot hover in one spot indefinitely. Physics aside, it's a *really* bad idea, tactically, to sit in one place for too long when you're in enemy territory. It was going to take a while for the men to find and move everything they were hoping to take back with them and Diego just couldn't get the warm fuzzies by sitting still for an hour or more.

The plan was to find and bring back as much aviation fuel as they could, along with as many full sets of external fuel tanks for the Black Hawks as they could find. If all went well, they would be able to outfit all thirty birds when they got back to Promised Land.

Ten minutes after Diego had dropped off his load of troops, he got a call from the Sergeant in charge on the ground.

"They're finally mounting some resistance," Sergeant Steve Nichols said. "Only a few shots fired so far, but that's probably not going to last long."

"I'm not going to second-guess you, Steve," Diego said, "but where are they?"

"Other side of the base," Nichols said. "We have a half-a-dozen patrols looking for anyone putting up a fight. I think we surprised them."

"Any casualties," Diego asked.

"Not yet," Nichols said, "on either side. You know how it goes, ninety percent of the rounds are going to go wide or be fired in haste. We were a little more entrenched when we ran into them, but it's almost like they're only putting up a token resistance."

"Depending on where they're from," Diego said, "that may actually be the case. Bragg was in on the raid and they're as deep in the rebellion as we are."

"Point," Nichols said.

"Any luck finding the base commander," Diego asked.

"Not yet," Nichols said, "we're looking, though. If we can find him, then maybe we can keep this from turning into a bloodbath."

...

It took almost an hour for Diego's and Nichols's men to gather external tanks–and the associated hoses and couplings that turned their stub wings into the Extended Range system–onto pallets, and load it all onto the five flatbed trucks they would be...liberating from the base. They had also identified three 10,000 gallon tanker trucks of JP-8 jet fuel that could be used by both the Black Hawks and virtually *all* of the current military vehicles currently in use back at Promised Land.

Having the full JP-8 tankers would free up the diesel they had for any civilian vehicles, and the farmers. The Black Hawks would be providing air support and cover for the drive back, which Diego sincerely hoped would be as uneventful as the flight up had been.

The first thirty minutes of flying cover over the base had been more than a little stressful. Diego's biggest worry usually came from his threat indicator, but being inside the base's perimeter and so low to the ground, he knew he and the rest of his birds were particularly vulnerable to shoulder-fired surface-to-air, or in some cases even surface-to-surface missiles. If someone decided to take a shot at him, those shoulder-fired missiles would give him absolutely no warning prior to the inbound warhead.

Nichols radioed in to let him know about a new minor skirmish on the ground every five minutes or so. Several times, Diego could make out gunfire on the ground from the muzzle flashes in the dark. The defense was hasty and, while fairly well organized, ultimately almost totally ineffective; after all, they really hadn't expected someone to do exactly what Diego and his men were doing right now.

Half of the engagements had ended when the defenders were caught from behind by some of Nichols's men. The other half were still going on when they found the base commander, who had been leading a squad of defenders, and convinced him to call off the defense. The longer it had gone on, however, the more convinced he was of what he'd told Nichols earlier.

It really did seem like the defenders were only putting up a token resistance so they could, in good conscience, say that they'd fought for the base. Of course not *everyone* seemed to be playing by those rules, but the overwhelming majority appeared to fall into the category of 'just enough to make it look good…and for heaven's sake, don't *kill* anybody.'

Egress would be the tricky part, as it always was; getting everyone back into the birds while keeping them covered, and not letting the defending guards get a shot off while they left. Diego didn't have any delusions about the guard that had tried to prevent him from landing in the first place. It wasn't often that you got knocked on your butt by prop-wash, but when you did it had the tendency to create a little animosity between you and the pilot who'd knocked you down.

…

Diego was a firm believer in not asking his men to do anything he wasn't willing to do himself. To put that into practice, he'd been the first to put his bird down and would be the last to pick up his troops. The last had just gotten in and the door was shut when he heard his co-pilot swear. He looked over to where his co-pilot was looking and saw that the original guard—the one who wouldn't stand down—was readying a shoulder-mounted missile.

"Designate," Diego said to his co-pilot, flipped the switch for the external loudspeakers again, and turned the Black Hawk to face the guard as soon as it cleared the ground.

"Don't do it," he said. "I swear you won't get the chance."

The co-pilot had designated the guard with a red teardrop that looked like a drop of blood.

"Nice," Diego thought. *"You have got one* sick *sense of humor."*

Diego had a pod of 70mm rockets and a 7.62mm machine gun on each stub wing on either side. The rockets were already active and tracking the designator. Realistically, if he launched one it would tear the guard apart as it went through him since it couldn't–literally *couldn't*–detonate at less than five-hundred-and-fifty yards.

"And if I unleash the 7.62's," Diego thought, and shuddered.

The guard and the Black Hawk faced off for several seconds until one of the trucks belched as the driver put it into gear. Apparently, he'd waited long enough and was getting out of there while Diego and the guard played chicken. The other trucks followed his lead and the movement seemed to break the guard's will.

Diego couldn't hear what the guard screamed at him but he could read his lips just fine. The guard hurled the missile launcher at the helicopter and it bounced off the nose.

"Gonna have to throw that one out," his co-pilot said, "probably cracked the propellant."

"May have cracked the man," Diego replied.

…

"Thirty thousand gallons," Mallory said and then muttered a thank-you prayer under her breath.

"And all of it JP-8," Diego said, "so we don't have to worry about the Hawks for the time being."

"That frees up a fair amount of the petrol diesel for farm work," Mallory said. "Not that we're going to lift the restrictions on fuel any time soon. Like you said, the helicopters *need* the JP-8. We're lucky we have so many multi-fuel vehicles though. We could probably run them on transmission fluid if we had to…not that we have much of that either."

"We have enough for what we have planned, though," Ben said. "That was the whole point of this raid and we got everything we needed, and then some."

Mallory nodded. "What else can you tell us about the base defenses," she asked, "and the defenders in general?"

"They didn't act that thrilled to be there," Nichols said. "I kept telling Diego that the defense, while fairly well organized was, well it was half-hearted. The base commander, Tippets was his name, wouldn't say a word once we found him, other than to call off his troops over the base PA system. I was half tempted to grab his dog tags because he wasn't even giving the old name, rank, and service number line."

"Tippets," Ben said and closed his eyes. "I know that name, but where from?"

"Most likely he's either from Bragg, Mackall or Stewart," Nichols said.

"Lieutenant," Ben asked.

"Captain," Nichols replied.

"That could have been yet another one of those field promotions," Mallory said. "From the sounds of it, Olsen's been handing those out like candy."

"I want to say he's from Mackall," Ben said. "If he was, then there's a good chance we could have a back-door relationship with the base."

"Are you thinking of anything specific," Mallory asked.

"No," Ben said, "just trying to keep our options open and put everything on the table."

"Let's not count our chickens before they've hatched," Mallory said.

Ben shook his head. "I'm not," he said, "believe me. I guess deep down I'd just really like to get my base back."

"One thing at a time," Mallory said.

Chapter Twenty-Eight

The plan was simple on its face…fly into an unknown area without having previously ascertained the loyalty of the troops on the ground, attempt to land, con them out of fuel, gather any intelligence they could, and then leave. Oh, and if they could not get blown out of the sky in the process that would be great.

Diego might respect Majors Franklin and Jensen for what they were doing–defying the Colonel and keeping the torch lit, and all that–but they had obviously never planned many, if any, air missions.

Diego had insisted that wherever and whenever possible, each leg of their trip would be no more than six-hundred miles, so that they would always have enough fuel to make it back to somewhere "friendly" to refuel. They were currently approaching Randolph Air Force Base, just north of San Antonio, Texas, after being in the air for a little less than four hours. They were coming in from the north to mask their original heading, but Diego was fairly sure that if the base had power they had already been painted, or at least hit with passive radar.

"Eagle flight," Diego said over the radio, "let me do the talking."

After a half-a-dozen affirmatives, Diego waited for the radio, the radar, or both, to come alive.

…

"Inbound lawn darts," the base radio operator said. "State your intentions and maintain your present heading at four-thousand feet. Hold station in fifteen klicks."

"Lawn darts," Diego laughed to himself. *"I haven't heard these things called that in a long time. At least it sounds like the Air Force is still in charge down there."*

"Wilco," Diego replied. "Can you get the head zoomie on the horn?"

"My birds, however, do not *fall out of the sky, thank you very much,"* Diego thought.

"You Army or Navy," the operator on the other end asked, not taking obvious offense to the epithet that had identified Diego as *not* being in the Air Force. "Not that it matters."

"Army," Diego said.

"Hold one."

…

"This is Major Dunkin. Who are you, and did Colonel Tweed send you down," a new voice demanded. "Never mind, maybe I should just shoot you down now and when you don't make it back Tweed will get the picture. We're not playing ball!"

"Negative, Sir," Diego said as soon as the line was clear. Dying before they made useful contact with the first base really wasn't his idea of a great way to end the day. "I have no idea who Colonel Tweed is."

"Well, you're coming from his general direction, son," Major Dunkin replied.

"In my defense, Sir," Diego said, "I'm coming from the general direction of quite a lot."

"I'll give you that," Dunkin said. "Maintain your current heading and speed. Follow the instructions we give you and maybe you can land

and we can have a chat. The radar is coming on now. If we sense so much as a *garage door opener* being used on your birds you can kiss your butt goodbye. Do I make myself clear?"

"As glass, Sir," Diego said.

...

The last fifteen minutes had been some of the most nerve-wracking stick time Diego had ever experienced. Usually in hostile territory you expected to encounter enemy radar and then maneuver to evade and prevent them getting a lock on you. Even the situation around Natchez Trace hadn't been this bad, because at least he'd known where the people on the ground stood in relation to their own Colonel.

This Dunkin character, he was a complete unknown. He hadn't just painted all of Diego's birds, he'd had multiple active locks on every single one, and the threat indicator had been going nuts. Diego had wanted nothing more than to turn tail and run, with every fiber of his being, but within a minute they were so far inside the radar envelope that none of them would have survived.

Now they were setting down inside a secured perimeter and it looked like Dunkin still wasn't taking any chances. There were guards everywhere, and at least a dozen .50 mini guns trained on his birds.

"At least they're taking us seriously as a threat," Diego said to his crew chief.

...

"No weapons," Lieutenant Glass said as he 'greeted' Diego and his group.

"Not a chance," Diego replied.

"You aren't going any further armed," Glass said.

"Fine," Diego said. "We'll sit right here. We aren't disarming. We've done everything you've said up to this point, but just like I'm not leaving the Hawks unattended, I'm not surrendering my sidearm. And neither is anyone else."

Glass was obviously gritting his teeth when he said, "Wait here."

"We're outnumbered fifty to one," his crew chief muttered. "It isn't like we're going to take over the base."

"No," Diego said, "but any one of us could take out the Major fairly easily and they know it. It's the principle, though, and they know that too."

Glass came back a minute later, accompanied by a tall, balding, red-faced officer who had obviously lost a *lot* of weight over the last year.

"Just what do you mean," Dunkin said, starting out loud and obviously planning to end with a yell, "disobeying an order."

Diego looked around, checked behind him and then pointed at himself. "Me," he asked. "You aren't in my chain-of-command."

"I landed at your base by invitation," Diego made a bit of a face, "okay, at gunpoint, but before the missiles had a lock I could have left at any time. I'm here because I want to be here, not because *you* want me to be here. You don't give me orders…*sir.*" The fact that the sir wasn't capitalized was obvious.

"And just why *are* you here," Dunkin asked, "if the Colonel didn't send you."

Diego was extremely aware of the number of guns pointed his direction and blocking the way between his men and his birds. "To find out how you're getting along," he said, "and what's really going on out here in the rest of the country."

Dunkin frowned at Diego as he thought about that for several seconds.

"You," Dunkin pointed at Diego, "and three others can come with me. The rest will be taken to the mess where they can at least sit down on something that isn't moving and get something to drink."

At the questioning look on Diego's face, Dunkin nodded. "You can keep your side arms," he said.

...

"Where are you from," Dunkin asked, "why are you here, and what do you want?"

"In that order," Diego asked.

Dunkin shrugged. "As long as you answer all three," he said.

"We're from further east," Diego started. "Home has changed for us recently due to circumstances similar to your own. We really are trying to find out what the situation is around the rest of the country, what's *really* going on, and not just what's being fed to us by some self-appointed regional commander."

Diego paused for a few seconds before he continued. He'd already said more than he had initially planned to, based on how things were playing out.

"As for the third question," Diego said, "*I* need some answers first."

"You haven't given me much to go on, Son," Dunkin said.

"And you haven't given me *anything*, Sir," Diego replied.

Dunkin sighed. "Fair enough," he said. "Colonel Tweed has all but declared himself Supreme Military Overlord of the Southwest. There were some orders that came down a little less than a year ago. ARCLiTE. Supposedly from Central Command. Seemed legitimate at the time, especially since he'd authenticated with the President's own call-sign and counter authentications."

Dunkin shook his head. "Since then," he said, "things have gone downhill fast. The Constitution's out the window. We've had over three-dozen Guard and Reserve units 'disappear' under *very* suspicious circumstances, and the Colonel is instituting more and more heavy-handed restrictions and laws."

Dunkin's eyes narrowed and he set his jaw as he looked at Diego from across his desk. "I've shot three men in the last six months for espionage and sabotage, Son," he said. "As much as I would have liked to give them a court-martial, I couldn't, and I wasn't about to run the risk of them getting away to cause more trouble. So, what do you want?"

"Allies," Diego said.

...

"Completely trustworthy," Dunkin said.

"But you said I could test them all," Diego thought to himself.

Dunkin nodded and went into the room with the fourth candidate.

"Airman," Diego said.

"Chief," the Airman replied, surprising Diego that he knew an Army Chief Warrant Officer rank from a hole in the ground.

"I just have a couple of questions for you," Diego said, without sitting down. "First, how long have you been in contact with Colonel Tweed?"

"Excuse me," the Airman said and started to get up.

Diego pulled his side-arm but didn't point it at the Airman, not yet. "Sit down," he said. "I'm not done and I have the full backing of the Major right now, so answer the question."

"I've never been in contact with the Colonel," the Airman said and the look of disgust and pure hatred on his face was almost enough to convince Diego. "He's guilty of treason and his body should be hung out for the buzzards. I don't know where he's getting his orders from, but regardless, he's broken his oath, and for that alone in this time of crisis he should be shot!"

Diego holstered his weapon. "Good enough for me," he said. "The Major will tell you where to go and I'll meet you there in a few minutes."

Instead of shaking Diego's offered hand the Airman swung a roundhouse that Diego was only partially able to dodge and that would leave his jaw bruised and sore for a week.

"You've got a lot of nerve coming in here and accusing me of…" the Airman said.

"And the Major has already shot three moles in the last six months," Diego said, rubbing his jaw.

The look on the Airman's face said he hadn't been aware of the moles.

"And what I'm going to be telling you is sensitive enough," Diego continued, "that I can't take *any* chances. It's even worth getting sucker punched."

Diego worked his jaw. "Which won't happen again, by the way," he said.

…

"So, Airman," Diego said to the last candidate. "How long have you been in contact with Colonel Tweed, and how did his last orders change now that Dunkin is executing the traitors?" Diego had no idea why he had changed up his script, but he'd gotten bored after fourteen interviews so he figured he'd toss this guy a curveball.

Instead of outrage and an immediate protestation of innocence, this last one narrowed his eyes. "How do you know the orders have changed," the Airman replied.

Diego couldn't keep the look of surprise off his face and the Airman realized he'd been had. Diego barely got his side-arm out of his holster before the Airman was out of his seat and coming over the table at him.

They were wrestling for Diego's .45 when the door flew open and three Air Force MPs stormed the room.

"*Drop it!*" The lead MP shouted as all three trained their weapons on the Airman. The struggle continued for a few seconds as he strained to point Diego's pistol at the guard nearest him, but that ended as soon as an MP made his way behind him and slammed the butt of his M16 into the back of his head.

Major Dunkin came into the room after the struggle was over and Diego had holstered his .45. "How did you know," he asked. "What made you ask him a different question?"

"Nothing," Diego panted, trying to catch his breath. "I was bored and tired of asking the same thing over and over again. We got lucky–I got lucky. Thank you."

"Thank *you*," Dunkin said. "Heaven knows how many more there are, but maybe they're the ones deserting. The rest of the group is in the room at the end of the hall. I'll meet you there in a few minutes."

Diego nodded and left the room. He was halfway down the hallway when he heard a gunshot and spun around. A few seconds later Dunkin came out of the room, holstering his weapon.

Dunkin caught the look on Diego's face and answered his question before he could ask. "I told you, I wish I could court-martial them," Dunkin said, "but I can't. I'm not going to have their deaths on anyone else's conscience, either. That might make me hard, it may even make me evil, but that's for me to deal with. They're waiting for you in there."

The news that Diego had, in fact, found another mole was sobering and caused three of the Airmen to walk to the front of the room and formally apologize to Diego for hitting him, taking a swing at him, or cussing him out. Once that was out of the way, Diego opened the duffle bag that one of his men had been holding on to and pulled out the ugliest HAM radio any of them had ever seen.

Chapter Twenty-Nine

After leaving Randolph Air Force Base, they headed to Kirtland, in Arizona, and then Luke, in New Mexico. Major Dunkin had been in contact with both of them, and they were both either in open rebellion against Tweed or near enough as made no difference. They would be expecting his people and he could use them as staging points for California and heading north, which was a good thing.

California had almost gotten them all killed. Southern California was lost, for a number of reasons. First, there was no longer a southern border. It simply didn't exist. And what was left of Mexico had decided it wanted California back. Second, Tweed's puppets were completely in control of what forces remained. Diego's thin excuse of performing a nationwide, hands-on check for Central Command had been met with requests for authorization from Colonel Tweed, and then a patch through to the man himself.

When Diego wouldn't–because he *couldn't*–validate his orders, they had to vacate the area back to Luke Air Force Base.

Hill Air Force Base in Utah had been a total unknown because they had simply dropped off the map. Several hundred miles from any other major military installation, except for the Dugway proving grounds and the Toole Army Depot–both of which were more storage or test facilities than military "bases"–Hill had apparently decided it was going to be an island unto itself.

Diego almost wished he'd decided to forgo Hill when they were buzzed by four F-16s with absolutely no warning, and then painted by so many active radar sources that it almost overwhelmed the threat indicator. It turned out that Hill's commander, Colonel Amy Holmes, had in fact decided to disconnect after receiving the first download of information regarding ARCLiTE.

The *original* orders were good enough for her–if you ignored the 'suggestions' tacked onto the end. She had listened to, but never logged into, the conference call that was requested several weeks after ARCLiTE was instituted and determined that someone, somewhere was making a power grab. From that point on, nobody on her base had answered any communications requests from their regional command, another Colonel somewhere in the northwest she assumed.

Six transmissions had been sent at random intervals, though, and six of her people had quietly been made to disappear shortly thereafter. Colonel Holmes felt the same way about traitors that Major Dunkin did.

Now, after another half-dozen bases that had been split four-to-two, with more rebelling bases than those loyal to whoever was pulling the strings, Diego was about to make his last stop before heading home.

This would be the last on their list for a number of reasons, not the least of which was the fact that the area was most likely controlled by at least two–and possibly as many as four–Army bases and an Air Force base. That didn't include the Marine Corp barracks or the massive nearby U.S. Naval presence. They were on their way to Washington D.C.

...

"So," Major General Pierce Sharpe said. "I think you'll find things are well under control."

Diego didn't trust himself to speak. According to the General, everything north of The Capital and east of about Harrisburg Pennsylvania was basically pacified. He admitted that there were still a few civilian holdouts, but that they were few and far between, and that they were being dealt with swiftly–and thoroughly–whenever they were found.

Diego seriously doubted that rural New York and New Hampshire were anywhere near under control, unless they were devoid of human life, but didn't say anything.

"For the most part," Sharpe said, "the people embraced the stability and order that we were able to provide, and temporarily relinquishing a few liberties hasn't been a problem. Now, a year later, nobody's saying anything about the fact that we're in complete control of virtually every aspect of their lives."

"They get up when we tell them to," Sharpe continued, "work on what we tell them to work on, eat, sleep and even have sex when we say. We only had to banish a couple-dozen people, and an entire family in one case, to drive home the point that we mean business...for their own good, of course. It goes without saying that we *took care* of the ones we banished, and made sure everyone inside knew that they'd come to a horrible end without the protection we're providing."

Sharpe laughed and Diego attempted to smile ...conspiratorially. This man made him sick and he wanted nothing more than to put a round between his eyes, step over his cooling corpse, find the next in charge, and do the same thing over and over again. The fact that the people, the citizens, had apparently embraced their chains–and that ultimately it would make no difference and he would just die for the effort–kept him from acting.

"You understand," Diego said, "that I need to speak to some of the residents in the camps." Diego almost choked on the last word.

"Of course," Sharpe said. "I do wish we'd been notified ahead of time though."

Diego just looked at the General, wondering how far he could push it. "That would have defeated the whole purpose of a surprise visit," he said, "now, wouldn't it?"

Sharpe nodded but the look on his face told Diego he was treading on thin ice. He may be acting on someone else's behalf but that authority only went so far.

"Would you like to speak to them here," Sharpe asked, "or at one of the work camps?"

"I think at one of the camps," Diego said, "once the Black Hawks are refueled."

...

The flight to Albany, New York took a little over an hour because Diego didn't want to appear too eager. He also didn't want to push his birds too hard, because they hadn't had any proper maintenance in over a month and he wanted to save any hard flying in case he really needed it. General Sharpe had offered to accompany him, but Diego had politely refused, again, in case they needed to leave in a hurry.

Four of the other pilots were interviewing individual citizens and he was interviewing a group with the remaining two. He'd insisted that the guard remain outside during the interview.

"And how are the conditions," Diego asked. "Generally, how have things been?"

"Fine," said one of the middle-aged men in the group. He'd started out doing most of the talking and had taken on the role of spokesman for the group.

"Just 'fine'," Diego asked. "Care to elaborate?"

"We're safe," he said, "there's food and water. Better than what must still be going on outside with all the shootings and attacks we hear about, and the reports we get."

"Reports," Diego asked. "Reports of what, and how do you get the reports?"

"All the roving gangs," the man said. "What else? We have a, kind of a newspaper that comes out once a month. I don't have one with me but…"

"I've got one," one of the other men said. He was older and looked like he'd been a farmer, or worked a ranch, all his life. He pulled the single sheet of folded paper out of his back pocket and handed it over to Diego.

"Mind if I hold on to this," Diego asked as he unfolded it.

"Please do."

Diego glanced at the paper which was printed on both sides and looked like it had been copied. He was reading it while one of the other pilots was asking a question when he realized that there was some writing at the end of a paragraph. It was small, neatly written, and it made the paragraph look fully justified instead of left justified. If he hadn't actually been reading the paper instead of just scanning it, he would have missed it altogether.

On three lines, the message was "Get me…out…of here."

Diego glanced at the top of the newssheet and realized that the date was almost six months past. This man had been carrying his note around in hopes of being able to pass it on since March.

Diego folded the paper up and put it in his flight-suit pocket and then looked up to see the older man watching him. He made brief eye contact with him and then continued asking questions.

How old was everyone? How large were each of their families? Were they being treated fairly? What were they being told about future plans? How were they handling money?

After the first few questions, Diego had had enough of the first middle-aged guy doing all the talking and told him so.

"I appreciate your willingness to take the lead," Diego said, "but I think I'd like to hear what everyone else has to say."

"Well," he said, "we all feel the same way, don't we?" He looked around and everyone nodded, including the older farmer.

"Then you wouldn't mind if someone else did the talking now, would you," Diego said. It wasn't a question.

"I don't see why…" the man started.

"You don't have to," Diego interrupted, "but just for the sake of argument, let's say I have a question about female reproductive health, are you comfortable answering that question, much less *qualified*?"

The man turned red, either from embarrassment or frustration, but two of the women in the room smiled. Apparently, Diego wasn't the only one tired of hearing this guy run his mouth.

Now, unfortunately, Diego felt he had to put up or shut up. He looked at one of the women who'd smiled and hoped she hadn't started menopause early.

…

"So, has there been any talk of when things should go back to normal," Diego asked. "At least a little bit like how they were before the power went out?"

"Once it's safe," one of the other men said. "It's still crazy out there. You read the paper, people have turned to *cannibalism*."

"Obviously not until its safe," Diego said, biting his lip to keep a serious face after the word cannibalism. No, he hadn't read that because he'd gotten an old paper, but how gullible were these people?

"You don't expect to live the rest of your lives in a pen do you," Diego asked, trying to make it sound like a normal question.

"What's with the questions," the first man asked. "You know what it's like out there. You should know what the plans are. Are you trying to start some kind of revolt or something?"

The older farmer hid a smile but had a twinkle in his eye.

Diego laughed. "Hardly," he said. "Yes, I know some of the future plans, but I'm obviously not in the inner circle. Let's just say that I'm from the Government and I'm here to help and leave it at that, shall we?"

The first man who'd been the spokesman for a while had a sour expression on his face and folded his arms, but didn't say anything more.

"Honestly I don't see any problems," Diego said. "I think we're done here."

On his way out he made brief eye contact, again, with the old farmer and nodded slightly.

…

Diego gathered his other pilots and headed back to the helicopters. On the way back he noticed that the spokesperson for his group was talking to one of the camp guards who was looking his direction.

"Uh oh," Diego thought. *"Looks like I might have gone too far with the questions."*

The guard spoke into his radio while keeping an eye on Diego and his men and began shadowing them off to the side.

"Definitely not good," he thought.

"Go ahead and get the Hawks prepped," Diego said to his second in command. "Thru-flight 'em."

Diego leaned into his second without making it obvious and whispered, "If I'm not there by the time you're done, get out of here. Now go."

With a lengthened stride, his second in command was about half-again as fast as the group and he would get to the helicopters with just about enough time to have the co-pilots thru-flight them by the time the group arrived.

Diego heard the radio on one of their guards come to life and he stepped to the side to talk without being overheard. A few seconds later, he stepped over to Diego.

"Sir," the guard said, "if you could come with me."

"You guys go on ahead," Diego said to the other pilots. "I'll be there in a few minutes."

Their postures didn't change, but the looks in their eyes told Diego they knew what was going on.

"Actually, Sir," the guard began.

"What can I do for you," Diego looked at the soldier's sleeve, "Corporal?"

"Sir," the guard said, "I'm afraid I need you..."

Diego interrupted him again to keep him from stopping the other guards and detaining the rest of his pilots. "Corporal," Diego said, "spit it out. I need to be on my way back to D.C."

"That's the problem, Sir," the guard said. "I'm not supposed to let you leave."

Diego's men were far enough out of earshot not to have heard that, but the guard was focused enough on Diego not to notice. Things had been running so smoothly for so long that he had been caught totally off guard by the need to detain this pilot.

"And why is that," Diego asked, noticing that the guard that had made the original call was walking up to join the two of them.

"It doesn't matter, Sir," the first guard said. "You won't be leaving until we get orders from D.C. to release you."

Diego sighed as he heard the engines of the first couple of Black Hawks spin up. "Then we need to tell that to my pilots," he said. "They aren't going to take your word for it."

The Corporal who had stopped him looked indecisive, but the Sergeant who had made the call nodded. "Let's go," he said, "you first."

"I may just get out of here," Diego thought to himself.

...

Diego walked onto the tarmac as a prisoner, just as the first two Hawks were lifting off. His second in command had taken him at his word and done exactly as he'd asked. As he stepped into the open he saw the heads of the co-pilots in the other five birds turn his way. He made a face that looked resigned and held up his arm like he was going to give a signal and then twirled his hand counter-clockwise.

Two of the remaining three Hawks took off within seconds of each other.

The fifth Black Hawk only had a co-pilot and a Flight Engineer, it was his bird. The side door was open, waiting for him.

"What did you do," the Sergeant guard yelled over the engine noise.

"I told them to get out of here," Diego yelled back.

The guard pulled his side-arm and put it to Diego's head. "Tell them to power down and exit the helicopter," he said.

Unlike the raid on Fort Campbell, the Black Hawks were armed with an anti-personnel weapon for this trip...technically. A .50 machine gun really is overkill on a human being, and at less than one-hundred feet, it's like turning out the light with a sledge-hammer...powered by a stick of dynamite.

Diego noticed that his flight engineer was no longer visible through the cockpit window and wondered for half-a-second where he'd gone.

The .50 swiveled up, with his flight engineer manning the trigger, and leveled at the three of them—the two guards and Diego. After all, one of the flight engineer's jobs was door gunner.

"I have a feeling that won't be happening," Diego said.

Slowly, Diego turned around to face the two guards, and the muzzle of the 9mm.

"If you shoot me," he said, "he lets loose and you will both be torn apart. If I drop to the ground, he lets loose and you will both be torn apart. Either way," Diego nodded his head back towards his helicopter, "they *are* taking off and *you* are dead."

"*Or*," Diego said after a second, "I walk to the helicopter, get in, tell my man to stand down, and I leave. In that case, they still take off but you are very definitely not dead."

"How do we know you won't," the Sergeant started, still aiming at Diego's head.

"Because I didn't have to tell you anything," Diego said. "All I had to do was drop and we'd already be in the air. I've seen him shoot. I trust him with my life. I have no doubt that he could hit you," Diego looked at the Corporal who was now off to his left, "right now, with a two or three-round burst, without touching me. That's why."

Emotions warred on the Sergeant's face, but eventually prudence won out and he lowered the gun. Diego started walking backwards.

When he felt the prop wash hitting him just right, he ducked out of instinct and put his hands out behind him until he felt the side of the helicopter, and hopped in.

"They let me go," Diego said. "Close the door and let's get out of here."

Diego yelled up front, "Peck, you're flying, my nerves are shot."

Chapter Thirty

August 1, 2013 - Fort Rucker, Alabama

"Sir," Sanford said as he came into Olsen's office and shut the door.

Colonel Olsen looked up in annoyance at both the breach of protocol and at being interrupted, but stopped short of reprimanding his Major at the look on Sanford's face. "Can I help you, Major," he asked.

"Why didn't you tell me sooner," Sanford asked. "Sir, I'm closer to the men than West is, I've even been trying to diffuse the situation with them as much as possible, but you chose not to trust me."

"I'm afraid I don't know what you're talking about, son," Olsen said. "But you need to start making sense, and quick."

"Denver, Sir," Sanford said. "I've worked out some of what's really going on and I want in."

Olsen's eyes narrowed a bit but he gave no other outward indication of what was going on inside. As soon as Sanford said Denver, however, his heart-rate almost doubled, the hair on the back of his neck stood up, and he could feel the adrenaline start coursing through his system. Instead of jumping up or yelling, though, Olsen leaned back in his chair and folded his arms.

"What," Olsen said, "are you talking about?"

Sanford looked to the side slightly, as though he couldn't believe the Colonel was denying what he'd been working towards for the last year. "Sir, with all due respect," he said, "cut the crap. We both know where the orders are coming from and it isn't the C-in-C."

He walked the couple of steps towards Olsen's desk and leaned on it with both hands. "The insanely wealthy are the powerful and they *will* win, every time," Sanford said. "They always have and they always will. I have to admit, it took me awhile to figure out something was going on. But I definitely want in. There is going to be a whole new world, eventually, and I want to be on the winning side. Unfortunately, you didn't trust me soon enough and now everything's gotten out of hand."

"What do you mean," Olsen asked.

"The men are about to revolt," Sanford said. "They don't see any reason to keep doing what they've been doing. They're good men, but without an enemy or a cause, keeping them at this constant level of readiness is wearing them down. They can't, and won't, keep it up any longer. We have to go…now."

Things *had* been getting worse and Olsen *had* been hearing more and more rumors of complaints from the men. Still, he couldn't just admit everything–or even anything–to Sanford. What did he really *know*? How could he actually know *anything*?

"If we have a problem brewing," Olsen said, "it's your job to deal with it. If there is dissention in the ranks, take care of it."

"Unless I shoot every third man," Sanford said, "that's not going to work, Sir."

"There is no *way* it's gotten that bad," Olsen snapped as he stood up and slapped his desk, finally letting his emotions get the better of him. "If it was, I would know."

"No, Sir," Sanford said, not backing down, "you wouldn't. Not until they stormed your office and you were escorted past West's and my dead bodies to be hung or shot. Like I said, I'm close to these men. It's my job."

Olsen glared at Sanford, but was impressed with both the man's conviction and his determination. He'd apparently underestimated him for the last couple of years, this last year specifically.

Without admitting anything, Olsen asked, "What do you propose to do about it?"

"I already told you," Sanford said. "We need to leave, now."

"And just where do you propose we go," Olsen demanded.

"Hunter," Sanford said. "They're already expecting me."

"What," Olsen said.

"Sir, you aren't listening. This base is a powder keg," Sanford pointed out the Colonel's window. "Take a look around and *see* what's going on. Poor discipline, sloppy uniforms, open disrespect for their superiors."

Outside Olsen's window they could see two of those very same sloppily dressed troops of unknown rank, due to the fact that they were wearing untucked white tee-shirts and fatigue pants, engaged in a yelling match with a Sergeant First Class.

"Those two should be brought up on charges," Olsen said.

"And who would do it, Sir," Sanford asked. "Look carefully, both of them have fully automatic weapons slung across their backs and bulges on their hips."

Olsen considered for a few seconds. "When can we leave," he asked.

"Sir," Sanford said. "I've been saying *now* for the last five minutes because I have a bird on the tarmac ready to go. I came in here to *get* you."

"I'll meet you there in ten minutes," Olsen said.

"I need to know a few things first," Sanford said.

"No," Olsen said and shook his head.

"Then find your own ride and good luck not getting shot down," Sanford said and turned to leave. He heard Olsen move and assumed he was reaching for his side arm.

"Don't bother," Sanford said and reached for the door handle. "They won't go with just you and you'll be dead in a day if you stay here."

"What do you want to know," Olsen asked.

"I want to know who they are," Sanford said. "I want to know who they are, really, and what they promised, and what I can look forward to."

…

"What if we don't pacify the general population," Sanford asked.

"Then anyone who didn't get with the program dies," Olsen said.

"The men won't do it," Sanford said. "We don't have a big enough stick to drive them to wholesale slaughter of the remaining citizens or their fellow brothers-in-arms."

"I never said *we* would do it," Olsen said. "It's biological, and I haven't been vaccinated yet and neither have you. It would take a while, but these people are incredibly patient. Even without international travel they have it figured out. They will distribute the vaccine to those who will be allowed to survive–somehow, they haven't told me exactly how–just before this super bug is released, and then a couple of months later they would come out of hiding and take over what's left, because there would simply be no resistance."

Sanford nodded. "And a land, if not a whole world," he said, "fresh, clean, empty and ready to inherit. Ruthless in its efficiency, but," he shook his head, "brilliant nonetheless."

"We need to go," Sanford said.

"Give me a few minutes," Olsen said. "I have to get a few things."

As Sanford left the office, Olsen heard him on the radio giving an obscure code to someone. Hopefully the Black Hawk they were taking just needed a thru-flight and not a full pre-flight. They ran enough flights that one more bird taking off shouldn't raise any suspicion.

Olsen closed the blinds, disconnected the radio and encryption unit he had in the drawer of his desk, and put them in a locked and padded ammo can. Then he closed the door of his office. The antenna would have to stay, and getting a new one installed would be a bridge he'd cross when he came to it. Nothing else in the office or his quarters needed to come with him.

As he left the office he thought he noticed more than a few hostile looks. Sanford was right, it was time to go.

...

Sanford already had a bag loaded and strapped into one of the rear-facing seats behind where they would be sitting. Apparently, Sanford hadn't taken the time to strip out the extra seats from the Black Hawk before the flight. The Pilot, co-Pilot, and Crew Chief were busy readying for take-off and none of them so much as glanced Olsen's way as he approached the bird. Not that it mattered, he couldn't tell who they were with their helmets on and visors down. He was sure Sanford had chosen his flight crew wisely, as his own life was in their hands as well.

Sanford held the door for Olsen and climbed in behind him. It was a little darker than he remembered it being inside since the last time he'd been in one, but he'd just been out in the bright sun and Olsen figured he just needed a second for his eyes to adjust. He strapped himself in and in less than a minute they were airborne.

Sanford handed him a headset so that they could talk during the two-and-a-half hour flight to Savannah, Georgia.

"Nothing else to bring," Sanford asked, pointing to the ammo can.

"Nothing else worth bringing," Olsen replied. "Believe me, that's the only thing worth taking. Everything else can be replaced."

Sanford nodded.

…

Every five or ten minutes, Sanford would ask a question or say something to break the silence and they would talk for a couple of minutes. After almost two hours and forty-five minutes Olsen initiated the conversation for the first time.

"Shouldn't we be there by now," he asked.

Instead of answering immediately, Sanford looked over his right shoulder, looked at Olsen, and then undid his harness.

"No, Sir," Sanford said.

Olsen felt hands grab both of his biceps as a tug at his waist removed his side arm. Belatedly, Olsen realized that although his eyes had adjusted somewhat to the dimness in the back of the Black Hawk, it was still very dark. He'd also not gotten a very good look into the back because of Sanford's bag, and now he knew why it had been there—to *block* the view. How many people had been back there all this time?

"No," Sanford said. "Change of plans. We aren't going to Savannah, to Hunter Army Air Base; we're going to Hanahan, South Carolina."

At the look of confusion on Olsen's face, Sanford continued as two black-clad figures came around the seats to secure the Colonel. "Colonel Spencer Donald Olsen. You are under arrest subject to Articles 81, 92, 94, 104, 106a, 109, 118, 119 and not the least of which, 133. You are being delivered to the Naval Consolidated Brig in Charleston, where you will be detained until such time as a full court-martial can be convened. You have the right to remain silent…"

…

"Diego," Sanford said over the intercom, "how much longer?"

"About fifteen minutes, Sir," Diego said. "We just made radio contact and they have us on radar."

Sanford nodded to himself and reached over to start bringing up the lights in the cabin. Olsen was handcuffed and had leg restraints which held his ankles to the floor mounts for the seat. They had also duct-taped the handcuff chain to the seat, so he couldn't open his harness.

For his part, Olsen had remained silent since he'd received his Miranda warning, which was fine with Sanford. He'd heard all he needed to, twice over now, to convict the Colonel and condemn him to death on at least a half-a-dozen counts. It would be too good for him. He was grateful for the two MPs that Hodges had provided, who had now come around to sit in the jump seats facing them, to keep an eye on the Colonel. Sanford just wanted to be done with all of this.

...

Once they touched down and the engines were cut, Sanford opened the side door in time to see a group of people walking towards them. He motioned to the two MPs to prepare the Colonel and climbed out of the helicopter.

Once out from under the still turning blades, he stood up and walked to meet their welcoming party.

"Major Sanford," he said, and held out his hand.

"Major Jensen," Mallory said, and did likewise.

"Major Franklin," Ben said.

"Colonel Howard Maldonado," the commander of the Joint Base said, and shook Sanford's hand.

"Command Master Sergeant Rudy Page," Sergeant Page, the second in command at the base said.

"And here comes our boy," Maldonado said with more than a touch of regret in his voice.

Olsen was obviously stiff from sitting in the jump seat for three-and-a-half hours, but he brightened visibly when he saw Maldonado.

"Don't even think about it," Maldonado said. "Sanford here has had a radio on since the start of your last conversation, and before you say anything, Alabama, Georgia, and South Carolina are all single-party consent states for recording. Actually, South Carolina has no statute, but case law has set a single-party precedent. If I wasn't positive you would be found guilty on pretty much every charge and sentenced to hang or a firing squad, I'd shoot you myself right here, right now."

"Colonel," Mallory said, "I didn't actually come here today to see you; I came to meet Major Sanford. I'm glad I was here to see this, though. Even if you don't get the death penalty, you'll never set foot outside these walls again, of that I've been assured. Good bye, Mr. Olsen."

Mallory turned to Sanford. "Thank you," she said. "We all owe you so much, but we're not out of the woods yet."

"No, we aren't," Sanford said. "We still have one more thing to take care of."

Ben took a step towards Olsen. "I, on the other hand, *did* come here just to see you," he said. Olsen hadn't been there when everyone made their introductions, but had read nametapes as soon as he walked up and knew he might be in trouble.

"I," Ben said, "don't have quite as much faith as Colonel Maldonado here in our legal system; although he guarantees me that he has enough lawyers and a sufficient number of officers to convene a court-martial within a week."

Ben drew his side arm and raised it to rest the barrel on Olsen's forehead as he thumbed back the hammer. Everyone but Mallory and Maldonado took several steps back, but nobody made any moves to stop Ben.

"Let's see," Ben said. "Seven days' worth of food, plus the time of the trial, plus the lost time of putting together the paperwork versus one round of admittedly irreplaceable ammunition and a shallow grave."

Mallory put her hand up on Ben's and Olsen thought she was going to try to make him put the gun down. Instead, she put her finger in the trigger guard with his. Mallory and Ben pulled the trigger.

The hammer fell.

The gun went...

click

Olsen wet himself.

"I lied," Mallory said. "I came here to see you pee your pants."

Chapter Thirty-One

Colorado, somewhere between the Denver International Airport and the city of Watkins

"Ready, Sir," Hodges said.

Sanford took a deep breath and keyed the microphone on Olsen's encrypted radio. "This is Pillar Four," he said and completed the authentication the same way Olsen had, except for when he'd gone off on his handler.

"I am afraid I don't recognize your voice," the voice on the other end replied.

"Nor should you," Sanford replied. "That's completely irrelevant to this conversation."

"It is obvious that this node has been compromised..." the voice began.

"It would behoove you to stop talking," Sanford cut in, "and listen for once. This node has been compromised for a long time, friend. And the truth, the real truth about your little game has gotten out. Not just to us, either, but to the entire country. We know about the contingency plan, we know about The Outbreak, we know you've been lying to each of the area commanders and pitting them against each other to try and hurry your agenda along."

Sanford took a breath to see if he would be interrupted but he wasn't so he continued. "It's over," he said, "done. Starting right now we're doing to you what you've been having your boots-on-the-ground commanders do to us."

Sanford hit a key on his keyboard and one of the windows on his screen started scrolling. "You are now locked out of the satellite network to everyone but me," he said. "At the end of this conversation, even that link will be permanently severed. Hanging up on me right now would be a *very* bad idea."

"What do you want," the voice asked.

"Nothing," Sanford said. "I don't want anything from you. I'm dictating to you what you can and cannot do."

"Nobody…" the voice began.

"WRONG!" Sanford yelled into the microphone. "Your days of making the rules and calling the shots are over. Interrupt me again this conversation is over and you'll never speak to another person outside of your compound again, end of discussion. From this point forward I will ask you a question and you will answer. If you so much as interject with a 'but' I will drop this connection and as of right now, anyone who sets foot above ground outside of your compound in Denver will be shot on sight. Do I make myself clear?"

"As crystal," the voice said, obviously shaken but not as much as Sanford had hoped or expected.

"You are now surrounded," Sanford said. "We are setting up a perimeter of five miles around the Denver International Airport. I won't go into the security arrangements, but suffice it to say; when we are done we are relatively confident you won't be able to get out without us knowing. Nobody over the age of eighteen will be permitted to leave the compound, ever."

Sanford waited to be interrupted, but the voice on the other end had apparently taken him at his word.

"Like I said before," Sanford continued, "we know about The Outbreak and it's no longer a threat. Not just because we know about it, or because I've cut off your communications, but because it has actually ceased to be a threat. Do you understand?"

"Yes," the voice said, "but how."

"The people you had handling your contingency plan," Sanford said, "weren't the ones who knew how to do the work. There was no question that the handlers were your people from the very beginning. It turns out that the technicians, though, took you for all you were worth. In only one instance was there a super-strain of Ebola, and that was only in Atlanta, and it's been destroyed. The rest of the promised killer viruses were never engineered, or were destroyed as soon as the tests were run to show they had been completed and a placebo put in their place."

"But I mentioned that no one over eighteen would be allowed to leave," Sanford said. "It's interesting that you didn't ask about that. Doesn't that interest you in the slightest?"

"Yes," the voice said, "it does. I have two grandchildren, and I would like to know what your intentions are."

"That's interesting," Sanford said. "I was under the impression that you didn't have any children, which would be a prerequisite for grandchildren. Since I don't really care though, I won't ask."

Sanford went on, "We cannot, in good conscience, condemn children for the mistakes, for the *sins,* of their parents. But we also won't *require* that you give up your children, or that any minors that don't want to leave be forced to go. This is, however, a one-time offer, so to speak. Once the…barricades go up, nobody goes in or out and no communication. No exceptions, period. The world outside of your prison is *not* going to be the world you wanted so you will not be welcome in it. Make the most of what you've got squirrelled away in there; it's all you will ever have. I'll leave the connection open…"

Sanford heard gunfire outside the tent he was using for the radio and swore under his breath.

They had established the initial perimeter at five miles, just like he'd told the voice on the other end. What he hadn't told him was that they'd also established lookouts and snipers at one-mile increments from the fence surrounding the Airport proper. Someone hadn't believed him that anyone caught above ground over the age of eighteen would be considered an enemy combatant. From the sounds of it, they had been armed, too. He didn't feel bad about the result at all.

"Talk to me," he said into the squad radio he'd brought with him to Colorado. They were coordinating with three local paramilitary groups and two guard units, along with a platoon from Fort Carson.

"A small group," one of the patrols reported in, "four men armed with automatic weapons, I repeat *fully automatic weapons*, not single fire semi-automatic, emerged from the ground at about the four-and-a-half mile mark. This underground base is *huge*."

"Casualties," Sanford asked.

"It looks like three of the tangos are down," the patrol leader replied. "One of them is still alive and waving something that I think we're supposed to take as a white flag."

"Ours," Sanford prompted.

"One pair of soiled shorts," was the reply.

"Deal with it and don't lose anybody," Sanford said.

"Dumb," Sanford said into the radio connecting him into the compound. "Then again, you now have four less mouths to feed, so maybe not so dumb. As I was saying, though, I will leave the connection open while you let everyone know that children are allowed to leave. Anyone who doesn't look under eighteen will need proof of their age. You may speak now."

"You have destroyed the world," the voice said. "You may believe that what you are doing is right and just and good, but you are dooming the world as surely as it was doomed before."

"I'm doing it by choice," Sanford said, "because that's what really matters. It's not up to you to decide what's best for the rest of the human race."

"And yet there you sit, proposing to do the same thing," the voice asked, a bit of the self-assurance and haughtiness Sanford was used to hearing from the recordings creeping back into it.

"No," Sanford said, "not at all. You would take virtually every choice away from everyone. On the other hand, by keeping you where you are, everyone else has the ultimate freedom, to decide for themselves. I'm not deciding anything for anyone…but you."

There was silence for a few seconds. "But you know that don't you," Sanford asked. "Because it isn't about freedom or personal expression or any of the other platitudes that you and your ilk spout; it isn't even about money or wealth. It's about power and control, and everything else is just a means to that end. Without that, your life is meaningless."

"Go talk to your people and tell them about the children," Sanford said. "It's 11:30. Make the decision by 8:00 tomorrow morning. After that it's over and the gates close."

…

"How many," Sanford asked.

"I would like to propose…" the voice began.

"You really are a pompous windbag," Sanford interrupted. "You are going to tell me how many children under the age of 18 are going to come out or we're done, end of story."

"There is someone…" the voice started again.

"Smarter than you who I can talk to," Sanford asked. "Preferably someone to whom I won't have to repeat myself three or four times to make my point. For the last time…"

"The President," the voice said.

Silence from both sides.

"I thought that would get your attention," the voice said.

"Not for the reasons you think," Sanford said. "Put him on, I'll give him thirty seconds."

"Seriously," the voice asked.

"Keep screwing around and you're going to cut into his time," Sanford said.

"Major Sanford," a new voice came on the line, one that Sanford recognized immediately.

"Speaking," Sanford said. He could almost hear the eyebrows rise on the other end.

"A little respect, Son," the President said. "I'm your Commander-In-Chief."

"No," Sanford said, "you *were* my Commander-In-Chief until you abdicated that responsibility by being bought and paid for by men like the man I was just talking to, and then running and hiding while they put the wheels in motion to destroy this country."

"Son," the President began, "you don't understand…"

"I'm done," Sanford said. "Put your handler back on. You have nothing useful to say and I've said everything I wanted to say to you. Good bye, Mr. Clement."

"Now wait a mi…" the President began but Sanford pulled the headphones away from his ears and set them on the microphone, which created a horrible feedback loop.

"I said put your handler back on," Sanford said after he put the headphones back on.

"I am already here," the voice said. "What did you say? He couldn't get the headphones off fast enough."

"Don't worry about it," Sanford said. "How…many…children."

"Ninety-six," the voice said. "There are some who do not want to leave and some that the parents will not let go."

"Understood," Sanford said. "Bring them to the same exit that the squad of four used when they tried to ambush us. We'll be ready to receive them in two hours."

"Very well," the voice said.

…

Tensions were high around the opened exit door in the ground. Once the men had known where to look, it hadn't been that hard to find, but without a more detailed idea of where to focus their search, it would have been a needle in a seventy-five square mile haystack.

Everyone assumed that there would be other escape attempts at the same time as the children were being released– if the children were even let go at this point. Sanford was being hard, but he didn't want any of his men getting hurt or killed for no reason.

Overnight, they'd been reinforced by an additional three platoons from Fort Carson, and they had almost a dozen helicopters in the air in case someone tried to make a break for it by air or in some kind of vehicle. Sanford was serious about the five-mile limit though, and anyone above ground over the age of eighteen. It would give him nightmares, but he would "okay" pulling the trigger.

At a few minutes after 10:00 they heard a noise in the tunnel. A minute later they saw the first face, and it wasn't that of a child. A well-coiffed woman in her mid-thirties, who had obviously been trying to maintain the standard of living and lifestyle she'd enjoyed above ground, stood at the bottom of the ladder, looking up.

The effect of the makeup, clothes, and hair that had obviously recently been styled was only slightly spoiled by the fact that she hadn't seen the sun or the inside of a gym in over a year. Under the makeup she was startlingly pale, and while not overweight by any means, all sense of muscle-tone was long gone.

"Ma'am," the Sergeant responsible for taking charge of the children once they came up said, "step back and stay away from the ladder. The orders were clear. Only children, and only under the age of eighteen."

"But he's my baby," the woman wailed.

"Then keep him with you," the Sergeant said, "but only one of you is coming out and it's not you. Now stand back, *now!*"

The woman slowly moved back, but she took her son, who looked to be about nine, with her. It wasn't clear if he wanted to go with her or not.

After that, there were some heartbreaking goodbyes in the tunnel and some children came up the ladder. In a couple of instances, older children were carrying infants in slings in order to get them up. Some of the children were sullen or shivering from shock once they reached the top, others hugged the first person they encountered like they had just been rescued, which might be how they viewed what was happening.

About two thirds of the way through the group, a tall, heavily-built 'young man' started up the ladder.

"Stop!" The Sergeant said.

"What," the boy asked.

"How old are you," the Sergeant asked.

"I'll be eighteen in two weeks," he said.

"I'm going to need some proof of age," the Sergeant said. "That was the requirement."

"Can I give you my driver's license from before the power went out when I get to the top," the boy asked.

The Sergeant paused for a second, since he was over halfway up the ladder. "Ok," he said, and then yelled down to the tunnel, "but nobody else starts up until he's taken care of."

It turned out he was, in fact, still seventeen–barely–he was just big.

About ten kids later, the same thing happened, and the Sergeant let him get to the top to produce his pre-power-outage license when he asked the same question.

The boy got to the top and reached behind him to get his license. It never occurred to anyone to wonder why these boys might still be carrying their licenses in the first place, much less in their back pockets, or how much their looks might have changed in the last year.

The boy, who had said he was within a month of his eighteenth birthday, missed his back pocket, drew a 9mm from an in-waistband holster, and aimed it at the Sergeant's head. At the same time, the first boy did the same thing as he reached out and picked up one of the younger kids, who looked to be a six or seven-year-old girl, and held the gun to her head.

"Now," the one with the gun to the Sergeant's head said. "This is what's going to happen. A couple dozen of our guards are going to come up in a minute and take control of this exit and then we're all going to go away. As long as you don't get in the way, you won't grow a third eye."

…

"Problem," Sergeant Simmons said to his sniper. He was acting as spotter and watching the location where the children were coming out.

Sergeant Allen turned just in time to see the second boy pick up the girl he would use as a hostage. *"Which one first,"* Allen said to himself.

"Take the one with the hostage," Simmons said, reading Allen's mind. "The other one will flinch when his buddy's head explodes and that'll be before the sound even gets there. Top'll understand."

…

Half the kids were crying, but none as loudly as the one with the gun to her head, and nothing would shut her up. Threatening her hadn't worked, and even if he'd wanted to hit her she was over with that other guy who, somehow, he still didn't know after a year.

Then, all of the sudden, everybody was quiet. *"What the,"* the boy, who was actually one of the security guards for the complex, thought as he glanced over to where the boy holding the girl hostage was standing...*should* have been standing. He was toppling backwards, and he was missing the majority of his head.

That split second of inattention was all the First Sergeant needed to take his gun away and pistol whip him with it. Eventually, he would wake up in the infirmary, back in the complex, after receiving the worst beating of his life.

. . .

"Tango down," Simmons said as Allen brought the rifle back under control from the recoil, in case another shot was necessary.

"Nice shot," he said, "and Top is pissed. That guy's gonna need a nose job."

. . .

The guards from the underground complex arrived less than a minute later to find the top of the tunnel opening ringed with the muzzles of U.S. Army issue M-16s and two outstretched hands, each holding a hand grenade.

"New plan," the First Sergeant yelled from behind the rifle barrels, "all ID comes up before the person on the ladder, and if I feel the need, I'm dropping the maximum age to sixteen. Any more shenanigans like we just had and I seal this entrance; I don't care how many people are still down there. Oh, and I thought it went without saying, but no weapons. Clear?"

"Roger," one of the guards in the tunnel yelled, and there was a mad dash away from the opening. A grenade or two in the tunnel would have been a bloodbath.

Chapter Thirty-Two

Returning to Fort Rucker without the Colonel, and after locking down the airport in Denver, had been an... interesting experience. One of the biggest concerns that Sanford had going into this was how his and others' bases would react to the Colonel being stripped of authority.

The first, and potentially largest, problem was going to be West. Lieutenant Colonel West, technically Sanford's new commanding officer, was more than a little curious about where Sanford and the Colonel had gone and why the Colonel hadn't come back.

"Sir," Sanford said, "if you'll give me an hour or so to put a few things together, I'll explain everything."

"One hour," West said, "no more. And if it doesn't make sense then, you get to keep explaining until it does."

"Understood," Sanford replied. "I don't think any additional explanation will be necessary."

"Now if Tuttle can just finish getting everything set up in time," Sanford thought, *"I may just be able to sleep with both eyes closed tonight."*

Hodges and Tuttle had been editing together the more important parts of the recorded conversations between Olsen and his handlers while Sanford was gone. He'd been adamant that they only be edited for length and not meaning, however. He refused to start down the road the Colonel had been on by creating fake conversations to further his agenda.

The most important conversation, though, would be the one he'd had just a few days ago in which the Colonel explained everything—or at least as much as he could—to Sanford, in his own words. That had been pretty damning, and he hoped it would be enough.

His radio squawked. "Sanford," he said.

"Ready when you are," Hodges said.

Sanford looked around and decided to head to one of the briefing rooms so he could lock the door.

"How will I know it's live," Sanford asked.

"You'll hear a little bit of white noise, or static, from the base P.A. system," Hodges said.

"Let's do it then," Sanford said. "Showtime."

Once he heard the P.A. system turn on, he took a deep breath and tried to calm his nerves. It didn't work. *"Now or never,"* he thought, and pressed the send key on his handheld. The sound coming from the P.A. system changed, and he knew he was broadcasting live.

"Ladies and gentlemen," Sanford began. "This is Major Sanford speaking. I need your undivided attention for the next few minutes."

"What you are about to hear is a collection of recorded conversations," Sanford began. "These conversations took place between this base and individuals at a location that was, until very recently, hidden and unknown to us. They were intercepted, decrypted, and an investigation was initiated based on their contents. I will leave it up to you to draw your own conclusions as to whether or not appropriate actions have been taken."

Tuttle began playing back the set of recorded conversations between Olsen and his handlers, which would take about fifteen minutes. Hodges and Tuttle had whittled things down from when he had played them for Major Jensen at Promised Land as well, adding a few of the newer transmissions.

Sanford set his radio on the table and leaned back in one of the briefing room chairs. *"Please let this go well,"* he muttered to himself.

A couple of minutes into the playback someone tried the door knob and then began hammering on the locked door.

"Well," Sanford said as he got up, "that took less time than I'd hoped."

Sanford took out his sidearm, and ejected the magazine and the round he had been leaving in the chamber for the last several months. With all three sitting on the table and pointed in a safe direction, he unlocked the door, opened it, and took a couple of steps back. West was at the door with a half-a-dozen MPs.

"Wow," he thought, *"six guards for little old me?"*

"What in the *HELL,*" West started, but was interrupted when the playback changed to a different conversation.

"I thought you could rely on your people's sense of duty and honor. I thought you said that they would obey and get the mission done."

"There's obedience," Olsen said, *"and there's blind obedience. We cultivate at least some sense of critical thinking in our men. They aren't going to jump off a cliff just because I say so."*

West stopped and his eyebrows knitted together. He remembered making the same argument to the Colonel not that long ago.

"Then your people need direction," The voice said. *"They need an enemy they can see, touch and feel. You say you have been holding the threat over them for too long with nothing to show for it. Give them an enemy."*

"Who," Olsen said, almost plaintively.

"Haven't you been listening," the voice asked, scorn obvious even over the radio. *"It doesn't matter who. It doesn't matter how. All that matters is how you present it. Were there weapons of mass destruction in Iraq? It doesn't matter.*

Was the U.S. Government complicit in the attacks of 9/11? It doesn't matter. Are there UFOs at Area 51? It…doesn't…matter!"

West turned a pale face to the MPs. "Dismissed," he said, and closed the door.

…

The rest of the playback was more of the same, all just as damning, with the final recording being the last conversation between Sanford and Olsen in Olsen's office, before they left in the Black Hawk. Sanford picked up his radio as the final recording finished.

"Colonel Olsen has been relieved of command," he said. "He is currently awaiting trial at the Naval Consolidated Brig in Charleston."

As Sanford was saying this last bit, West stood up and drew his sidearm.

"I've done my part," Sanford thought, wishing he hadn't cleared and disabled his own firearm. *"Do it if you really think you have to."*

Sanford was willing to die for this, although he didn't really want to. West had always been the wild card, and now it looked like the base was going to come to blows with itself. Surely they wouldn't just fall back in line if West took him out now, would they?

West surprised Sanford by grabbing his sidearm by the barrel and presenting it to Sanford grip first. He didn't bother clearing it, and Sanford could see that the safety was on, but the .45 was cocked, which meant there was one in the pipe.

Sanford and West looked at each other for several seconds before Sanford accepted the pistol.

"For the time being," Sanford said into the radio, "and potentially only for the time being, command has fallen to me. Additionally, though we don't have any recordings to play back, the group that has been handling Colonel Olsen, as well as at least a dozen others for the last year, has been contained. I'll be holding a briefing about *that* later today or tomorrow. Sanford out."

...

Sanford escorted West to the on-base brig, without needing to call for the base MPs. Neither of them had said anything, but West had surrendered his sidearm and hadn't corrected him about who was in command of the base. West may or may not be released in the future, though, and if they could keep rumors to a minimum it would be best for all involved.

Once behind bars, West finally decided he had something to say.

"How long," he asked. "How long has it been going on?"

"Since a couple of days after the power went out," Sanford replied, "the communications between Olsen and his handler that is. As for how long he's been under their thumb, nobody knows, but these were *very* patient people. They didn't create this situation, but they had a plan to take advantage of it, or any of a hundred other crises, as soon as they happened. If Hodges can be believed, they've been waiting for over a hundred years."

Sanford shook his head, still somewhat in disbelief himself. "Haven't you ever wondered why the Government had a plan for *just such an event,* but didn't implement it," Sanford asked. "Or where all the leaders ran off to immediately afterwards, or even the fact that *everything* was being funneled through the Colonel and not one person has heard the President's voice in over a year?"

Sanford chose not to mention the fact that he'd actually spoken with the President less than two days ago. "We were played," West said. "And it was so easy for them to do."

"You should hear some of the other recordings," Sanford said. "In retrospect, I'm sure even the Colonel would look back and realize just how badly he was manipulated. At the time, though, I'm sure it all seemed perfectly reasonable, every step of the way."

"I wanted to believe," West said and shook his head. "That's the worst part; I wanted to believe that what we were doing was right."

"Stop," Sanford said, and then reminded West of his rights. Whether or not you agreed with Miranda, it was the right thing for *him* to do.

"I don't want an attorney," West said. "There's no defense, so it doesn't matter."

"I have to take care of some things," Sanford said, "but I'll be back later, hopefully today. Don't do anything stupid."

West snorted and then sat down on his bunk. "I think it's a little late for that," he said.

...

"I kind of did that already," Sparky said, "didn't I?"

"Not exactly," Stewart said. "You gave *us* a way to communicate relatively securely, but you have to know about it, to basically be invited into the system, and it really helps to be a HAM radio operator already."

Sparky bit the inside of his cheek. "So not just us," he said. "This is supposed to be for everyone? Nationwide?"

"That's the idea," Stewart said with a nod. "We lost telephone, commercial radio, cell phone, and even satellite-phone service over a year ago. We need something to take its place."

...

"But that's what you already did," Tuttle said.

"That's what *I* said," Sparky replied. "I'm completely tapped when it comes to ideas right now."

"No," Tuttle said and then repeated herself. "I'm serious, that's what you already built, and even then you didn't reinvent the wheel. You don't need to do it *again*, just tweak it some, maybe, and make it a little more user friendly."

Sparky tapped his lips with a finger as he thought about it.

"I'm *not* writing a Windows program," he said finally, which got a laugh from Tuttle.

"Well," she said, "that *would* be more user friendly. You're willing to disenfranchise eighty percent of the population?"

"Politics and religion aside," Sparky said, "if I have to make something that the average person can use, it has to run on whatever hardware we can find. Linux is going to be a whole lot less picky and resource intensive."

Sparky was quiet for a few seconds and then continued. "Maybe I could write it in Java," he said.

"Yeah," Tuttle replied, "like *that* wouldn't be a resource hog!"

"Heh, yeah, point," Sparky said. "Would we actually need to encrypt traffic though?"

He answered his own question before Tuttle could reply. "Yeah," he said, "we do, or at least it should be an option."

"Why," Tuttle asked.

"Fourth Amendment," Sparky said, "sort of. People have the right of a reasonable expectation of privacy. The encryption isn't necessarily there to hide the contents of the message but because the contents are nobody else's business. The FCC rules for a HAM operators were, I think, intentionally written to be a little vague on the topic of encryption so that people would err on the side of caution."

"Don't I know it," Tuttle said. "I've argued that very thing more times than I care to count. Technically, we could always use encryption as long as the *purpose* of the encryption wasn't to obscure the meaning, but to prevent non-licensed access to the 'network'. As long as we were using an encryption mechanism that was publicly documented, we weren't breaking the rules."

"So that gives me a couple of ideas," Sparky said. "Implementing it large-scale like this, though, that's going to be a *lot* of work. I don't know if I can do it, honestly."

"Maybe not," Tuttle said, "but *we* can."

"You don't need to get sucked into this," Sparky said.

"So you just called me to complain," Tuttle asked.

"No," Sparky started, and then paused for a few seconds. "Okay, that's fair. I'm not saying I wouldn't welcome the help, and I really was out of ideas. It hadn't occurred to me to just keep using what we have and maybe make it easier to use. I wasn't trying to dump this on you, though."

"You're not," Tuttle said. "But if it makes you feel any better, I'm volunteering to help, and frankly, I'm intrigued. It sounds like fun."

Sparky snorted. "You're sick," he said, "or we need to work on your definitions."

"Meh," Tuttle said, "guilty on both counts."

…

"That seems a little extreme," Stewart said, "don't you think? I mean, making people learn Morse Code?"

"With all due respect," Sparky said.

"Which means none at all because I'm too stupid to see the nose on my face," Stewart interrupted, "much less the glaring hole in what I just said?"

"With all due respect," Sparky repeated, "if I thought having people learn Morse code was excessive, I wouldn't have suggested it."

Stewart frowned a little and Mallory quirked her mouth into the not-quite-smile people make when they're trying not to laugh.

"Ok," Stewart said, "fair point, but that's not all there is to it, right?"

"No, Sergeant," Sparky answered. "It's actually just a very small part of it, but it's as important as having a phone that could send and receive text messages used to be in a disaster. Morse is…tiny, and uses hardly any bandwidth compared to voice. That's why it was so popular with HAMs on the lower frequencies."

"But to answer your question," Sparky continued when he realized he was on the verge of geeking out and losing everyone in the room, "we're suggesting that we simply extend the technology we've already deployed by making it a little easier to use."

"We," Mallory asked.

"Oops," Sparky thought and took a breath.

"Sergeant Tuttle and I," he said.

"This would be the same Sergeant Tuttle," Mallory began, "that found the setup at Fort Campbell?"

"Yes, Ma'am," Sparky said, "the same. She and I…"

"She," Stewart interrupted. "As in a girl?"

"Technically, she's a woman," Sparky said, used to the jibes about him being a geek and never finding a girlfriend. "There *are* female geeks after all–they're just…rare."

This time Mallory did laugh. "Ok," she said with a smile, "what's the first step? And it's ok to get your geek on if you need to."

"Power," Sparky said, pointing to the table where he had his equipment set up. "Every unit is going to need power. We've scrounged a number of solar panels over the last year, but I'm sure there're thousands more out there to be had."

"But that's only good during the day," he continued. "We'll need at least one battery for each unit, and each one will need a charge controller. If I had a fully stocked Radio Shack it would be pretty simple to make them. As it is I have to disassemble anything and everything electronic that we don't need to find some of the parts. The biggest thing holding me back from making more is the IC, or integrated circuit. It's simple, and if I have to I can *build* an alternative, but I'd rather not because that just means more parts that

I may or may not have, and would make the charge controller really big."

"How big is it now," Stewart asked.

"About one-and-a-half times the size of an old Altoids tin," Sparky said.

"How big would it be if you can't find all the parts you want," Mallory asked.

"Have you ever seen the movie Back to the Future," Sparky asked, referring to the giant replacement that the Professor had created out of vacuum tubes for the tiny, blown-out IC. "Ok, not quite that big, but the whole reason for ICs is to make things smaller. It would probably be about the size of an ammo can."

"Why make the whole system available to everyone, encryption and all," Stewart asked, and Mallory let Sparky answer, although she knew what he was going to say.

"The same reason we have encryption," Sparky said. "The same reason party lines replaced 'Mable the Operator' and individual phone lines eventually replaced party lines. By its very nature, radio is a shared medium, but people want to have at least *some* semblance of privacy when they communicate."

Stewart wanted to ask about allowing the military to have access to the private keys and certificates, but knew that was a path that none of them were willing to go down.

"Each unit will have the ability to create its own certificate, too," Sparky said, almost as if he could read Stewart's mind. "Users will have to share their public key in the open, but that's not a big deal. It will take some educating for people to trust the system, but what 'new' technology doesn't require that?"

"How long before you can start putting these together," Mallory asked.

"Sergeant Tuttle is already working on building more radios," Sparky said, "and trying to find laptops that we can use. And they actually did have a Radio Shack down there that had its inventory…appropriated about nine months ago. She's making a charge controller for each radio she's able to put together."

"Then I think we have our communications system just about worked out," Mallory said.

Chapter Thirty-Three

"Remember how you said we can't be making decisions for everyone without their input," Joel asked as he approached Mallory.

Mallory was caught completely off guard, and almost shook her head to get her bearings. "Uhm, yeah," she said, vaguely recalling the conversation in question.

"We need to throw a party," Joel said.

"Wait, what," Mallory asked. "What are you talking about, Joel? Slow down."

"Sorry," Joel said, "but it's just…" Joel paused for a second and took a breath.

"We've been at this heightened state of alert," he said, "on pins and needles almost since we got here, if you think about it. It's been one thing after another for a solid year and we barely remembered to celebrate Christmas for crying out loud! We really haven't been able to take any downtime, we've missed Independence Day…twice; we need to have that get together we talked about a month ago, but it needs to be a big bash–a *real* party."

"You've been thinking about this a lot, haven't you," Mallory asked.

Joel shrugged. "Kind of," he said. "Ok, yes, but that doesn't change the fact that we need to do it. People need the release. We need to mix more with the folks from the farms we're working with, and the horse ranch, and the dairy. Did you know that some of those people haven't been back to town or the base in almost six months?"

Mallory made a face, but nodded.

"Who do we invite," she asked.

"Everybody," Joel said, "why?"

"Are we including Eric and Kyle's group in our group of towns," Mallory continued.

Joel narrowed his eyes at Mallory. "What do you mean 'our group of towns'," he asked. "Do we have cliques of towns in America now?"

Mallory started to say something, but Joel didn't let her interrupt. "Cool towns and lame towns," Joel said, "or maybe acceptable towns and those that we find unsatisfactory."

"Okay," Mallory said before Joel could continue, "okay, I get it. Point made."

"Earl's group should be included too," Joel said.

Mallory nodded. "I'm sorry," she said.

"It's not me you need to apologize to," Joel said. "It's going to be a party though, and a time of healing. We've overcome a lot and we all need to recognize that. I'll get a committee together for the…festival. We'll come up with a name for it, pick a date, and get this thing going."

…

"Long time no chat," Eric said into the radio.

"Haven't really had much to talk about," Joel replied, "or the time, to be honest. I've been meaning to find out how things are going with you all, though."

"About as good as can be expected," Eric said. "Still living out of the trailers for now, but we've got some pretty good ideas going forward."

"How's the food situation," Joel asked.

"Better than it was," Eric said. "We've finally got something to barter with, and it's a doozey."

"Well," Joel said, "maybe you can tell me all about it in person in a couple of weeks."

"Which is the real reason for your call," Eric said with a chuckle.

"Yeah, I've never been good at small talk," Joel said. "Kinda figured you'd see through that, but I really have been meaning to check on you guys."

"So," Eric said, "what's this about getting together in person? Nothing was ever officially said, but Kyle and I figured we were pretty much persona-non-grata there at the base."

"First of all," Joel said, "this isn't a military dictatorship; which is another thing you need to be brought up to speed on. Secondly, I'm a grown man and I can choose who I associate with...as long as I have Rachael's approval. Lastly, I'm the Mayor, in case you forgot, and the *town* doesn't have beef one with you guys, regardless of your relationship with anyone else."

"Point," Eric said. "Sorry. Speaking of which, I know you aren't Mallory's keeper but..."

"She has her moments," Joel said, "but then again so do I. We call each other out if we need it. It isn't going to be a problem for you and your whole group to show up. We're having a festival and you're invited."

"Well, I can't speak for the whole group," Eric said, "but I appreciate that. Why the festival and why invite us, though?"

"Colonel Olsen has been arrested," Joel said, "and is awaiting trial in Charleston. There's a little more to it, but that's the important piece.

Equally important is the fact that those who were really pulling the strings, Olsen's handlers, have been taken out of the picture; hopefully permanently."

"Okay, that's going to require an explanation," Eric said. "The fact that there even *were* handlers is news."

"Yeah, I guess a lot's happened since the last time we talked," Joel said. "And I'd really like you all to be here to discuss a few other things."

Eric didn't say anything and eventually Joel decided he needed to let Eric know what he had planned.

"We're inviting you and Earl's group," Joel said, "and all the local farmers. The force that Ben brought with him has really put a strain on our current resources and we'd like to discuss future plans with as many people as we can. Chuck's come up with some proposals, assuming we can come to a consensus as a group, which would make much better use of the skills people are bringing to the table."

"You're thinking of starting more towns," Eric asked, "and maybe specializing a little bit."

"Pretty much," Joel said, only a little disappointed at having the wind taken from his sails. "So, do you think you can convince Kyle and the rest of the group to come? We're having it two weeks from Saturday."

"No promises, but I think we'll be there," Eric answered. "We may even have a little surprise of our own."

...

The fire wasn't too large since it was still warm outside, but Eric had wanted to get the majority of the adults together and by now, a fire in the central fire-pit was the unspoken signal to get everyone together for a discussion.

"But it was Joel who made the call," Kyle asked. "He's the one that reached out to us?"

Eric nodded. "But that just makes sense," he said. "What he's doing is almost purely civilian. It may end up affecting the Army, but I get the sense that he's the one driving this. He even said it was Chuck who came up with some proposals for specialization."

"So," Kyle asked, "what are we going to do?"

"I assume you mean long-term," someone from the crowd said.

"Yeah," Kyle said, "I meant in the long run. Obviously I think we should go because, well, what everyone else decides is probably going to affect us either way, so we may as well be there to represent our interests."

Eric raised an eyebrow and Kyle nodded. He and Kyle had been doing all of the back-channel work with Travis without having brought it up to the group. Now seemed like a perfect time to do so.

"I've been kind of working with the owner of the horse ranch on something," Eric said, "and with this meeting at the festival coming up and us deciding the course of action for the community ..."

One of the women said, "Just spit it out, Eric. Unless you've committed us to something ridiculous I don't think we're going to string you up."

"I've had him working on designs for wagons," Eric said, "horse-drawn covered wagons."

Several people in the crowd made faces, but nobody said anything.

"Originally I got stuck in the same rut most of you are in right now," Eric continued. "I asked him if his farrier turned blacksmith would be able to make iron bands for the outside of the wheels and everything. Instead, Travis and his farrier have come up with something *much* better."

Eric spent five minutes explaining the details of the wagons that Travis was actually already building. The looks of skepticism became thoughtful and, by the end, a few people were even nodding.

"As nice as some of these camping trailers are," Kyle said, "they just weren't meant to be lived in every day, year-round. Some of them are already starting to have problems with leaks and little things breaking. We could probably get another year out of some of them, and a lot longer out of a few of the really well-made ones, but ultimately we're going to have to switch from the trailers to something else."

"And until then," Eric added, "we can't pull these things around forever. For all intents and purposes we're out of gas, and we've all agreed that we can't even stay in this location long-term. Having the wagons, pulled by horses, would kill a couple of birds with one stone."

Amanda had just been listening up to this point, but realized her idea could actually work, especially if they weren't tied to the trailers and trucks to pull them with. "Gypsies," she said.

"Say *what*," one of the men closest to the fire said.

"Hear me out," Amanda said. "If we aren't tied to one spot because of the trailers and no way to pull them, then we could be on the move as often or as seldom as we wanted, right?"

A few people nodded.

"I don't know how heavy it would make them," she continued, "but what if the wagons weren't just covered, but were more of a solid box...kind of like a trailer." A couple people chuckled.

Kyle looked at Eric and got a nod. "One of the things we were going to trade for the wagons," he said, "was that windmill we've been working on. We've got templates made for all the parts of the gearbox and the blades. It won't be long before we've flooded the market here with windmills and would need to look for new...customers." Kyle shook his head at the thought of being a traveling salesman.

"There're other pieces of technology we could bring to people, too," Eric said and looked at Amanda. "We could even have a bit of a traveling school. Heck, if we can start gathering old textbooks and things like that, we could be a traveling University."

Amanda grinned.

"Everybody is going to be in the same boat we're in," Kyle said, "with regards to transportation. When they see the wagons, it'll probably set the wheels in motion, as it were, to start building their own. There have got to be some other forms of transportation that we aren't taking advantage of right now that we could bring to people."

"I'm out of shape because I haven't been mountain biking for a year, but if we can find bicycles," one of the men said, "I can fix just about anything on one."

He stopped to think and then went on. "In fact, anything that's beyond repair could be pillaged for parts," he said. "Bikes have been used for transportation for over a century. I don't know why we couldn't start using them again."

"Handcarts," one of the women further back said. "Every third-world, and even second-world, country uses them."

She looked at the mountain biker and continued. "The handcarts could even use the bicycle wheels that we salvage from ruined bikes."

Eric had been nodding up to this point and then remembered something he'd seen onone of his deployments. "When I was deployed to Afghanistan I had a chance to visit India," he said. "They use a…carriage; I think that's even what the word means, called a Tangah. It's a no-frills horse-drawn cart with wooden wheels. I know that wagon wheels were out of the question for Travis and his farrier, but we might be able to make something similar to the Tangah fairly easily."

"How out-there are we thinking," another man from the group asked.

"I don't know that we're discounting anything right now," Kyle said.

"Okay, how about hot-air balloons…"

...

"So, what's going to happen to us," Ben asked.

"I'm not thinking about that right now," Mallory said. "And don't spoil the mood."

"Sorry," Ben said, and leaned over to kiss her.

"You're forgiven," she said, and then sighed. "Of course now that's all I'm going to be able to think about."

Ben looked like he was going to apologize again but she stopped him with her finger on his lips. "It's not your fault," she said. "We'd have had to think of something sooner or later."

"Just because the people that came with me are most likely going to set up their own town," Ben said, "doesn't mean I have to go with them. I can almost guarantee that however we decide to do it, it's going to be more civilian than military-based."

Ben shook his head slightly and went on. "Not that there's anything wrong with that," he said, "it's just that I don't think I'm ready to walk away from the whole Army lifestyle just yet. Are you?"

"No," Mallory said with a small head shake of her own, "and we're going to need to keep the military around in some shape, form or fashion. I don't get the impression that Joel was trying to disband the Army."

"Good," Ben said with a smile. "I think he'd be in for quite the battle if that were the case."

"As long as it isn't anything like what we've had hanging over our heads for the last year," Mallory said.

"Are you willing to be relegated to law enforcement if that's what the world needs for a while," Ben asked. "Because I don't see us having to defend the borders any time soon."

"Yeah," Mallory said, looking up at the ceiling. "Over the last year I've come to realize something that was a real shock and a bit of a rude awakening."

"What's that," Ben asked.

"We, us, the military," Mallory said, "we don't produce anything. We're consumers, and before the lights went out we didn't even always provide a service.

Mallory rolled over to face Ben. "That's a hard thing to realize about yourself," she said.

"We *made* the world a safer place," Ben said. "No one would have been able to enjoy everything they *produced* without us. That's not 'nothing'."

"Over the last year, though, most of what we've done—most of what the Army *here* has done—hasn't had anything to do with soldiering."

Ben nodded. "It was getting that way for me up at Campbell," he said. "It was…good I guess you could say, to feel useful when push came to shove and we were needed to fight back, even if we did end up losing the battle, if not the war. It's what the Army is for, what we're put there to do."

He sighed. "Don't get me wrong," Ben said, "I'm not looking to fight a war, but I'm not quite ready to hang everything up and walk away from it all just because everything's changed and we may not be needed anymore, at least not like we were. That's a hard pill to swallow."

"But we can change," Mallory said. "We're flexible. We'll make it work."

"And I'd like to stick around if it's all the same to you," Ben said.

Mallory pulled him into a kiss. "I think," she said, "I'd like that very much."

…

"Is that the same uniform you were wearing yesterday," one of Ben's Lieutenants said to him on his way to breakfast.

"Son," Ben said, "it's the same uniform I've been wearing for a *year.*" Then Ben smiled.

"And not that it's any of your business but, yes," he said as he continued on to the mess hall.

Chapter Thirty-Four

"Are you going to be ok," Rachael asked Joel as he paced around the house looking for heaven only knew what.

Joel stopped and looked at his wife, and then shook his head. "I have no idea," he said. "I thought I knew what I hoped to accomplish with this festival, but now I'm not so sure."

Rachael put a hand on either side of his face and made him look at her.

"*It* will be fine," she said. "I didn't ask about the festival. I asked if *you* were going to be ok. The festival is all I've heard anyone talk about for the last week and a half."

Joel closed his eyes and tried to calm himself down. "You're right," he said. "It's supposed to be a celebration above anything else. We've finally got a chance to relax a little."

Rachael smiled and kissed her husband. "Focus on that," she said. "And remember, you're the Mayor of Promised Land and Redemption, that's it. The others, while important, really aren't your responsibility."

Joel nodded and turned his head to kiss her hand. "Thank you," he said. "How long do you think that'll work for?"

"Ten," Rachael said with a snort, "maybe fifteen minutes, tops."

...

The windmill had been up for almost a week and was providing all the water they could use at the ranch. Kyle had worked with the farrier to fashion a new pump cylinder for the smaller well pipe at the ranch, but now that everything was installed it seemed to be working just fine.

Eric and Kyle were there with another dozen people from their group to pick up the first three wagons and horses. They would be bringing the horses back after the festival, but the wagons would get towed with them back to the airport. Travis didn't have the room to keep more than a couple of finished wagons and build new ones at the same time.

"Keep in mind," Eric said to Kyle, "that I have *never* done this before and I haven't the first clue what to do."

"Bet you never thought you'd say that again," Kyle said and slugged Eric in the arm.

Eric just shook his head. "What has gotten into you," he asked. "You've been on one for the last week."

"Nothing, just glad things are finally moving forward," Kyle said, "that's all."

...

"The first thing to remember," Travis said to the group, "is that horses are *not* stupid. They can be stubborn, they can decide they don't like you and refuse to cooperate, they get tired just like we do and they can *act* stupid, but they are, in fact, very intelligent."

"Once the team is in harness to the wagon," Travis continued, "they'll get the hang of what they're supposed to do pretty quickly. Unless the two in the team don't like each other, they'll work together because they realize it makes life easier on them if they do."

"What if they don't want to move," one of the group asked. "Or don't want to stop when you tell them to?"

"Two good questions with completely different answers," Travis said. "If you want to go and the horses don't, there's not a whole lot you can do. They're bigger, stronger, and can be meaner than you if they set their mind to it. If they don't want to go, try to figure out why. They may know something that you don't. Check the area ahead and make sure there isn't an obstruction or something else that might be causing them to stop. Check the horses over and make sure there isn't a problem like a thrown shoe or rocks in their hooves."

"Lastly," Travis said, "make sure the brake isn't on, especially on these wagons. Which brings me to the next question, what if they don't want to stop? In that case, put the brake on."

Travis directed everyone's attention to the wheels on the wagon he was using for the demonstration. "Four-wheel drum brakes," he said. "I know the front looks like it has disc brakes, but believe me, there's a drum in there too. We used drum brakes because that's what an emergency brake in most cars uses."

He pointed out the brake lever in the middle of the split bench seat where the driver would sit. "That," he said, "is connected to all four emergency brakes, and unless you're in the middle of a stampede, it *will* stop the wagon."

"Again," Travis continued once everyone was looking at him and not the wagon, "horses aren't stupid. When they feel the resistance of the brakes, they'll slow down or stop. The one possible exception is in the winter. If you're on ice or thick snow, the horses may be able to pull you along even with the wheels locked. At that point, you're in a sled and not a wagon. The horses most likely won't run off a cliff…again, not stupid, but they may do something unexpected or try to turn too tight and tip the wagon. There's not much to be done at that point but either hold on and pray, or jump off…and pray."

"Now," Travis went on to the next part of his lecture.

…

"Are you sure you're ok with this," Chuck asked Sheri for the fiftieth time since they'd made their decision. "I'm not married to the idea, I'm married to you and I can always teach somebody else to run it."

"Who are you trying to convince," Sheri asked, "me or you? Honestly I'm getting bored here. It's not that there isn't enough work to do, but…I haven't been challenged since the Framework and this would at least let me contribute again. I don't mind hard work, but I think I've had enough of *dull* for a while."

"Well, I can almost guarantee it won't be dull," Chuck said, "at least for the first while."

"Any idea how many people would come with us," Sheri asked.

"Not really," Chuck said. "We haven't really discussed it outside of the few times Joel and I have gotten together with Mallory and her staff. I think Joel is afraid of getting people's hopes up."

"If anyone can do it," Sheri said, "I'm sure you can."

"I wish I had your confidence," Chuck said, "but we won't know until we try."

…

The festival was scheduled to start at eleven, to give everyone enough time to get to Redemption after finishing up any early-morning work. Lunch would start around noon, and there would be activities and games, and even face-painting for the little kids.

The wagons—with Kyle and Eric's leading the way—along with a good portion of the residents of the ranch, were the first to arrive and, true to his word, Eric surprised Joel.

"I'm not entirely sure what to say," Joel said. "How long have these been in the works?"

"A little over a month," Eric said. "We found and fixed a broken windmill and put it up at the ranch in trade. When Travis is done we'll have seventeen wagons and thirty-four horses."

Joel whistled. "Remind me never to trade with you," he said with a grin.

"It was mutually beneficial, and I'm also working on a solar project for the ranch," Eric said. "Panels are the first thing on my list to find once we have enough wagons to be mobile. I'll bore you with the details later, though."

Kyle had pulled up with one of the other wagons, with Amanda on the seat next to him and William in the back with some of the other kids.

"Any chance we could find a place to park these," Kyle asked.

Joel gave them directions to the temporary paddock they'd erected for the horses being ridden in from the ranch. "There should be room off to the side to park the wagons," he said.

As they were negotiating turning, Amanda saw a group of trucks approaching. "Looks like Earl just showed up," she said, and Joel excused himself to go greet the next group.

...

Joel had assembled the main leaders of the groups they'd invited to the festival for what he hoped would be a productive meeting of the minds. They were gathered outside, in front of the old Post Office, using a mixed bag of chairs and a few tables that had been brought to the town common by the residents.

"I don't want to spend all day on this," Joel said, "and I'm not really even expecting to get to a lot of the details sorted out today. I *would* like to go over some proposals and hear what everyone has to say about being involved, though."

At nods from everyone, Joel began going over the revised list of priorities and suggestions for specialized towns.

"Joel," Chuck said once the floor was opened up to discussion. "I know it wasn't on the list, because you didn't have an answer from me yet, but Sheri and I would like to go ahead and take on the power plant."

Nobody said anything for several seconds, and it was Earl who broke the silence. "Do you mean you're going to try to bring one of the power plants back online," he asked.

Chuck nodded. "The operative word being *try*," he said. "It'll be at least a couple of months before we know for sure if it's even feasible, but if it is, we could have limited power back online no later than this time next year."

"We can make an announcement later today," Joel said, "so people can start thinking about where they might want to move and who they'd be going with."

"Sounds good," Chuck said and sat back down.

"Well," Eric said, "I don't think we can compete with that, but we've got an announcement too. The wagons and horses are the first step, but ultimately we're going to be, well, nomads. Amanda came up with the idea to be like Gypsies. We're going to be mobile. We've got a few things up our sleeves to trade with, on top of being a traveling school. It's going to be a couple more months before we have all of the wagons we need, so we probably won't start moving until next spring, but that's our plan."

The meeting continued with discussions of how an industrial town might work and whether or not anyone was willing to start it up. After the discussion turned to skilled trades, Earl agreed to get a better idea of what his people had done before the power went out and what trades they might be able to contribute.

The farmers agreed that with only a little additional work, the production of just about every farm should be able to increase a fair amount. There really wasn't any reason they couldn't be generating a pretty fair surplus by this time next year.

...

Eric made his way over to Chuck once the meeting broke up.

"Got a minute," Eric asked.

"Sure," Chuck said. "What's up?"

"We need to talk about the coal at the power plant," Eric said. "Specifically, I've kind of promised Travis that I could get him more once what I've already delivered is gone."

Chuck let out the breath he'd been holding from the point Eric had said 'coal' and visibly relaxed. "You have no idea how glad I am to hear you say that," he said. "How much did you…bring back for Travis?" He'd almost said 'take', but realized at the last second how that might come across.

It wasn't his coal, yet; it was simply railroad car after railroad car and a couple of *really* big piles. Chuck had realized that a noticeable amount had disappeared between visits and he'd been worried about securing the plant from raids ever since.

"A couple of pickup trucks full," Eric said.

"That would make sense," Chuck said. "I'm so glad it wasn't some random group that I was going to have to guard against."

Chuck shook his head and focused on Eric. "It's found goods," he said. "I can't in good conscience say no, you can't have any more coal. Up until now, it was everybody's, and really, it needs to stay that way. Obviously the plant will need to use a lot of it, but we had already talked about ways to use it in town. I don't know if I really have the right to ask, but could you just let me know when you need to pick up a bunch?"

"Absolutely," Eric said, relieved that this hadn't turned into a pissing match. "And the only thing Travis is using the coal for right now is the forge, and he's said he's going to continue supplementing it with charcoal."

"At that rate," Chuck said, "we may have found another source of coal before he needs more."

…

Mallory had been dreading this moment ever since Joel had called her out for even *asking* if Kyle and Eric would be included today. She knew she'd been wrong at the time, and she knew she needed to bury the hatchet with Kyle, she just hoped it didn't get buried in one of their backs.

"Kyle," Mallory said as she walked up to him and Amanda. "Can I...talk to you for a minute?"

"Sure," Kyle said with a slight shrug.

"Alone," Mallory asked.

"Major," Kyle said, deciding to keep things formal on his part, "anything you need to say to me you can say in front of Amanda."

Mallory took a breath and pursed her lips and decided to push it just a little bit. "I don't doubt that," she said, "but I'm still asking to just talk to you."

It hit Kyle at that point that Ben was nowhere to be seen. Amanda realized the same thing at about the same time and squeezed Kyle's hand. "It's ok," she said with another squeeze, "I'll go get us something to drink."

"I'm really not trying to be difficult," Mallory said.

"I know," Kyle agreed, "and I didn't mean to be either. I'm sorry."

"Whoa," Mallory thought. *"He's really changed. You really screwed that one up, didn't you girl?"*

"No, Kyle," Mallory said, "*I'm* sorry."

Kyle started to protest, but stopped when he realized Mallory wasn't finished–he knew from years of experience that she *would* finish, whether he liked it or not. In this instance, it wasn't that hard to hold his tongue.

"I was wrong," Mallory said. "I was bitter and angry, and frustrated at you and Eric, but that doesn't excuse how I acted or reacted. I'm sorry. You didn't deserve to be treated that way, and although you don't need my permission or validation, you were *well* within your rights to put me back in my place."

Kyle thought he could see Mallory's eyes glisten a little as she took a breath. "I know you've moved on," she said. "The Army will miss you; I know I already do. I'm sorry I hurt you, in more ways than I realized at the time. I hope you can eventually forgive me because I hope we can be friends again, Kyle, I really do."

The silence stretched out for several seconds before Kyle said anything. "I can't let you take all the blame," he said. "I'm a big boy, and I let my temper get the better of me. I shouldn't have let that happen and, with anyone else, I don't think I would have. It was partially my fault for never saying anything, although how that would have done anything but make matters worse I don't know."

"It was for the best," Kyle said, and then frowned a little. "I'll forgive you if you can forgive me; for being stupid and for how I acted."

"Done," Mallory said, and held out her hand."

Kyle ignored the hand and stepped forward to give Mallory a hug.

She was surprised, and almost resisted, but realized that it was just a friendly hug and returned it.

"Thank you," she said. "And now, if you'll excuse me, I think there's someone who would like to join you again."

Amanda came back and handed him a cup of apple juice. "That certainly seems to have gone well," she said.

"Yeah," Kyle said and wiped a tear that he hadn't realized was there until just now. "I'm glad it's over, though."

Kyle put his arm around Amanda's waist and pulled her close. "I love you," he said, and gave her a kiss.

"And I love you, too," she said and returned the kiss with interest.

Chapter Thirty-Five

The bulk of the festival was being held in the 'downtown' area of Redemption. Traffic wasn't an issue, and the streets were wider here, with a small park running in-between the roads.

"Well, Mr. Mayor," Rachael said, as she put her arms around Joel from behind and put her chin on his shoulder. "It looks to me like you didn't really have anything to worry about."

Aurora was napping, and there seemed to be no shortage of tween-age girls just chomping at the bit to look after her.

Joel nodded and hugged her arms. "The meeting even went well," he said. "Assuming anything actually comes of it, things could really take off and start getting back to…normal?"

"I don't think normal is in the cards for us," Rachael said. "Or at least, this *is* the new normal."

"It's not too late to change your mind," Joel said to Chuck as he and Sheri walked up.

"Nope," Chuck said with a grin. "This will be a welcome change. I know I said I was up for a vacation when this all began, but it'll be good to get back to what I really know."

Joel nodded. "How about you," he asked Sheri.

"Pretty much the same," Sheri said. "I know we're all contributing and making a difference, but this is really going to help out a lot and hopefully help us get back some of the things we lost."

"Hey," Rachael said to Sheri, as she disengaged herself from Joel. "Let's go see what's for dessert after that lunch, huh?"

Sheri's weak smile was more of a grimace, but she nodded and they headed towards the cluster of tents where the baked goods were set up.

"We're two lucky guys," Chuck said.

"Don't I know it," Joel replied. "I don't know how she puts up with me but I *know* I couldn't have done this without her."

Chuck just nodded.

. . .

"I heard somebody mention that they still needed judges for the pie contest," Rachael said.

Sheri closed her eyes and shook her head. "Not today," she said. "Just the thought of pie…" She stopped talking and clenched her jaws.

"You okay," Rachael asked.

"Just been queasy off and on for the last couple of days," Sheri said. "Nothing sounds good at all, and even some smells set me off."

Rachael hid a small smile. "Have you been to see Ty or Dan," she asked.

"Not yet," Sheri said. "I don't think it's anything serious, just kind of run down and pukey."

"I'm willing to bet it's a little more serious than you realize," Rachael said.

Sheri gave her a worried glance.

...

"Will J.B. get as big as *those* horses," Jessie asked Travis when she saw the pair of draft horses he'd brought along.

"No, honey," Travis chuckled, "J.B. is a Quarter Horse. When he's grown up he'll be a little bigger than his mother, most likely."

"When is he going to be big enough to ride," Jessie asked. It was something she asked at least once a day when they visited the ranch.

Instead of giving the same pat answer he'd been using for the last several weeks, Travis told Jessie the truth. "Jessie," he said, getting her full attention, "J.B. probably won't be old enough to ride until he's three."

Jessie's jaw dropped and her face fell. "Oh," she said with a little sigh. Then she stood up straight and squared her shoulders.

"Okay," she said with a nod, "I can wait."

Travis was impressed with her reaction and made a quick decision.

"I tell you what," Travis said with a glance towards Dan and Marissa. "If it's okay with your parents, if you keep coming to the ranch and helping out with J.B., I'll teach you to ride so you'll be ready when your horse is old enough. Deal?"

Jessie's eyes got big and she turned to her parents. "Please," she said, "pleasepleaseplease? I'll help take care of him every day, and anything else they need me to do. *Please?*"

Marissa and Dan both had small smiles when Marissa said, "We need to talk it over with Mr. Travis. Now go play with Bekah."

Jessie nodded and ran off, and Dan and Marissa turned to Travis.

"I mean it," Travis said. "Both about you having to agree and me teaching her to ride. I know a lot of girls go through a phase where they're horse crazy, but I really don't think that's the case with Jessie. First of all, she's still a bit too young for that and, well, she really does seem to have a way with the horses. I think she's got a future there."

Marissa shook her head. "If you'd told me two years ago that my oldest daughter had a potential career in hunting and marksmanship," she said, "and that Jessie had a future in horses, I'd have laughed in your face."

"I have a question about something you said, though," Dan said. "You referred to J.B. as 'her' horse."

Travis smiled. "That I did," he said. "I think he's been her horse all along. If it keeps her interest, and again if it's okay with you, J.B. will be her horse when she's old enough."

"That's," Marissa started. "That's incredibly generous of you."

Travis shrugged. "Maybe," he said, "but I'd much rather he go to someone that'll truly appreciate him than sell him as part of a team. That, and I guess I consider it an investment. In the long run we're going to need more people like her."

...

Shortly after 2:00, the festival got a little bit of a scare. The inbound Black Hawk had radioed ahead and gotten clearance to land, but almost nobody at the festival knew it was on the way. Once it landed just outside of town and let off its passengers, an announcement was made to calm any fears that they were under attack.

"I thought you said you weren't going to be able to get up here," Mallory said to Sanford. "Something about there being too much to do getting things pulled back together."

Sanford just shrugged. "These guys," Sanford said with a nod towards Hodges and Tuttle, "weren't going to let me hear the end of it if we didn't at least try."

"Well, let me introduce you to a few folks," Mallory said, "and then you're free to just...relax."

Sanford stepped up beside Mallory as they began walking and asked under his breath, "Is Sparky around?"

Mallory smiled. "He should be," she said. "He was actually still working on something until about a half-an-hour ago, when I had to all but order him to take a break."

Sanford caught himself before he looked over his shoulder at Tuttle. "I know what you mean," he said. "We would have been here a little earlier but Tuttle had her head buried in a couple of laptops."

"And speak of the devil," Ben said from Sanford's other side.

"Sergeant Lake," Mallory hollered to get Sparky's attention, and he obediently trotted over to the group.

"Ma'am," Sparky said, once he was close enough to salute, but didn't because they were outside. Old habits die hard.

"I believe you have at least heard mention of Major Sanford and Lieutenant Hodges," Mallory said.

"Actually," Sanford said, "at the risk of starting down the same path as Colonel Olsen, I've taken the liberty of promoting Hodges to Captain. It was far past time."

Mallory looked again and felt a little color rise on her cheeks. She hadn't noticed the double bars on his collar.

"Please don't worry about it," Hodges said. "I'm still not used to it myself." To his credit, however, he kept from fingering the new pins like he'd been doing the entire way down in the helicopter.

Mallory nodded and continued. "And of course you already know Sergeant Tuttle," she said.

Sparky struggled to keep a straight face. He'd had no idea that Tuttle was going to be coming and was equally unprepared for the fact that she was...*gorgeous*!

"Man, and I really hoped I might have a shot," Sparky thought. *"Oh well. But DAMN!"* He'd always been partial to redheads and she was... *"I'm not looking, I am so not looking. Eyes up soldier!"*

Sparky held his hand out for the three, Tuttle being the last.

"Might as well just go back to the base and work on the radios," Sparky mused. He wasn't so much depressed now as…disheartened.

"We've been working together on the civilian radios," Sparky said with a nod towards Tuttle. "We've been fine tuning the software, and Sergeant Tuttle has a couple of ideas on how we can make them even more user-friendly."

…

"He's cute," Tuttle thought to herself. *"Thank goodness."* She'd been afraid that he would be what she envisioned as the typical computer nerd—glasses, shy, unwilling to make eye contact. *"I think he's checking me out,"* she thought with a small smile.

Little did she know he'd had laser eye surgery done about five years ago, otherwise he *would* have been wearing coke-bottle bottom glasses in the standard-issue Buddy Holly frames. What armies the world over referred to as "birth-control goggles".

"Sergeant Lake," Sanford started.

"Please, call me Sparky," he said. "Only the Major calls me Sergeant Lake and usually only when I'm in trouble. My mother doesn't even…hadn't called me Evan for a couple of years before the power went out."

"Sparky then," Sanford continued. "I'm sure you and Sergeant Tuttle can talk shop, or not, for a couple of hours.

"Absolutely," Sparky said. *"Please don't screw up,"* Sparky prayed, *"please."*

…

"Have you had lunch yet," Sparky asked as he and Tuttle headed off, away from the Officers.

"A little before we left, but," Tuttle blushed, "I hate flying, always have."

"Well, if you're up to it now," Sparky said, "there're a couple of folks that still have food at their stand. Barbecue, fresh coleslaw, deviled eggs."

"I love living in the South," Tuttle said with a smile. "Although, I'll have to hit the gym to work it all off."

"What are you talking about," Sparky asked. "You look great."

Sparky felt the heat rising on cheeks and the back of his neck as soon as the words were out of his mouth.

"Fifteen seconds," he thought. *"I didn't make it fifteen seconds before I blew it."* He was surprised by Tuttle's response.

"Thank you," she said. "You haven't let yourself go, either."

. . .

"I am so bad at this," Tuttle thought. *"He probably thinks I'm the biggest dork now."*

"She's just being nice," Sparky thought. *"Nothing else to do while* They Who Must Be Obeyed *are busy."*

. . .

"I can't believe the Colonel, or his handlers, thought their whole deception would work," Sanford said. "Obviously ARCLiTE wasn't the miserable failure they claimed it was just to advance their agenda."

Mallory nodded. "For us," she said, "the orders were validation for what we'd literally been doing since the second day." She looked at Ben for confirmation.

"Things didn't go quite as smoothly up at Campbell right away," Ben said, "but it wasn't ever an utter failure there, either. Hindsight is twenty-twenty, though. Now that we know what they were up to, it's easy to see how it was all about disinformation and, ultimately, pulling the strings in secret."

"Not everyone is happy about Denver," Sanford said. "They're definitely the minority, and in the long run I don't think they'll be a problem, but, well the Northeast is a good example. It isn't just the military that bought the story hook, line, and sinker. The civilians are being willingly subjugated."

"You can't free someone who doesn't see their own chains," Ben said.

"As long as they keep to themselves," Mallory said, "and don't try to break the security around Denver, I really think they'll burn themselves out in a couple of years; especially without any direction or reinforcements."

"We've certainly got enough on our plates for the time being as it is," Sanford said.

...

"As long as you're still sure," Dan said.

"Why wouldn't I be," Ty asked. "This isn't a spur-of-the-moment decision for either of us."

"What isn't," Joel asked as he walked by, "a spur-of-the-moment decision, that is?"

"Go ahead," Ty said to Dan.

"Ty and I are going into practice together," Dan said. "Ty's going to stay with the military for the time being, and he's going to have his hands full trying to turn me into a doctor but, we're going to give it a shot."

Joel was grinning from ear to ear. This is what he'd originally hoped for when Dan had first showed up.

"That is great news," Joel said, shaking both men's hands. "How's Marissa taking the decision?"

"Well," Dan said, "it was *our* decision, Marissa's and mine. She's good with it and thinks Ty and I can make a difference, setting up a regular practice and having both of us available…once I get up to speed."

…

"So I've opened the satellite back up to everyone," Sanford said, "except for Denver. They're permanently locked out. I didn't even know we had the ability to segregate communications like they'd been doing, although it makes sense that we could."

"With the handlers locked out," Mallory asked, "how is everyone taking the truth?"

Sanford shrugged. "About like we figured," he said. "There've been some midnight disappearances of senior officers once things started getting out and communication was restored for everybody. The change in command at a couple of *large* units was…violent to say the least."

"Everyone that was in a position of ultimate authority was in on it," Mallory said, "in one way or another. How do we trust any of them now?"

"With only a few notable exceptions," Hodges said, "they aren't in charge anymore. They're the ones making themselves scarce in the middle of the night before someone else takes care of them permanently."

"It's left a bit of a leadership vacuum in a few places," Sanford said, "but for the most part people are dealing with it. They're picking themselves up by the bootstraps and moving on."

…

"Dan helped with Aurora's delivery," Rachael said to Ty and Dan. "How about you, Ty? How many babies have you delivered?"

"I've delivered a few," Ty said. "No Caesarian's, though."

"And to be fair," Dan said, "I was there for Aurora's birth more for moral support. The midwife did most of the work."

"We aren't trying to run you off," Ty said, "just trying to paint an honest picture. Either way, I think you'd be in good hands, but I'm not going to dismiss the midwives either."

"Well, I need to know for sure if I'm even pregnant," Sheri said.

"Oh honey," Rachael said and shook her head a little. "What you need to do is come to grips with the fact that you are, although I think either Ty or Dan could confirm it for you fairly quickly."

...

"Thank you again for coming," Mallory said to Eric as the festival was winding down and people were starting to head home.

"We're all still in this together," Eric said. "Have you talked to Kyle?"

Mallory nodded. "I think we've buried the hatchet," she said.

"I'm glad," Eric said. "And I know he'd never ask for it, but when the time comes, I know he'd appreciate your blessing."

"For," Mallory asked.

"He and Amanda are engaged," Eric said.

...

After dinner, Joel got on the PA system and made a few announcements.

"The festival is almost over," Joel said after a couple of minutes recapping some of the decisions made during the day, "and we still don't have a name for it. The plan is to do this every year, but we can't just call it 'the festival'."

Someone from the crowd shouted something that Joel couldn't hear, so he asked them to repeat themselves.

"The Phoenix Festival," they shouted again.

Joel's immediate thought was of the city in Arizona, although he was sure that wasn't what they had meant. It only took a second for him to make the right connection and look at the members of the committee that had set up the festival in the first place.

"Phoenix," Joel said with the beginnings of a smile. "Rebirth, rising from the ashes, renewal, recommitment, triumph …"

Joel paused to let the crowd consider the idea before continuing.

"Unless we have any other suggestions," Joel started, but was interrupted.

Chants of "Phoenix, Phoenix, Phoenix" from the crowd made it obvious that at least for now, people liked the suggestion.

"Then I declare today," Joel said, "September 28, 2013, to be the first annual Phoenix Festival."

Cheers erupted from the crowd again and Joel stepped down from the small stage that had been constructed at the end of the town center.

"Why didn't we think of that," Marissa asked to nobody in particular when Joel was back on the ground.

"Personally," Joel said, "I used up all my imagination on 'festival'. It fits, though. The longer you think about it the more…*right* it sounds."

Joel looked at their one resident pastor, Sergeant Stanton. "You don't suppose we've just started a new pagan religion, do you Marci," he asked.

Marci laughed. "Joel," she said. "Look around. I think it's okay for you stop worrying quite so much now."

Acknowledgements

Once again, I owe my family a huge debt. To my wife, not the least of which for editing, but while I was "plodding", she was plotting and helped me even more on this book than the previous one.

Then there are my kids. I know I can be grumpy when I'm trying to write and things are either coming along too slowly for my taste or, worse, not coming along at all. They have been real troopers. I've finally paid the ice-cream debt for the last two books, but I owe them…again.

Next, I feel the need to thank all of our men and women in uniform, past and present. I can't express my gratitude sufficiently for all you have done and continue to do. While I've never served, I have a long (and current) family history of military service in the Army, Navy, and Air Force. Our country doesn't celebrate you nearly enough but I thank you.

The author of this quote is unknown, but this sums up the honor of our Veterans and active-duty armed forces:

A veteran - whether active duty, retired, or national guard or reserve - is someone who, at one point in their life, wrote a blank check made payable to "The United States of America," for an amount of "up to and including THEIR LIFE."

I have nothing but the deepest respect for all members of our armed forces. You are all Heroes. Thank you, from the bottom of my heart.

And finally, to you, the reader, thank you. This book seemed like it was a long time in the making, even though I only started working on it in January of this year (2013 for future generations...ha!). Nevertheless, I'm sure that some were wondering if I would *ever* be done.

While the books don't come nearly as quick as I'm sure everyone would like (myself included), you need to know that I want to give you all a good read. My goal is to create a story that's thought-provoking, well-thought-out, and worth *your* time and hard-earned money.

It takes time, though; with a day job that pays the bills, a family that needs me and that I love very much, and all of the other distractions of daily life. So, to everyone who stuck with me, nudged me on Facebook, or posted on one of the several Author pages out there, this one's for you.

--David

http://www.davidcwaldron.com
http://www.facebook.com/AuthorDavidCWaldron

Made in the USA
San Bernardino, CA
10 December 2013